ARCHIE MYERS

REQUIEM

Copyright © 2022 by Archie Myers

All rights reserved. No part of this publication may be reproduced, stored or transmitted in any form or by any means, electronic, mechanical, photocopying, recording, scanning, or otherwise without written permission from the publisher. It is illegal to copy this book, post it to a website, or distribute it by any other means without permission.

This novel is entirely a work of fiction. The names, characters and incidents portrayed in it are the work of the author's imagination. Any resemblance to actual persons, living or dead, events or localities is entirely coincidental.

Archie Myers asserts the moral right to be identified as the author of this work.

First edition

Editing by Becky Wallace

This book was professionally typeset on Reedsy. Find out more at reedsy.com

For Azzie,
Without you, this book would not exist.
I Love You.

"Act well your part; there all the honor lies."

— Alexander Pope, An Essay on Man

Contents

I THE INTROITUS

Prologue	3
Chapter One	8
Chapter Two	12
Chapter Three	17
Chapter Four	22

II THE SEQUENTIA

Chapter Five	27
Chapter Six	36
Chapter Seven	42
Chapter Eight	48

III THE KYRIE

Chapter Nine	53
Chapter Ten	57
Chapter Eleven	67
Chapter Twelve	75
Chapter Thirteen	80

IV THE CREDO

Chapter Fourteen	83
Chapter Fifteen	87
Chapter Sixteen	92
Chapter Seventeen	96

V THE COMMUNIO

Chapter Eighteen	107
Chapter Nineteen	121
Chapter Twenty	126
Chapter Twenty-One	131

VI THE SANCTUS

Chapter Twenty-Two	139
Chapter Twenty-Three	148
Chapter Twenty-Four	158
Chapter Twenty-Five	163

VII THE BENEDICTUS

Chapter Twenty-Six	167
Chapter Twenty-Seven	172
Chapter Twenty-Eight	182
Chapter Twenty-Nine	189

VIII THE GLORIA

Chapter Thirty	199
Chapter Thirty-One	208
Chapter Thirty-Two	215

IX THE AGNUS DEI

Chapter Thirty-Three	231
Chapter Thirty-Four	240
Chapter Thirty-Five	246
Chapter Thirty-Six	261
Chapter Thirty-Seven	266
Chapter Thirty-Eight	270

X THE REQUIEM AETERNAM

Chapter Thirty-Nine	277
Chapter Forty	282
Chapter Forty-One	293
Chapter Forty-Two	300
Chapter Forty-Three	305
Epilogue	306

Acknowledgments	311
About the Author	313
Also by Archie Myers	314

I

THE INTROITUS

Prologue

8:00 PM - Wednesday, 3rd November 2021

A chill slowly settles on the town of Telluride, Colorado.

As winter looms on the horizon, families stock up on blankets and firewood, and some even begin putting out Christmas decorations. Surprisingly, there is also a high demand for door locks, weapons, and alarm systems.

When the first murder happens, people don't worry. They let the family grieve, maybe bake them something just so they can feel like they're good people, but inevitably, they move on with their lives.

But when the second murder happens, then the third, and the fourth, hysteria sets in. People feel guilty because they don't feel sympathy for the victims. All they can think about is how grateful they are that it wasn't them. It's interesting to watch. Seeing neighbor turning on neighbor, watching friends gradually grow suspicious and eventually stop trusting each other while I sit back and blend in. Funny, even.

It does make my job harder when everybody starts barricading their doors and locking their windows. Oh well. Where there's a will, there's a way.

The family that lives in the house across the street seems to be having a good night. A mother and father are on the couch with their two younger children, a boy and a girl, cozied in between them. The perfect victims. Their other daughter doesn't seem to be with them. She must be in her room. From what I've gathered over the past five days of watching, she tends to avoid them—always walking five feet behind or ahead, on her phone at the dinner table. Maybe she's embarrassed by them? Perhaps she's just a typical teenage girl.

Or maybe, there's more to the story.

I subtly scan my surroundings to see if anybody will witness my next act. I walk across the street and toward the house. The unlocked side gate allows easy access to the backyard. I've been watching them long enough to know they keep a spare key behind a flimsy board in their wooden fence. God knows why they keep a spare key outside while the local serial killer is still on the loose.

They're practically asking for it.

After double-checking that the family is still on the couch, I slip in through the back door, locking it behind me. I am careful to avoid stepping on floorboards and causing a creak, so I walk on the narrow carpet runner to get from room to room. Luckily all the bedrooms are carpeted. I creep up the stairs and make my way into the boy's bedroom, crawl under the bed, and I wait.

—

I've been patient enough.

The family is sound asleep and won't be woken by the little noise I make. I slither out from under the bed and look at the little boy who occupies it. I giddily unsheathe my knife and hold it mere inches from his neck.

I pause. I contemplate whether I should spare the child. Killing children has never been my M.O. Maybe I take care of the others and then see how I feel.

Eh.

The hunting knife slides effortlessly through the layers of skin and muscle until it finally stops at a bone. The boy's eyes dart open, and it's apparent he wants to scream, but it's difficult when there's a knife in your throat. The life drains from his eyes along with the blood from his neck. I move out of his room and into the hallway. I stand there, examining the family photos on the wall while taking in the silence. Mattresses squeak as they adjust their sleeping positions is the only sound to be heard. There are two doors to choose from.

Eeny, Meeny, Miny, Moe. The left one.

I nudge the slightly opened door. It creaks. The mounded bed covers insinuate life underneath, and as I near, I can now see the fifteen-year-old girl. I make quick work of her, plunging the knife deep into her chest. She tries to scream but my hand is planted firmly over her mouth, but still, a few squeaks manage to escape. I press down on her throat with all of my weight as I repeatedly stab her chest. Her ribcage becomes loose and the knife makes a harsh scraping sound as it grates against her bones.

I've found it quite effective and a little more enjoyable to twist and push the knife. The girl gurgles, and blood gushes from the hole in her chest until finally, the gurgling stops, and the only sound that indicates she was ever alive is the faint plink of the blood dripping onto the floor. Typically, I like to attack while my victims are sleeping. If they're asleep, they can't overpower me. But for children, I like to make an exception. Especially young, weak ones like this. No matter how hard they try, they will never be able to win.

I exit the room and walk straight into what I assume is the parents' room. Without thinking, I thrust my knife deep into one of the mounds. Judging by the scream, it was the father. I quickly shut him up by slashing his neck open. The mother shrieks, dragging herself away from me like a wounded deer, and screaming for help; little does she know her precious babies are already lying in pools of their own blood. I would say they went peacefully, but they didn't. Just because someone makes little noise doesn't mean it didn't hurt. It just means they were caught off guard. Poor woman. But what she doesn't know won't hurt her.

I slice away at her husband's neck, half decapitating him, as she rushes to open her bedroom window and for a second, I let her think she can call for help before I quickly jam my blade into the side of her throat and kick her through the glass, out the window. She lands on the cement with a surprisingly loud thud.

I know I haven't got long until the police show up. That screaming *must* have alerted someone. I leave the mutilated body and walk down the hallway towards the final door, the eighteen-year-old girl's bedroom. She'll be awake and prepared, so I must be ready for her. I push my ear up against the door and listen for signs of life—the sound of clothes rubbing against each other or a heavy breath. Maybe even a faint whisper as she calls 911. That's always my favorite because it gives them a sliver of hope, one that I know will soon be dashed.

But there's no sound. I grab the handle, pause, and swing it open. Again, nothing. Bed-made. Nobody in the closet. She's not here. Or she was here and called for help—no time to ponder.

I need to leave. I hastily walk out of the room and head down the stairs. I almost get to the bottom when I hear the back doorknob turn and the hinges creak as the door begins to open. I duck around the closest corner. The eighteen-year-old girl sneaks in, careful not to step on that creaky floorboard. Great minds think alike.

I clasp the handle of my knife, ready to attack. She slowly walks in my direction. Closer and closer. Until she freezes and spots something in the distance, and then I notice it too. Red and blue flashing lights from down the street. For a second, they illuminate the room, and I stare into the eyes of the eighteen-year-old. In a panic, she screams and stumbles to the back door. I want to kill her then and there, but the flashing lights stop in front of the house, and the and the wail of the sirens is so close. The girl opens the door and screams as she runs to the front of the house. I race out the back door and halt. I want to hear the sound she makes when she sees her mother on the front lawn. I want to revel in my work, because if I can't then what's the point? Well, I guess I'll have plenty of time to soak it all in when the news outlets arrive. But a little glimpse won't hurt.

Three ... two ... one ...

There it is. I use her high-pitched shriek as an opportunity to sprint in the other direction. As I flee, the girl's wails follow after me.

I laugh to myself. *Wait until you go upstairs.*

Chapter One

Willow - 7:00 AM - Thursday, 27th January 2022

I'm never prepared for the alarm.

Sometimes I hear it in public, and although I know it doesn't mean I need to get up, I still shudder. I often set the alarm on weekends to feel the pleasure of going back to sleep. I've been told that's not normal, but whatever, it feels nice. I could use some relief in my life. But today is a day I need to get up for.

No, I'm *excited* to get up.

Today, the cast for our last high school play will be announced. My boyfriend Hugh has been writing the script for two years. He's so incredibly talented and intelligent that I have zero doubts it will be amazing. I got really lucky with him. He's pretty much the only straight boy in the entire theater department and we look perfect as a couple.

We're similar to Rachel Berry and Finn Hudson from *Glee*, my favorite show. And also, well ... okay, he reminds me of Finn from *Glee*. *But* he does write incredible scripts and has always given me a significant part, so there is a reason to keep him around. However, he's been very secretive about this play, maybe even overly secretive. But he says there's a great role for me, which honestly, is what I expected. I've been the lead in every high school musical and play for the last four years, so I don't see why this year would be any different.

Not to brag, but I do have incredible range, both in my vocal skills and acting abilities. At least that's what Ms. H, our theater teacher, tells me. In my freshman year of high school, I played Elle Woods in *Legally Blonde* and in my sophomore year, I got to play Maria in *West Side Story*. Noa was upset about it. She said it was "cultural appropriation," and that I shouldn't be playing her because I'm white but I was clearly better than her, and I think the role should go to whoever is the best. When I said that in rehearsals, it was met with a great uproar, and I was silenced. It's almost like you can't have an opinion anymore.

But she was great as Anita's understudy.

She has been completely off the grid since the attack. Nobody knows where she really was. People thought she moved states or fled the country, but a few weeks ago she started showing up to school occasionally. I wonder if she'll be here today.

Walking into the kitchen, I see the news is on. I find the remote and cautiously turn up the volume, careful not to wake my mother. She's been going to bed later and later since dad left. I guess a bottle of wine or two also has something to do with it. She doesn't believe dad would just leave her. She thinks he's one of the unlucky souls taken by the alleged serial killer roaming our town. But I know he's not a victim. Before he disappeared, he was drinking more and more and would get really angry and would take it out on Mom and me, so honestly, I wouldn't mind if he didn't come home.

I listen intently. There has been no further information about the killer the town has dubbed "The Telluride Maniac."

He's had 24/7 news coverage, so I assume they have nothing else to say. Everybody in Telluride has been bouncing off the walls with fear since he started his spree.

But the attacks have seemed to stop after the new year.

We have one of the few houses in Telluride that isn't worth one billion dollars, so we don't have a built-in alarm system, and we weren't lucky enough to snatch any alarms before they sold out. By lucky enough, I mean they're expensive, and we hardly have enough money to cover my school fees. I mean the only reason I'm able to go my prestigious private school is because of a Theater Scholarship *and* a staff discount because of my dad's position. He's an Assistant Principal for Fine Arts. Well, he was. He obviously hasn't shown up to work since he disappeared, so I don't know how long it'll take before that gets taken away too.

I watch as the news report displays family photos and sketches of the supposed attacker given by Noa, the surviving daughter. She actually used to be one of my good friends before she ditched me for Caleb and Kaya, but to think she was mere feet away from the maniac makes my skin crawl. He almost got her. They must be close to figuring out who did this. They *have* to be. Unfortunately, she only saw him in the middle of the night, peering out from behind a wall, unmoving. In her statement she said he was wearing a deer mask with huge antlers. She hasn't spoken much about it, though. She hasn't spoken much about anything, really.

I do my morning vocal warm-ups in the shower: an arpeggio lip buzz, a hum up and down the scale, and a breathing exercise. Once dressed, I grab my phone, pack my lunch bag, and get in the car. Black ice covers the roads as winter rages on, so I've got to be careful of my speed.

CHAPTER ONE

The radio is on, still talking about the maniac, even after a month of no attacks. I hate to sound disrespectful because I tend to pride myself on being quite woke, but I'm really sick of hearing about it. It's depressing. I thought people would *want* to move on. As usual, I put on my show tunes playlist to make myself feel better, which is something else I'm very proud of. Years and years collated from different eras of the genre. It has fifty thousand likes on Spotify, so I'm basically famous. I pull in to my senior parking spot, and as I get out of the car, I see Noa walking in the main door.

"I knew she wouldn't be able to miss this. Bitch."

I cover my mouth and look around, praying nobody is close enough to hear me. It's just she's always been trying to snatch the lead from me, even though she's not good enough to do it.

No. Her family is dead. I should be nice.

I watch as Noa is greeted at the doorway by Caleb and Kaya, two other theater club members. Caleb is Hugh's best friend, and they spend almost all their time together. When he's not with me, of course. And Kaya is Noa's best friend, goth-looking, really weird. They don't like me whatsoever, even though I've done absolutely nothing to them. Ugh, just look at them, smothering her with love and hugs. I bet they love this. Being friends with the traumatized girl gives them a lot of sympathy points and attention and—oh my god. They're looking at me. Shit.

I quickly snap my head around, open my car's backseat, grab my school bag, and walk toward the doors. The trio has gone inside by now, thank God. I walk through the halls and make my way through the crowds of teenagers towards our theater class. I take a deep breath, place my hand on the doorknob, twist it and walk inside.

Chapter Two

Caleb - 8:30 AM – Thursday, 27th January 2022

I am really not in the mood to put up with Willow today. I mean, I never really am, but she is particularly unbearable on cast announcement days. She already knows she'll get the lead role, and I don't know why. Oh, wait, yes, I do. Her recently missing father is the head of the theater department.

That is the *only* reason because when she tries to sing, it sounds like someone *trying* to be bad or a dying seal. Either-or. She's the high school equivalent of a Hollywood nepotism baby. One time in junior year, she told me she was "the only one who could delve into a character's mind and deliver a truthful, *honest* performance." Then she realized I was looking at her funny and quickly corrected herself by saying, "I mean, *you* and me, of course."

The sad thing is that Noa is *actually* talented and would do ten times the job Willow does, but she gets nothing.

Noa is too sweet to say anything and stand up for herself, but oh my god, have I been waiting to say something and today might be the day. We have a few talented people in this club. Kaya, who is a fantastic alto with an unbelievable range and, like Noa, gets nothing. Samuel and Arthur are incredible comedic actors. When we did *Heathers*, they played Kurt and

CHAPTER TWO

Ram, and I genuinely laughed so hard I wet myself one of the nights.

It was funny at first, but then I realized I had to go onstage and had a huge damp stain. I was playing JD and was wearing black, so it wasn't very noticeable, but the smell was. Evelyn has a beautiful classical voice, which means she usually gets shoved into the "mother" or "old woman with wisdom" roles, but she kills it every time. Riley is an incredible dancer. She's not the strongest singer, but she knows that. She doesn't give in to her delusions like a certain somebody. And then there's Fergus, who ... well. He's extremely weird. And not just in a quiet sense, but in a *he could possibly bring a gun to school to "take revenge on everybody who made him feel invisible" way.* Hugh, my best friend, has written a few of the plays we put on. Most of them have been dogshit, but there have been a few alright ones. He wrote one when he was a freshman, about women in the 1800's and the parallels to today. As if he would know anything about that. Kaya took great delight in telling him how far off the mark he was. And yet, that was one of the better ones.

Apparently, he's been working on this most recent one for two years. Seems a bit excessive.

"What do you think it's going to be?" asks Kaya, taking a seat next to me.

"I have no idea," I respond.

She glances at me, a look of confusion on her face. "Wait, he hasn't told you? I would assume you tell each other everything."

"I've got no clue. He was super secretive about this one. Like *overly* secretive."

"Yeah, I heard," she chuckles. "Well, there aren't many

minority groups left that Hugh hasn't spoken for. It's probably one of them."

We sit silently for a few awkward seconds as our quiet giggles die out. "Is Willow going to get the lead?" I finally ask, even though I already know the answer.

"What do you think?" she asks sarcastically. "Although I would love to see her reaction to getting in the ensemble."

We both laugh—louder this time. I can picture it. The absolute theatrics that would ensue. A storm out, an attempted boycott, and then finally, some threat about her dad being the head of theater. It's fun to think about, but I know deep down that would never happen. Even though her dad apparently left the school, it's too late to change the way this department works; and frankly, I don't have the energy to be assaulted by the real life Sharpay Evans. Besides, Hugh is choosing the roles, and he would never not give her what she wants. I hate that about him.

It's extremely difficult, impossible even, to get on Willow's good side. Many have tried and all have failed. She's utterly self-serving, so if your friendship doesn't completely consist of compliments about her then it may as well not exist. That's what Noa says. They used to be friends, but it ended when Noa realized this.

I haven't even tried to be friends with Willow. She hates me because I'm Hugh's best friend, and she thinks he spends too much time with me. Which is ridiculous and I take no notice of it. I don't really want to be her friend and it's clear she has no interest in becoming mine either. She certainly wouldn't want to be if she knew what I've done.

I notice Noa hasn't come in yet. She left Kaya and me to go to the bathroom before class. Coming back to school is hard for her. She's tried a few times, but the stares and attention from total strangers are too much, and she goes back into hiding. I don't blame her. I cannot even imagine what she's been going through these past couple of months.

Everyone seems to be celebrating the "disappearance" of the Telluride Maniac, but she's been grieving his—or her— or their last victims. People forget that the day the maniac disappeared was the day she lost her entire family and was almost killed herself. She had been extremely depressed and suicidal in the weeks following the attack. She had called Kaya one night, in the middle of a panic attack, wishing that "she was dead" or that she "wished he just killed me as well." It shattered Kaya to hear so she called me for advice, but I had no idea how to make her feel better. That night saw her first suicide attempt. It nearly broke Kaya, and it still makes me squirm even thinking about it. She's been living with her aunt and cousins since it happened, and I think it's helped her to be with family and not all alone. It hasn't *fixed* her, not in the slightest, and I'm not sure anything will, but I shudder to think what would have happened if she didn't. She's eighteen after all, she could have easily started living on her own.

When she told us that she was coming back to school today, I told her maybe she should wait a little longer. I knew people would still stare, and she would be uncomfortable, but she told me, "Eventually, I'm going to have to come back. I need to graduate. People are going to stare however long I delay this." It was surprisingly self-aware of her, and I was shocked to hear her speaking so rationally. But I knew the real reason she wanted to return. Especially today.

The door to the room opens, and Noa walks through. She's done it. Finally, she's made it to the first period. Our class stops talking and looks up at her. Except for Willow, of course, as she's probably too wrapped up in her conversation with Hugh. Most likely about whichever part she will be playing. To avoid any awkwardness and to help Noa feel as comfortable as possible, Kaya and I leap up from our seats and go over to her. She stands with her arms crossed, gives a faint hint of a smile, and lowers her head to the ground.

"I don't know if I'm ready," she chokes out.

"If you need to go home, nobody will blame you," Kaya suggests softly as she rubs her arm.

"No," she says very matter-of-factly, "I have to do this. I can't hide forever." The last thing she says is tinged with a sliver of hope, and I can't help but smile.

"Okay. Well, come sit with us. We're so excited to have you back!" I say. This is true, but I meant it more for comfort. She follows us down the stairs to the first row of seats and sits down. Just as we do, Hugh gets up and claps his hand twice, giving us all a fright.

"Alright, everyone. Let's get started."

Chapter Three

Noa - 8:45 AM – Thursday, 27th January 2022

Every stare feels like a constant reminder of what's happened to me.

People don't think they're doing anything wrong just by looking, but the truth is that absolutely nobody would be looking at me if my family was still here. The first time I returned to school, I thought I was ready. Then I had a panic attack about five minutes after walking through the door and had to go back to my aunt's house immediately. The second time, I did a little better … two minutes better. That time, my Aunt decided to check me in to in-patient care. I called it the "looney bin." Nobody knows that's where I was except Kaya and Caleb. People just kept staring, and I couldn't handle it. I knew they would, and I can hardly blame them, but all it made me think about was how I was just a tragic story and a girl that nobody would ever treat the same. That's how I feel sitting in this circle of chairs. I can see people glancing over at me in my peripheral, but when I look at them, they conveniently need to look anywhere else.

I mean, except Fergus. When I looked over at him, I realized he was looking at my boobs. I'll give it to him. No shame.

"Alright, Belinda is out sick today, so she's put me in charge of going through the script and giving out roles." He means Ms. H. Hugh is the kind of guy who thinks using a teacher's first name makes him seem cooler, but it just makes me cringe. And judging by Kaya's unsubtle eye role, she relates. I suppress a laugh. It feels nice being at school with Kaya. For a few seconds, everything feels normal. Then, I remember my mother lying dead on the pavement and quickly realize nothing will ever be normal again.

"So today, I'm going to be giving out the roles for our play, and we're going to read through the script and make sure everybody is okay with it. And if anyone is concerned, all the roles are equal in importance."

Kaya gives a faint scoff, which earns her a sharp glare from Willow. Sort of like what she was giving me in the parking lot, but with more malice behind it. Willow and I used to be close friends in middle school and freshman year.

When we used to watch *Glee* together, she took an unhealthy liking to Rachel Berry. I think she missed the point that Rachel is a mockery of try-hard theater girls, but she idolized her anyway. As we grew apart, all her flaws that I used to brush aside became unmissable, unavoidable, and unbearable. Some days I couldn't even look at her. As I became closer with Kaya, we had fun bitching about Willow and giving each other looks of "did you just hear what I heard?" anytime she said something questionable. It was because of Kaya that I realized what real friendship is. She cared about me. She asked me questions about *my* life. She listened to *me*. It wasn't all about her.

After the ... attack. Willow reached out once. And it was to ask if I still wanted to be in the play. I was expecting more, seeing as she knew my parents really well, even though they never liked her and constantly told me to cut ties with her. She felt completely blindsided that I dropped her. She thought it was all Kaya's idea and since then, she has hated both of us. I initially felt guilty about everything, but I'm pretty comfortable with my contempt for her after that.

"Alright, everyone," Hugh pipes up, "The title of our final high school play is, drum roll please ..."

Willow plays the snare on her thighs, but she's the only person who participates.

"*Requiem*!" Hugh looks at us expectantly.

My first thought is that it's a pretty name, but I have absolutely no idea what it means.

Hugh catches on to everybody's confused stares, so he continues, "Oh, a requiem is a song for the dead. The story is about a woman who commits multiple murders in her town and then writes the requiems the town will sing at the funerals. It's kind of a historical fiction."

Oh no. It plays out in slow motion in my head. Silence fills the room. A few heads slowly turn to me, not even trying to hide the fact they are staring directly at me. Even Willow looks shocked. That's when you *know* something isn't acceptable.

I mean, a girl in your class lost her entire family to the town's serial killer, and you put on a show about a town serial killer? I always thought Hugh wasn't the most excellent writer, but this is purely tone-deaf.

"Are you fucking kidding me, Hugh?" Evelyn asks. Hugh looks taken aback, clearly not anticipating such a negative response. His eyes follow other people's gazes until they lock onto mine.

"I-I think I'm going to go," I stutter, shakily grabbing my things and walking toward the door.

"Wait!" Hugh says, calling for me to stop as he races over, "I'm so sorry. I know that this story may pull a few heartstrings considering new circumstances that were not present when I wrote it."

"Making me relive the moment of finding my parents and siblings dead is not *'pulling a few heartstrings,'* Hugh!" I spit.

"But this story doesn't entirely revolve around the actual murderer; instead, it focuses on the town and how the people this person hurt turn their trauma into something useful or productive."

It doesn't help. Not in the slightest. He clearly has no social awareness and didn't think about how this would affect me. I want to turn on my heel and leave the room. I want to escape to the parking lot, run away and never turn back. But I can't. If I leave, if I break down again, my aunt is going to call my therapist and I'm going to end up back in the looney bin. That's something I can't risk. Not anymore.

"Please, sit. We can read through it, and if it's too hard for you we can pick something new," he says with a smile.

I've never been crazy about Hugh because of the whole connection to Willow thing, but I gain some respect for him at that moment. He's willing to scrap the play he has been working on for years to make me comfortable. I think he's hoping for me not to take him up on that offer because as he waits for my response, he fiddles with the silver cross around his neck. I drop my bags and cautiously walk back to my seat, and Hugh lets out a relieved sigh. The class goes back to normal, despite some tension lingering in the air.

"Are you sure you're okay with this?" Kaya whispers.

"Yeah, I'm fine. Sorry about that," I whisper back.

Hugh hands each of us our scripts with our name and

character labeled neatly on the front cover with his near perfect handwriting. On the inside cover is the cast list, and what do you know? Willow is the main character. The woman who commits the murders. Typical. She can't even hide the obnoxious grin sprawled across her face. A part of me wants to tell him to scrap it just to watch her crumble. The rest of us are subjected to being townsfolk, except for Fergus, who plays the executioner—a part with no lines and who wears a mask the entire time. I'm okay with that. I flip through the pages, and to my surprise, it's not as triggering as I thought it would be because we don't get to see any of the murders. But I can't shake one thought from my brain as I flip through it.

This took two years to write?

Chapter Four

Willow - 9:20 AM – Thursday, 27th January 2022

For the remainder of the class, we lightly blocked some scenes, seeing as Ms. H isn't here to direct us. I thoroughly enjoy the play, and my character, Abigail, has a lot of emotional moments with a great character arc. A genuine meaty part, just like Hugh promised.

We block a scene where Abigail stands trial before the town as they seek vengeance for all they have lost. Five minutes before the bell rings, Caleb stands on a chair and loudly claps three times. We all turn around.

"Hey everyone. I just wanted to say how excited and sad I am to be doing our final play in high school, and a huge thank you to Hugh for writing an excellent script. Going out with a bang!"

He and Hugh chuckle. They are best friends and all, but my god, they kiss each other's asses every chance they get. I bet Hugh hates it. He continues, "I know we've had our ups and downs as a group."

I notice Noa and Kaya share glances. Eff off.

"But I'm really going to miss you guys. I truly mean that. So, I have been doing some thinking, and I thought it could be a cool idea if we all went up to my family's lodge in the

CHAPTER FOUR

mountains this weekend—"

"Your family has a lodge?" Hugh interrupts.

"Hugh, how do you not know this?" Caleb shakes his head. "It would be an amazing chance to do some final bonding, reminisce about our time together, or make amends with people you've had issues with over the years."

I can feel Noa's eyes stabbing me in the back. I even notice Caleb's subtle glance over at me.

"We can even work on our characters and try to make this the best play we've ever put on. Whaddya say?"

There is a moment of silence, which is broken by Samuel and Arthur, "Hell yeah!" "When do we leave?"

"Tomorrow," Caleb says directly after. "After school."

"Sweet," Samuel responds.

One by one, everybody agrees. Hugh couldn't sound more thrilled. "I'm dying to see this lodge."

Finally, it's just Noa and I who haven't said anything. I look over at her when she softly says, "I guess," followed by a cheer from the class.

Then everybody's eyes turn to me. I don't know what to say. I can't just leave for a weekend trip with a day's notice. My dad would have never allowed that. But then again, he isn't here. I should stay. These people don't like me for some reason, and I'm not too fond of them either. But then I think about what else I would be doing—probably picking up wine bottles left around the house. I turn to Noa, and I see a comforting smile. Just the corners of her lips are upturned. I missed that smile.

"I mean, sure. Why not?"

Another cheer from the class, and I can't help but grin.

Caleb speaks again, "Okay, it's settled. I'll text you all the details tonight. But probably meet at my house at 3:30 p.m.

after school tomorrow. My parents own a few vineyards around Colorado, and we have a Sprinter van for tours. We'll take that up. This is going to be great."

The bell rings, and people begin walking out. My stomach flutters as butterflies erupt inside me. Excitement about seeing my theater class outside of school is a new feeling. Maybe this could be the start of something new. Maybe this is when people will decide to give me a chance and stop blindly hating me because they've been told to. I find myself walking out of the classroom, just waiting for it to be tomorrow.

II

THE SEQUENTIA

Chapter Five

Willow - 3:30 PM – Thursday, 27th January 2022

When the bell rings, I basically run out of my last period of the day, AP Psychology. Although I'm definitely more of an artistic individual, I love psychology and found out last year that I am excelling at it. It's something about how the brain is wired, and its complexity intrigues me. Mr. Riley believes I have what it takes to be a successful psychologist, but I genuinely have no interest in that.

"It could be a valuable backup plan," he tells me.

I don't want a backup plan. No, I don't *need* a backup plan. From years of training and receiving feedback, I have zero doubts that I will be a performer. In class, we learned about psychopaths, sociopaths, and narcissists and the differences between each. Of course, there was an unusual silence and a few objections when the term "psychopath" was brought up. A few people who haven't been directly affected by the maniac got anxious and offended on other people's behalf. Again, I understand that this whole Telluride Maniac business is upsetting, but we have to move on. We need to learn the curriculum. Life doesn't give out trigger warnings for any sensitive topics.

While learning about narcissists, I couldn't help but think of Kaya and Caleb, smothering Noa in an attempt to make themselves look good in front of everybody. It's disgusting. They probably don't even care about her; they just want the attention that comes with being connected to the sob story. They don't know Noa like I did. The Noa I knew would hate all of that attention. She was usually more comfortable fading into the background.

I walk down the hallway, the exit in sight and a slight skip in my step. I'm meant to be meeting Hugh in the parking lot to get frozen yogurt. I pass the group of popular girls standing at their lockers. They give me their usual side eye, and then I hear the familiar laughter that follows. Noa and I used to be friends with our school's "Regina George," Andi, in freshman and sophomore years, but as we went into junior year, she deserted us for a new group of friends. Now they all laugh at us—the "weird, cringe, theater kids."

It was fine for Noa because it's true for her. She was already friends with Kaya, Caleb, and the rest of the theater class, but I wasn't. Being seen with them is embarrassing. They need to know we're not friends.

"What?" I say, turning around to face the group of girls.

They abruptly stop snickering, and some even look a little guilty. Andi doesn't.

"Nothing," she says as a smirk spreads across her face. "We're just wondering where all your friends are."

I feel my face burn with embarrassment.

"They're not my friends," I inform the group.

"Oh, okay," Andi says. "So you have none?"

Then, they all laugh, and my stomach sinks. I don't know why I'm letting them affect me like this. Nobody affects me.

CHAPTER FIVE

My eyes lock onto Andi, and I can't physically stop myself from saying, "Hey, Andi, do you remember when we were friends in freshman year, and you told me you and your brother practice kissing?" I ask her. "Do you guys still do that?"

Andi's smirk is replaced by pure horror. Then, she chuckles and looks around at her friends. "That—she's lying," she says, her chuckle fading as she realizes her friends aren't laughing.

"You know, if you delete texts on your phone, I can still see them on mine," I say as I wiggle my phone in front of my face. Then, I turn around, triumphant, and walk towards the exit. As I push open the door and walk outside, Hugh is nowhere to be seen and I am instead greeted with the sight of Noa and Kaya standing against the wall, talking to each other. I manage to sneak past them and make it halfway across the parking lot when Noa speaks up.

"Hey, Willow!" she yells.

I stop in my tracks. I could keep going and pretend I didn't hear, but I'd already stopped. I take a deep breath and slowly exhale through my nose. Then, I turn around. "Hey," I shout back.

Noa wears a nostalgic smile as she beckons me over. Grudgingly, I approach them. Noa's warm but Kaya is ice cold. She's clearly confused as to why Noa is reaching out like this.

"Hey," I say awkwardly, "Um—I really have to head home."

Noa's face sinks a little, clearly disappointed with my lack of effort, but Kaya looks pleased.

"Oh," Noa says. "Well, anyway, I'm excited to have you on the trip."

I have to force my smile as I say, "Thanks. You too" and begin to walk away. But I stop and turn back around.

"Hey, have you guys seen Hugh?" I ask them.

Kaya makes direct eye contact with me and then looks away, completely ignoring me. Oh my god, she's so rude. Noa thinks for a bit until she finally says.

"Yeah, I think he's with Caleb."

I feel a rush of betrayal flow throughout my veins. I understand they're best friends, but we made these plans days ago. Why does Hugh always pick Caleb over me?

"Oh, okay," I say, trying my best not to sound disappointed. It doesn't work. So, I turn around and walk towards my car without saying anything more.

"Bye," Kaya calls. I'm not sure if it's just because I hate her, but she sounds incredibly bitchy. I pretend I don't hear her and open my car door.

I get into the driver's seat and throw my backpack in the back. I lock the doors and let out a sigh of relief as I rest my head on the steering wheel. I haven't talked to Noa in such a long time. It feels strange that she's finally reaching out. More than strange. It feels too late.

I want to ignore her and continue with my life, but as I pull out of the car park, I catch a glimpse of her being picked up by Kaya's mom. A pit opens in the depths of my stomach. I miss her.

I'm annoyed at Hugh. If it wasn't for Caleb's weird obsession with him, I would be eating frozen yogurt with my boyfriend, not having to drive home and spend the afternoon with my most likely inebriated mother. It's fine. I'm sure it's just a misunderstanding. But those are becoming a more common occurrence.

The drive home isn't long, and it feels shorter with my show tunes playlist playing. I want to sing along to "She Used to

CHAPTER FIVE

Be Mine" from *Waitress,* but I'm distracted. I can't focus on anything except Noa. I hadn't even considered that we could ever restore our relationship, but today made me feel like there was a chance. I'm sure Kaya will have some sort of objection against the two of us, but at the end of the day, it's not up to her.

At least we have a weekend trip to talk things out. *Maybe.* Most likely not.

I pull my car into the garage, step out and grab my bag, all while the garage door comes to a deafening close. I throw my backpack over one shoulder and walk inside. My mind is full of conflicting emotions. Everybody seemed excited to have me at Caleb's lodge, and that made me feel wanted for the first time in a long time. However, if I go, I'm trapped with Noa for a whole weekend, and that makes my stomach churn.

Slow down. I don't even know if I'm going yet. I stop by my room and throw my bag on my bed. As I'm leaving, I catch a glimpse of my closet. It's open. Why is it open? Has my mom been in my room today? Panicked, I practically run towards it and slam it shut before stomping down the hallway to the living room. There she is. My mother is sitting on the couch with a glass of wine in her hand. At first glance, it doesn't look too bad. One glass is fine. But when I look at the kitchen counter, I see the empty bottle of grocery store Pinot Noir.

"Did you go in my room today?" I ask my dazed mother.

She doesn't respond right away. "Hm? Oh, no. I didn't, honey," she slurs.

I know I won't be able to get a clear answer out of her anyway, so I drop the topic. Besides, knowing her, she wouldn't have left the living room at all today.

"Hey, Mom," I begin. She doesn't acknowledge me, but I

keep going anyway. "A few of my friends are going to a lodge this weekend and invited me. Can I go?"

I wait for her answer. Part of me wants her to say yes, and the other half wants her to say no so this whole awkward situation can be solved without me having to do anything.

"Um," she groans. "Ask your father."

I feel my face go red. I wasn't expecting that, but I guess I should have been.

"I can't," I say, "He's gone."

This catches her attention, and she swings her head around to face me. She looks hurt. As if I'm the bad guy for not allowing her to live in these twisted delusions.

"He isn't, Willow," she says through tears she's trying to choke back.

"He is, Mom," I tell her as my voice gradually rises. "He's gone. He left."

"He'll come back," she says, sounding completely delusional. "He'll come back for me."

My anger escapes my body in a laugh. "No!" I shout. "No, he won't! I get that you're grieving, but it doesn't give you the right to shut down and forget about your daughter!"

"I'm not grieving!" she rebuts. "He's not dead!"

"Just give it up," I say, defeated. "Please."

My mother looks at me, and for a second, she seems remorseful. Then, she scoffs and shakes her head. "You wouldn't understand."

"Really?" I ask. "I wouldn't? Has it ever occurred to you that I lost a father? Oh my god, you're so fucking selfish!"

"Language!" she slurs.

"Oh, fuck your fucking language!" I scream. This always happens. Every time I try to talk to her, it ends in a screaming match. The one good thing about this is that now I want to go to the lodge. I need to get away from her.

"Whatever," I say. "I'm going to the lodge with friends. People who want to spend time with me." That's a lie, but I want to make her feel guilty. I can tell by looking at her that she's not processing anything I'm saying, so I turn around and walk back to my room, slamming the door behind me. I want to scream. I hate that woman. I can't believe I'm related to her.

I stay in my room all night, not even leaving to get something to eat. I can't bear to have one more conversation with my mother. I grab my suitcase from my wardrobe and lay it flat on the floor. I fill up the entire thing and grab another smaller bag, which I have to sit on to close the zip. It takes about fifteen minutes, but the whole time I want to claw my eyes out and cry.

I finally get it closed and lie on my bed, completely out of breath. I look at my phone and realize it's almost nine o'clock. I've been so busy that when I get a free night like this, I need to use it. I go to my bathroom, put my hair into a ponytail, wash my face, and brush my teeth. Then, I get into bed. I switch my lights off and am about to plug in my phone when it starts ringing. I think about declining the call and going to bed, but I answer. Hugh.

"Hello?" I say, accentuating my groggy voice, hoping he will get the hint.

"Hey, babe," he says. "What you up to?"

"I'm just trying to sleep," I tell him, but again, he misses the cue. "What do you want?"

"Just wanted to know what you thought of the play," he says. "Did it live up to expectations?"

I can't help but roll my eyes.

"I loved it," I say with fake enthusiasm, and I hear his sigh of relief from the other line.

"Oh, good!" he says. "And the part?"

"Yes, Hugh, I love the part," I tell him. "Thank you for giving it to me."

"You're welcome," he says. "You'll do amazing."

"Thanks," I respond.

There is a pause in the conversation. Sometimes I wonder if the only thing we have in common is theater. I really have to think. If it wasn't for us being forced together almost every day, would he still want to hang out with me? All these questions twist and turn at my insides, along with the unresolved annoyance at him ditching me earlier today.

"What did you do today?" I ask him.

"Nothing," he says, almost too quickly. "Just chilled at home."

This strikes me as odd. I know he was out with Caleb. Why would he lie to me?

"Hugh." I sigh. "We had plans, remember?"

His goes silent on the other line for a few seconds before I hear him groan.

"Oh god, Willow, I'm so sorry," he says. It sounds genuine but I can't really be sure. If he could lie to me so easily before, why couldn't he do it now?

"It's fine," I say, interrupting him before he gets a chance to explain. It's occurred to me that I don't care to know where he really was. I just care about the fact he lied.

"No, it's not fine," he continues anyway. "I had a church thing my family forced me to go to."

I go silent. He just said he "chilled at home". He's lied to me once again. Why would he lie to me about being with his family instead of just telling me he was with Caleb? I am thinking about how to bring it up when it occurs to me that maybe Caleb is the one who is lying. Maybe he lied to Noa and Kaya, and Hugh is innocent. Yes, that sounds more correct. Hugh wouldn't lie to me.

"Hugh?" I say. "Do you think this trip is a good idea?"

"Of course I do," he replies. "Why? Do you not?"

"It's not that. It's just …" I falter. "I don't know. I feel like it'll be weird."

"How so?" he asks.

"I don't think anyone likes me," I admit.

Another pause.

"What? No, that's not true," Hugh says, sounding shocked. Another lie. "Babe, don't stress about it. It'll be so much fun. Just… try to be nice while we're there."

"What's that supposed to mean?" I ask. I already know. I tend to be a little hostile towards, well … people.

"Just don't be mean to them, that's all," he says. "I know they're not your favorite people in the world, but please promise to try being friendly. I don't want things to be weird when we're stuck on a mountain."

I can feel a smile on my face. He's being reasonable. "I promise to be on my best behavior."

Chapter Six

Caleb - 9:30 AM – Friday, 28th January 2022

I'm the first one in the theater classroom. On Fridays, I have a study period first, which basically just means extra time to sleep-in. I'm going to need that sleep for the weekend that's about to happen. I have a feeling a lot of late nights will ensue.

But this morning I was grateful for the extra sleep in. I was with Hugh last night. We were driving around for a while, just hanging out, but eventually, he had to go home and call Willow. They have such a strange relationship. She has him completely wrapped around her finger, and he doesn't even realize it. It's like she's his mother. He can't be out too late. He has to call her five hundred times a day. It's uncomfortable. But, him leaving early wasn't so bad as it gave me a chance to make sure everything was perfect for this weekend.

I walk down the small auditorium aisle and take a seat against the wall on the left side. A minute of waiting passes when the door opens, and Samuel and Arthur walk in.

"Hey, bro," Arthur calls.

"Hey," I reply.

The two of them walk between the chairs, and when Arthur reaches the bottom, he walks over to me and sits down. I like Arthur and Samuel. They're really sweet, well, Arthur is. Samuel can be kind of a jackass, but it's all in good fun and neither of them cause any issues. They're like brothers, always bickering and have a crazy back-and-forth banter full of inside jokes, so it's entertaining to be around them.

"Have you read through the script *ten times?*" Samuel asks sarcastically.

We all laugh. Yesterday, after class, we all received an email from Hugh.

'*Hey Team,*

Quick update! Belinda and I have been talking about the play and rehearsals, and we think the best thing for you to do right now is to read through the script at least ten times so you can fully understand the plot, themes, your character's intentions, etc.

Very excited about the trip!'

I love Hugh of course, but god, can he be pretentious. He doesn't even realize he does it sometimes which for some reason makes it slightly endearing. I don't think anybody needed to read through the play ten times to grasp its concept. I mean most of the story feels slightly redundant because the concept is so easy to grasp on the first page. I would never tell him that out of fear of being shunned. Fergus made that mistake once, now look at him. Destined to a life of lineless characters. Also, character intentions? Samuel and Arthur have about five lines, most of which are shared. They're purely there for comedic effect.

"Okay," Samuel starts. "Serious question ..."

"What?"

"What do you bet Hugh and Ms. H are fucking?"

I snort. The question seems so ridiculous, yet completely reasonable.

"I mean, come on," he continues. "*"Belinda"*? Who does that?"

"Does what?" I reply through my giggling. Even though I know it's not true in the slightest, I'm unable to get that idea out of my head—that poor sixty-five-year-old woman.

"Call a teacher by their first name *so* frequently and in your face," he says. "So cringe."

"I guess Willow doesn't fulfill his needs," Arthur says with a shrug. This makes me smirk, but I don't let it show.

"Yeah, and you just know Ms. H knows what she's doing," Samuel adds.

"Oh yeah?" I question. "Why is that?"

"She's old," he explains. "She's done some stuff."

The image in my head is starting to become a little less funny, and now I just feel gross.

"Ew," Arthur groans. "You're fucked up. Besides, Hugh would never cheat on Willow. They're endgame."

I quickly stop smiling and swallow the saliva that is pooling in my mouth. Why is it that every time you're trying to be subtle, you suddenly need to gulp very loudly? I really hope they're not endgame. I think Hugh will come to his senses soon enough.

"They make me want to end my game," Samuel utters. I just stare at him until he clarifies. "Kill myself, I mean,"

"That was terrible," I say as Arthur and I start laughing, and Samuel tries to explain how it was actually funny, but in an understated way.

Then, the auditorium door opens once again, and Riley walks through. She gives us her usual little wave and walks down the steps. However, her smile fades when she takes her eyes off us. Something is up. She is as pale as a ghost. Is she sick?

As she reaches the bottom of the seats, Samuel shouts, "Hey, Riles, Caleb wants to know if you think Hugh and Ms. H are fucking?"

I turn around and hit him so hard. That was too loud.

"Samuel, you're so nasty," she groans. Good, she knows I didn't say it, at least. But when she walks over to us and sits down, she continues, "But, like, yeah, I do." She gives a chuckle and a weak smile. Something is off, but I can't put my finger on it, so I lean over to her.

"Hey," I whisper. "Are you okay?"

"What? Oh, yeah, I'm fine," she says unconvincingly. "Just a scratchy throat, I guess."

"Oh no," Arthur says. "Will you be okay for this weekend?"

"Yeah," she quickly responds. "I'll be fine. Don't worry."

After a few minutes, the class floods into the room, and the usual cliques form almost instantly. Hugh and Willow stand far away from everyone, but I can see what looks to be Hugh pleading with Willow. Willow stands with her arms crossed, unbothered. What kind of information is she holding over his head to make him stay with her? He's clearly miserable. I realize that not only have I been staring at them for a while, but my eyes have also naturally narrowed at the sight of them together. I turn my head away before they notice me, but my eyes land directly on Arthur, who has been watching me with furrowed brows. He quickly looks away when I notice him. Embarrassment rushes over me, and I immediately feel the need to play it off.

I grab the nearest chair, bring it to the stage and stand on top of it. I speak loud enough for everyone to hear and I notice I am successful in stopping Willow and Hugh's conversation.

"Guys, about this weekend," I begin. "We want to leave my house at around 3:30 p.m., so get there for at least 3:25 p.m. That alright?"

Everyone makes faint sounds of agreement. It's a little dull for my liking.

"Also, my parents are out of town this weekend, so it will just be us!"

This invokes a cheer, which is the response I was looking for.

"And remember to bring your scripts!" Hugh adds.

The cheering stops. I roll my eyes. "Yep. Remember your scripts."

When I look over at Willow, there is a trace of a smile on her face, but she looks uneasy. Then, Hugh puts his arm around her shoulder, looks at her and mouths, *"You'll be fine."*

I don't think she believes him, and neither would I. If everyone hated me the way they hate Willow, I'd be very uncomfortable going on a weekend getaway with them. Surely even she has enough self-awareness to understand that.

The classroom doors fly open again, and Ms. H walks through them. She flows down the aisle like an A-list celebrity walking the red carpet. She's so dramatic. Last year, when we were auditioning for the musical, her feedback was incredibly rough. Like *really* rough. She told us, "That's what the real world is. You're going to face rejection. I'm just preparing you for that."

I guess that's true, but I think when she called Fergus an "Unsettling little boy," she crossed the line. When she finally reaches us, she lifts her arms and authoritatively claps twice to get our attention, even though we are all already silently looking at her. She stands there for a few more seconds. It's so long that I don't know if she's expecting us to say anything. Then, she speaks,

"Why aren't you rehearsing?"

Chapter Seven

Willow - 9:45 AM – Friday, 28th January 2022

I love my part in Hugh's play. Yesterday, we didn't get around to blocking that much of it without Ms. H, but she's back, so we can properly get started. Ms. H doesn't usually talk to us about her personal life unless it concerns an audition or her bragging about some "exciting opportunities." So, she told us that she wasn't in class yesterday because she was attending an audition for a quote "big project."

Apparently, she flew four and a half hours to Los Angeles for a half an hour audition and then flew back. I think Ms. H thinks we're stupid. We have all seen her acting work on terrible student projects and short films, and it's safe to say that she isn't good. She's not even close to being good. There is no way she was called in for an audition of that supposed scale.

Fishy. I guess the phrase "those who can't do, teach" perfectly relates to her.

Before we started rehearsing, Ms. H praised Noa for being back at school. She was talking so loudly we had no choice but to listen. It felt so fake, and Noa looked immensely uncomfortable. She started rubbing Noa's shoulders and was saying things like, "I completely understand what you're going

CHAPTER SEVEN

through," and "I'm here if you ever need to talk." Every single one of us was cringing.

We're rehearsing a scene where my character, Abigail, is being tried, and she has a beautiful moment where she calls out the town for neglecting her and forcing this upon themselves. It's compelling. Considering Ms. H's lack of acting ability, she actually makes a decent director. I am placed at center stage while everybody else surrounds me. The scene is about the town finally gaining the strength to overcome its fear or whatever. Honestly, I think it would be a much better story if Abigail got away with it.

"Stop!" Ms. H calls from the seats. "Just stop. This is making me want to take up drinking again."

She stands up, walks towards us with a chair, and sits down, gesturing for us each to grab one. I thought the scene looked terrific. Well, I thought *I* was terrific and like I was finally connecting with my character. I can't speak for the others. We all sit in a semi-circle, looking at Ms. H, but she just sits there with her head in her hands until she finally looks at us.

"I don't believe it," she says flatly. "I don't believe any of you. When I look up there, I don't see a group of talented actors, I see students. I see children. Talk to me. What's not clicking?"

She rubs her chin as if she's concentrating. A quick glance around the room reveals that everyone is perplexed. I don't know why. Surely when they act, they can tell they're not good.

"Um," Arthur starts to speak up. "I don't know, maybe, this is the first time we're doing it."

I keep a poker face as I groan on the inside. I have always hated that excuse. They should have read the script like Hugh said and come in with a thousand different ideas. It's lazy.

"No," Ms. H says softly with a condescending smile while shaking her head. "That isn't a good enough reason. I think I know what it is. I think you guys aren't connecting with your characters. *I'm* not believing it because *you* don't believe it."

That's probably right. I know the others need to do some serious work, but she can't possibly mean me. My performance was excellent.

"As someone who has years of experience in this industry," she begins, and I can see Kaya choke back a laugh, which would have made me laugh if it was anyone else, "You must fully immerse yourself in your character to tell their story truthfully. You have to live as them. Hugh has written such a beautiful script, and it would be a disservice not to give it your all. I mean, the only one I'm believing is ..."

Here it comes—my recognition.

"Noa," she says.

What? The word doesn't even register with me at first. Is she serious? How is that possible? I dart my eyes to Noa, who looks caught off guard. She must be confused as to why I'm not being recognized either.

"Noa is the only one who I believe," Ms. H continues. "Noa understands what this is about. She's experienced it firsthand. I can see the anger in her eyes as her character looks at Abigail. I want that from all of you."

Noa goes red but Kaya turns even redder. Typical. Noa digs her nails into her thigh and looks like she is about to explode. I understand why the comment could be seen as a little *insensitive* or some other buzzword, but I don't know why she is getting this upset. She just complimented her.

"Are you serious?" Caleb begins. "You want us to almost get ourselves killed by the Telluride Maniac just so that we can seem *believable*?"

"Not *seem*. *Be*," Ms. H responds.

"Are you fucking kidding me?" Kaya spits. "How dare you trivialize her trauma for a school play?"

"That's good, Kaya," Ms. H replies, ecstatically. "Use that. Use that anger."

Kaya seethes. It's pretty entertaining but that's typical Kaya, constantly in a state of second-hand offense. She has nothing to be upset about on her own but loves the attention, so she forces herself into other people's business and gets upset on their behalf. I mean, my father has gone missing, and I'm not offended. She hasn't even dared to ask me about it. For all she knows, my father could be another victim of the maniac. It's unfair we all have to walk on eggshells around Noa, but I don't get that same luxury.

The bell rings, and Noa runs out of the room immediately. Ms. H tries to tell her to stop, but she doesn't listen. Kaya, of course, runs after her.

"Okay, before you go, your homework for this weekend is to meet your character. Befriend them. Be like Noa." Ms. H tells us as she smiles at Noa for an uncomfortable amount of time. When she dismisses us, we all leave without saying a word to her.

I exit the classroom and head for the bathroom, not lifting my gaze from the ground. This is so humiliating. In one of my most significant scenes, I wasn't able to pull focus. Noa took it from me. I would typically work on improving my craft by myself, but now I have to go to a mountain with everyone and work on the scenes together, and everybody is going to know that Noa did better than me. It's okay. I'll just have to show them I can do better.

That I *will* do better.

I enter the bathroom and head straight for the furthest stall from the door. I lock myself in and sit down to pee. My mind is racing with different ways I could have improved. Maybe she simply wasn't watching me. Maybe she didn't notice. But she should have. I am so disappointed in myself for letting somebody else outshine me. A background character of all people. I snap out of my spiral when I hear the bathroom door open and two pairs of footsteps enter.

"That was so fucked up," the familiar voice of Kaya scoffs. "Are you okay?"

"Kaya, I'm fine," Noa reassures her. "She's not trying to be malicious. She's just weird."

I stop my flow of urine, not wanting to alert them that anybody else is in here. The last thing I want is to see Noa right now. I'm so angry at her for getting noticed during *my* scene. Besides, talking to anybody while your pants are at your ankles isn't the most ideal situation. I can see through the slight crack in the cubicle door that Noa is standing with both hands on the sink as she bends over. She's clearly stressed about something. I suppose it must be a little challenging coming back to school after everybody witnessed your breakdowns. I lean a little to the left and Kaya comes into view. She's holding a brightly colored vape and takes a puff from it every thirty seconds or so. I shiver. I hate those things. They're so bad for you. And as a singer, I know how detrimental they are to your vocal cords.

"We don't have to do this," Kaya says softly to Noa. My ears perk up. She's whispering as to not let anybody hear. "Go to the mountain, I mean. We could do it another time."

"No," Noa snaps back. It's strange to see her like this. Every time I've seen her since we stopped being friends, she's been nothing but calm. Except for when she screamed and cried in the middle of the halls, obviously. But this is something else. This is frustration. This is anger. "It has to be today. I need people to stop thinking I'm crazy."

She stops talking suddenly and turns her head to look directly at my stall. The unanticipated movement startles me and I sit back, accidentally knocking the side of the stall. Now she definitely knows someone is in here. I expect them to knock on the door but instead, the girls turn around and hurry out of the room.

I sigh out of relief and lean against the back of the toilet, letting the rest of my pee flow. I'm still grappling with the idea of going to the lodge. I wish Noa had taken Kaya up on her offer to move the lodge trip to another time. I know it's important to Hugh, and I want to be able to spend time with him while his psycho parents aren't around. But everyone else, however, I wouldn't mind avoiding.

Especially Noa.

She seems to be on edge, and I'm not sure I want to be around her when she finally breaks.

Chapter Eight

3:25 PM – Friday, 28th January 2022

It's been almost three months since my last attack, but like many days before, I find myself standing on the sidewalk, looking into the window of a family's home. A woman is standing at the kitchen counter, preparing dinner for her two kids. They look so happy. As Telluride begins to heal, the alarms have been activated less and less often. More and more windows are being left unlocked. It's almost like the town is inviting me back.

It's too easy.

It's not the first time I've been standing outside a stranger's house, waiting for the right time to attack, since I killed that family. I tried once more a month later but somebody caught me. I had to run but they chased me. Eventually, I lost them, but it was too close. After that, I didn't try again. Maybe it was because that was too close of a call, or perhaps it was the police roaming every street, making sure no unwanted guests were making themselves at home in strangers' houses. But I don't think of it like the killings have stopped forever. It's more like they're on hold. And they will begin again eventually. When they do, they will be worse than ever. It's what the town

CHAPTER EIGHT

deserves. They need to be reminded of who I am. They need to remember who is really in charge. They need to experience fear like never before.

I hear chatter and laughter coming from down the road and turn to face it. A group of high schoolers seem to be packing a Sprinter van with small suitcases and travel bags. Where are you going? I step away from the house in front of me, taking one last look at the mother in the kitchen.

I'll be back. Don't worry about that.

"This is going to be the best weekend ever!" one of the boys shouts.

I glance around the neighborhood and watch the kids pile into the van. A tall blond boy gets into the driver's seat. No parents. Then I see her. Noa Ortiz. The one that got away.

They leave the van door open, allowing room for a few more people. They are waiting for someone. With a honk of the horn, I know it's my time to go, and as I walk, I can't stop thinking about how fun this will be.

III

THE KYRIE

Chapter Nine

Willow - 4:00 PM - Friday 28th January 2022

I forgot how carsick I get while driving up a mountain.

My parents used to take me skiing all the time, and I would never be able to make it the whole car ride without vomiting. But this trip hasn't been bad. When we left Caleb's house, I fell asleep almost instantly on Hugh's shoulder. But when I woke up half an hour later, Hugh had moved to sit next to Caleb in the front.

I know it's probably only me being jealous, but Hugh spends *a lot* of time with Caleb, and I think Caleb wants their relationship to be more than just friendship. Again, I do pride myself on being woke, but I would be skeptical if Hugh was spending this much time with another girl. I brought it up to both of them when they were hanging out once. They took it poorly, especially Caleb.

"Just because I'm gay doesn't mean I want to fuck every guy I see, Willow! We've been best friends since before he was dating you!"

I didn't mean it like that, obviously. He overreacted, and I thought he'd get over it. I didn't understand why he had to bring up our separate relationships with Hugh as if it was a competition. I still feel as if I deserve an apology, but I've never gotten one. I pinch my nose and blow out to unblock my ears, since we've climbed in altitude since I fell asleep. And now that I'm awake, I can feel the tiniest bit of nausea growing in my body. I look out the window in an attempt to distract myself from the sickness, and I'm glad I do because it's beautiful. As far as the eye can see, there are sprawling mountains covered in snow, with a frozen river weaving through the trees and heading toward town. I unbuckle my seat belt and slowly walk to the front of the van, trying not to fall over.

"Hey Caleb, do you know how much longer till we're there?" I ask, sticking my head through the front seats.

"Um ... it should be about another thirty minutes?" He responds, not taking his eyes off the road.

Part of me knows he needs to watch the road, especially when that road is on a mountain and covered in ice, but part of me also thinks he should acknowledge me with a hint of eye contact. Even if it's through the rearview mirror.

I give a short, "Thanks," before pressing my lips to Hugh's and giving him a long, *passionate* kiss. When I'm done, I glare back into the mirror and see that Caleb is apparently now okay with looking at me, and he can barely suppress the snarl on his face. It feels great. Now he knows that Hugh is mine, not his. As I stand back up and turn around, I see that most of the class is asleep. Noa and Kaya seem to be tangled in each other's arms, their *clearly* self-dyed hair blending into an eruption of "alt." Evelyn sleeps next to Samuel but they couldn't be further apart, both upright in their chairs. Samuel keeps taking quick glances at her and even tries to put his hand on her thigh, but when he realizes I'm watching, he pretends to go back to sleep. I shudder. I really hope this trip doesn't consist of everyone trying to hook up with each other. The thought makes my nausea even stronger.

Arthur rests against the window while Riley is hunched over in her chair, nervously biting at her nails. I guess she doesn't like mountain drives, either. Arthur has his headphones on but they're blasting so loud I can hear his listening to "The Blue Danube" by *Johann Strauss II*. So pretentious. And then there's Fergus. Sitting upright on the single seat in the front row. That boy scares me. He doesn't even have his phone, a book, or even the script in front of him. I mean, I guess he doesn't have any lines, so that's fair enough. As I walk back to my seat, the van makes a sharp turn, sending me toppling onto Fergus's lap. My already present nausea mixed with Fergus's unique scent brings me close to puking. I pick myself up and brush off my sweater, glaring at Fergus. He smirks at me, as if anything I just did was on purpose. I scoff and glance back to the front seat, where I notice Caleb grinning from the rear-view mirror. Asshole.

I stomp back to my seat. I try to go on my phone, but the service is spotty as we ascend higher up the mountain, constantly going in and out. It's not like anybody will be trying to reach me, anyway. I put my phone away and turn my head to stare out the window once more. Thinking about how close my head was to Fergus's nether regions and the smug look on Caleb's face makes me more and more nauseous by the minute. I take deep breaths, trying to remember my breathing exercises from this morning. I watch as the cliff's edge gets further and further away, as Caleb takes a turn down a quiet road covered with trees on both sides. The van becomes livelier as more people wake up, which might have something to do with what seems like the thousands of potholes Caleb insists on hitting. Which really makes me want to throw up.

"Caleb!" I call instinctively. "Can you pull over, please?"

"We're like five minutes away, Willow. Hold your pee."

I wish it were pee. Oh god, I wish it were pee. "No—" it's too late. I can't speak. Something's coming. A look of understanding flashes on Hugh's face, and he whispers to Caleb.

"Shit," Caleb says as he quickly pulls the van off to the side of the road. Noa gets up to open the door for me. Just in time, too, because the second I get a hint of fresh air, it's over. As I release what feels like ten gallons of liquid into the ditch beside the road.

From inside the van, Arthur yells, "I've heard of yellow snow but never orange."

To which Samuel replies, "Nah, man. That's green."

Chapter Ten

Hugh - 4:30 PM - Friday 28th January 2022

The van sits in front of a ginormous wrought iron double gate attached to magnificent stone pillars, with a driveway stretching across a snowy clearing and neatly trimmed hedges and Ponderosa Pine trees on either side. The lodge appears to be hidden behind the foliage, quite a distance down the drive, but the triangular peak of the building peers out invitingly.

"Caleb, this is incredible," I stutter, utterly astonished at what I am seeing.

"What? This old thing?" Caleb says with a smirk while climbing out of the van.

How have I never heard of this place before? Caleb is usually quite humble and always has been. He never talks about the incredible things he does. He's the complete opposite of Willow. Anytime someone tries to compliment him, like after a performance, he goes red and laughs it off with self-deprecating humor. So, it doesn't wholly shock me that he never mentioned his family's second home. Trees engulf the van and cover us from both sides. The only thing peeking above them is what I think to be a fire tower on a hill, far off in the distance. I watch through the windshield as Caleb opens the gate manually. I think it's strange as there is a keypad perched on the stone pillar, so I open the van door and step out, walking towards Caleb.

"Why can't you use the keypad?" I ask.

"Um, well, the mechanism freezes over in the winter and they won't open. It's a pain in the ass, but oh well," he says with a shrug. "Hey, could you help me with the other one?"

I gladly do. I wrap my bare hands around the metal bars but pull them back quickly. The metal is freezing cold. Caleb laughs at me from behind the bars and when I look at his hands, I realize he's wearing gloves. My palms feel like they're on fire and the cold air is already making them go stiff. I rub them quickly against my chest which brings a little life back. It's icy on this mountain, about sixteen degrees Fahrenheit, and even my ski pants and puffer jacket aren't enough to shield me from the wind. Every second my hands are exposed they grow stiffer and stiffer. I hope the lodge has good heating. I pull my hands into my sleeves and use them to grab the gate. As I'm about to start pushing, I notice a cleanly shoveled patch of snow behind the gates. Just enough has been cleared to give room for the gates to be opened. Almost like someone was just here.

"Caleb, has anybody been here recently?" I ask him. "Anyone that could've shoveled this snow?"

The question catches Caleb off guard. I don't think he'd even noticed the snow behind the gate. He looks past the gate and studies the snow. His face looks alarmed but it soon relaxes and he begins speaking.

"Oh wait, yeah. My dad was here yesterday or the day before, picking up some things Mom needs for work. It hasn't snowed much so it's still visible. Fuck, you scared me for a second."

CHAPTER TEN

I scared *myself* for a second. I thought our weekend trip was about to be thwarted by Caleb's parents. Although, when I think about it, I know his parents are far more laid back than mine. Caleb's parents understand that seniors drink, and they would just urge us to be careful. They probably would have let us do whatever we wanted. My parents, however, do not understand that. They always expect perfection from me. No drinking, no parties, no fun. All they think people should need is school, work, and church. There's no need for all that other stuff. I used to subscribe to that way of thinking. I used to believe that was obvious. But it's not, and as I grow older and realize that's not what kids my age do, I have started to question it. Not to them, but to myself. Yet, even after all my research and forming my own opinions, I still hear their voices in the back of my head, telling me what to do. And sometimes, I listen to it.

I push the second gate back, beginning to make room for the van. It slides effortlessly thanks to the pre-shoveled snow but as it clicks into the open position, my feet lose grip and begin to slide. I'm going down. I hit the ground with a thud, landing on my side, and Caleb rushes over to me, half laughing and half asking if I'm okay. But I just lie there, making peace with my embarrassment. The snowy rocks burn my cheek, and I quickly roll onto my back. I let out a single chuckle. Caleb grabs my arm and tries pulling me up, but I've already gone total dead weight. We laugh as he drags me around in circles until finally, his feet give out too, and he lets out a high-pitch shriek as he falls to the ground, his face mere inches from mine. We cackle loudly until the laughter fades, and we are left staring each other in the eyes. A few seconds, or minutes, go by until our trance is interrupted by the sound of the van's horn blaring. We look towards it to see Kaya's face staring out of the windshield.

"Are we going to drive or what?" Kaya's muffled voice calls from the van.

"Coming right away, your majesty," Caleb calls back, getting up from the ground. I can't help but smile at his playful, lighthearted nature. It's so freeing. He walks to the van, not before looking back at me, still on the ground.

"Get your ass up."

He climbs into the van and shuts the door, and I follow suit. I slam the door and exhale. The warmth of the vehicle makes my fingers and left cheek begin to tingle as my temperature slowly rises. Caleb drives up the driveway, and as he drives further and further, the trees on either side of us disappear and the lodge finally reveals itself, and it's beautiful. Rows and rows of pine logs create the towering walls, with black steel lining the windows, door, and roof. The pure white snow emphasizes the black timber that makes up the roof. Everything about this house is perfect.

Caleb parks the van just in front of the garage doors, and one by one, the whole group clambers out of the van, stretching their legs, not seeming as impressed by the house as I am. The lodge sits in the middle of a snowy plain that stretches for a hundred yards in every direction. Then, there is nothing but trees and mountains. The sight alone takes my breath away and all I want is to see the inside of the cabin. Caleb opens the back of the van and hands people their luggage. Evelyn and Riley get theirs first and then trudge through the snow to the front porch. Everybody seems to have appropriately sized bags considering the length of the trip, except Willow, who, of course, has a suitcase that looks like she's moving in permanently. Watching her fall behind the group while she's trying to wheel her case through the snow is amusing. Finally, she gives up and looks at me in agitation, insinuating help is required. I grab her suitcase, lift it, and … holy shit, this is heavy. Has she put bricks in here? Perhaps she's planning on building another lodge. The walk to the porch is about twenty yards but her bag makes it feel like twenty miles.

We catch up to the group as Caleb struggles with the keys. I drop the bag on the wooden floorboards and for a second, I think the entire lodge is about to collapse.

"Huh, I think the lock is frozen."

This is met with numerous groans from the group, including me. It is unbelievably cold outside. My nose has already started streaming and my eyes keep watering. So, while the rest of them stand helplessly on the porch, I step down onto the front lawn and glance around the property, hoping that moving around might warm me up. I halt. I see something in the snow. Are those fresh footprints? I blink a few times and wipe my eyes to make sure I'm not imagining it, but I'm not. They're there. They lead from the back of the lodge all the way to the woods by the front. I find myself involuntarily following them, but before I can get any further, I hear Caleb call, "Got it!"

I hesitantly turn around and head back toward the house, occasionally glancing behind me. I try not to think about it as I instinctively fiddle with the cross around my neck. Maybe they were just animal prints. But deep down I know what I saw was from a human. What would somebody be doing walking away into the forest?

As I walk through the front door, all my concerns fizzle out, and I am again amazed. The mix of dark wood and gothic fixtures really gets me going. There is a small entry hallway from the front door to the main room. Bare walls and empty side tables lead us into the great room and when we walk in, my jaw drops even further. A gorgeous black antler chandelier fixed with candles hangs in the middle of the room, and one wall is dominated by a black marble gas fireplace. *Exquisite.* I walk around the open living room that merges seamlessly into the kitchen. It's beautiful—forest green cabinets with a black marble countertop. There is a door on the other side of the kitchen that I assume is a pantry, but when I open it, I find a set of stairs leading towards a basement. I'm about to walk down when Caleb notices me.

"Hugh, don't go down there. It's not finished, and there are wires everywhere. It's dangerous."

Fair enough. I shut the door and walk back into the living room. Walking around the lodge, I feel so inspired. I picture different stories that could be told here. It's so magnificent, that it could belong to a royal family, yet it's so isolated and gothic that it could be home to a vampire. I pull out my phone and open the Notes App, creating a new note called 'Cabin Story'. I stare at the screen, my fingers hover over the keyboard but nothing comes. I put the phone back into my pocket. I'll come back to it. Maybe I should focus on the play I've just written.

Caleb begins taking people to their rooms, and I'm back on suitcase duty. He leads us into a hallway and of course, Noa and Kaya share the room just off the great room and Riley and Evelyn take the one on the opposite side of the hallway. We walk further down the hall, and Caleb gives Fergus the smallest bedroom to himself. Caleb made it seem out of kindness, but I know Caleb. He knew everybody else

CHAPTER TEN

would feel uncomfortable in a room with him. I know I would, at least.

We walk up a flight of stairs to a landing and arrive at Arthur and Samuel's room. To the right of that is mine and Willow's, with Caleb taking his parents' room on the other side of the lodge. Willow shuts our door and immediately, the room goes quiet. I drop our bags and begin unpacking. Our room has one tiny closet that Willow fills up within seconds, still leaving half of her suitcase unpacked, so I decide to keep my things in my bag. With a great sigh, as if she's worn herself out, Willow lies on the bed, inviting me to join her. I'm not really in the mood. All I can think about doing is exploring this incredible lodge.

"Come on Hugh," Willow pleads. "We haven't done it yet and this is the perfect place!"

"Maybe later," I say distractedly, still fiddling with my cross. I don't know how to tell her I'm not ready. She's right. It is a perfect place to finally do it, but something is stopping me. I can't tell whether it's my parents in the back of my head, or that maybe I don't want my first time to be with... her.

Willow looks annoyed and turns her back to me in what I believe is an attempt at the silent treatment, but I couldn't care less right now, so I turn around and walk out of the bedroom.

As I walk down the stairs and back down the hall towards the great room, I notice some doors are shut, but others are wide open, and the rooms are empty. From one of the windows, I see Kaya, Noa, Evelyn, and Caleb deep in conversation outside while building a terrible excuse for a snowman, all holding vapes. I open one of the large sliding-glass back doors and walk over to them.

As I get closer, I see Kaya look over at me and say, "Hey,

Hugh!" very loudly, which stops the conversation dead in its tracks.

"What are you guys up to?" I ask, wiping my nose and making it very clear that I am looking at the snowman.

"Building a snowman, duh," Kaya replies sarcastically, offering me a puff of her vape, which I politely decline.

"Well, *attempting* to make a snowman," Evelyn interjects. "It looks like shit right now." She chuckles, and I join her.

"Woah, Evelyn," Noa says, covering the snowman's nonexistent ears, "Don't say that about Lil Piss Baby. He can hear you." She's pretending to be upset, but the smile on her face suggests otherwise.

"I'm sorry, Lil Piss Baby, that was rude of me," Evelyn says jokingly as she gives the thing a hug.

"Lil Piss Baby?" I reply with a mix of shock and amusement. "Y'all are sick."

"Hugh, this is a judgement-free zone," Caleb remarks. "If you're going to be a hater, then you can leave."

"No, I'm sorry. It's a beautiful name." The five of us laugh until Noa stops. She is looking at one of the bedroom windows. I notice her smile fade. I follow her gaze to see Fergus staring directly at us, not moving.

"What's he doing?" Noa asks sheepishly.

"Oh, he's harmless. Just a little strange," Caleb explains. As a joke, he waves his arm at Fergus, offering for him to join us outside, to which Fergus responds with a blank stare, and then he closes the curtains. There's a moment of confused silence before we all erupt into cackles. The girls get back to talking about random things that I don't care enough about to pay attention to when suddenly, "Hello?" A strange voice calls out from behind us.

CHAPTER TEN

We all jump at the sudden loud noise. When we turn around, we see a burly, lumberjack-looking man. My heart gets stuck in my throat. What is he doing here? Caleb walks over to him with a confused look. I want to pull him away. We have no idea who he is or what he's capable of. I turn to look at the girls, and they look like they're thinking what I'm thinking. Their eyes are wide and horrified. Caleb talks to the man, and soon the confusion spreads to the man's face. I see Caleb give him a handshake. I start walking over there in an attempt to hear the conversation.

"—this is my family's lodge." I only catch the last part of Caleb's sentence.

"I didn't think anybody would be here this weekend. Nobody let me know," the man replies.

"Yeah, very sorry about that. This trip was kind of a last-minute idea," Caleb explains to the man with a slight chuckle, clearly attempting to be friendly.

"Oh. Okay," the man says hesitantly. His face shows he's still confused but is reluctant to continue the conversation. "Well, it was nice meeting you," the man says as he begins to walk away.

"You too," Caleb calls back to him.

"Who was that?" I ask.

"That was the groundskeeper, apparently. I've never met him, but he knows my parents." As Caleb speaks, I watch the man walk past the front lawn and into the woods, exactly where I saw the footprints earlier, filling my entire body with concern and skepticism.

"Don't worry about him. He seems really nice," Caleb reassures me. "Anyway, I have to show you something I think you'll love." Caleb walks towards the house, but before I follow, I watch the tree line for a few more seconds. The 'groundskeeper' is gone. The idea of an older man lurking somewhere in the nearby forest unsettles me, but I don't have time to dwell on it because Caleb leads me back into the house. We walk down a different hallway and up a more extensive flight of stairs, stopping at a door. There's only one room on this floor. His parent's bedroom.

"What is it?" I ask, following him into the bedroom. Caleb shuts the door and locks it behind him. He approaches me. His lips meet mine then the sweet taste of his tongue crosses my own. Any stress or anxiety fades into nothingness. All I can think about is the person I love standing right in front of me. I know it's wrong to cheat on Willow, but at this moment, nothing matters. I grab his lower back, and we fall back onto the bed.

Chapter Eleven

Noa - 7:00 PM - Friday 28th January 2022

The sun begins to set over the mountain, and the sky turns bright orange with specks of lavender. The service on the mountain isn't great. It works but it's incredibly slow, so we had to get creative. We have spent the day making snowmen, playing cards, and discussing plans for the weekend. However, we found a sweet spot for signal in the living room so naturally, the first thing we did was karaoke in the living room. It was exactly what you'd expect. A bunch of theater kids doing karaoke is usually a recipe for cringing, but it was actually really enjoyable. Kaya, Evelyn, and I sang "Meet the Plastics" from *Mean Girls.* Caleb sang "Out There" from *The Hunchback of Notre Dame* which blew everybody's minds. It made me realize it was the first time all of us have hung out as a group outside of school, and I'm shocked we haven't done it sooner. We had such a great time and then Willow emerged from her room for the first time today, clearly in an attempt to "impress" us all with her voice. She sang four songs in a row to nobody's delight. After that, the activity was pretty much dead, so we started making dinner.

We make pizzas and as we sit down, Hugh begins speaking.

"I think now is the perfect opportunity for us to revisit the play."

There is a collective eye roll. Everybody here but Hugh, and Willow, understand that the play is not the real reason we came up here. Still, Hugh disappears into his room and quickly reemerges, holding the pile of scripts. Caleb has the idea to break into his parent's alcohol cabinet, which all of us secretly agree would be the easiest way to get through this. Riley, however, seems very nervous about the idea.

"Won't they notice?" she asks.

"They'll be fine," Caleb says, putting Riley at ease. "I'm sure they know what we're doing."

He sets multiple bottles of expensive red and white wine on the table and gives everybody a crystal wineglass. Kaya goes wild, pouring glass after glass, switching between a Pinot Noir and a Pinot Grigio. Evelyn and Riley show far more restraint, only sipping their first glass. Caleb is right along with me, on our second glass but not rushing. We haven't been talking about the script, as Hugh is currently not at the table. He has been forced on butler duty for Willow, making her an Aperol Spritz. She insisted on Hugh making her that because wine makes her "swell up." Jesus Christ.

As Hugh makes her drink, Kaya leans over to me and whispers in my ear, "God, is she trying to look more sophisticated than she actually is? We all know she's broke as shit."

I chuckle at her comment, but I feel a pit deep down in my stomach. That comment was mean and unnecessary, even if it was about Willow. I do not like the girl, but I feel like commenting on her socioeconomic status is entirely inappropriate. I love Kaya but sometimes she tends to take things too far.

"So, Willow, what are you planning on doing next year?"

CHAPTER ELEVEN

I ask, trying to end the painful silence, and trying to put off actually working on the script. It works because Willow lights up at the opportunity to talk about herself.

"Well, I think I might take a year off next year and just do some work around town. Earn some money. And then hopefully I'll be accepted into Juilliard in 2024," she states robotically, almost like it was a memorized answer, spat out to anybody who dares to ask. This response is met with a scoff from Kaya, which Willow notices.

"What was that, Kaya?" Willow asks with a subtle undertone of annoyance.

"Hm? Oh, nothing," Kaya replies. "Just had something caught in my throat."

I roll my eyes. Willow hasn't spoken for more than thirty seconds and a fight is already beginning to break out. I would rather be working on the script.

Never mind, no I wouldn't.

I look around the room to see Evelyn is very much enjoying this. I know everyone hates her, but they should be playing that on the down low.

"Oh, okay," Willow replies, leaving a long pause. Then, "It didn't sound like nothing."

Here we go.

"That's strange. What did it sound like, Willow?"

"It almost sounded like you don't think I could get into Juilliard."

"That's an impressive assumption to make from me clearing my throat."

Just as Kaya says this, Hugh walks back into the room, holding Willow's Aperol along with two six-packs of beer and a glass of water for himself. Arthur, Samuel and Fergus take a bottle of beer each but stay silent, wanting to catch every word of this brawl. Hugh hands Willow her Aperol, for which she thanks him, and then goes back to scowling at Kaya.

"Okay, I want to read through this script and understand our characters and their motives," Hugh tells us.

Ugh, that didn't last.

Most people at the table look disappointed that Hugh has put an end to the conversation, but we follow his instructions anyway. We sit at the table for hours, asking questions and going through scenes. And sure, the play isn't Shakespeare, but it *is* better than I first thought. But the question that's been on my mind for a day has been answered. Did it need to take two years to write? Absolutely not. It's very elementary. Each act named after a section of Mozart's Requiem. I groan on the inside. A child could come up with that.

After all the wine disappears and Willow is halfway finished with her Aperol Spritz, I feel the urge to ask a question. "Hugh, I know you said the play focuses more on the town, rather than the killer. But there are a lot of scenes with just the killer, kind of making us feel bad for her. I think, just, you know, maybe some of those scenes should be cut down. Considering what happened to... in our town."

I had wanted to ask it as soon as we read the last page of the play. It's something I noticed throughout the entire readthrough. It all felt a little too glamorizing. I know that some people may not be happy with what I have to say, and by "some people" I mean Willow. I sneak a look at her and see that she has turned red.

"But every character needs human qualities, or they'll be one-dimensional," Willow retorts. She sounds significantly more aggressive than my calm and composed tone.

"But the issue is that the story spends a lot more time focusing on the woman with murderous tendencies rather than the actual townspeople we're supposed to be uplifting. Half of us don't even have names, let alone 'human qualities.' Maybe the killer could be the personification of evil and represent everything wrong with the town."

I know I'm right. Half of the characters in the play don't even have names. We're known as "Townsperson #1, Townsperson #2" and so on. Reading through it triggers me slightly. It reminds me of Telluride and how the media has dealt with the "maniac" situation. They all focus on the killer, rather than the victims. The only thing people care about is the person behind the killings, not the people directly affected by them. I can see everybody around the table nod agrees, although I can't tell if it's because they agree with me or because they want Willow's part to be cut down.

"I think the killer is simply the more interesting storyline," Willow begins. "I understand what you're saying, and I get where you're coming from, but as someone who has gone through a similar thing, I'm not sure I agree with you."

My blood boils as I listen to her speak. This entire night, I have tried to give her the benefit of the doubt. Every time somebody has made fun of her, I haven't supported it, but holy shit she makes it hard. I know what she's referring to. Her dad's disappearance. It's almost like she wants a slice of all the unwanted attention I've received from our peers and the media. So, she's using her dad leaving her as a means to obtain it. She has been going around school saying her dad might have been one of the victims, fishing for sympathy. But everyone knows that he was a drunk.

"It was just a suggestion," Arthur says innocently, coming to my aide. I'm sure he can see how much I'm seething at the moment. If I try to respond right now, I doubt anything remotely positive will come out.

"Okay, well, the play is already written, so we can't just change it now." Willow chuckles, glancing at Hugh, hoping for support, but instead, Hugh has a look of contemplation on his face, something Willow was not expecting.

"I think we could," Evelyn says, backing me up and struggling to hide a smirk.

"I see what you're trying to do, Noa," Willows spits out, leaning towards me with her eyes narrowed. "You just want my part to be smaller because ... because you're jealous of me!"

Kaya laughs. "Oh my god, Willow, absolutely *nobody* is jealous of you—"

"Shut up, Kaya!" Willow squeals, interrupting her. "Nobody was talking to you!"

Oh my god, this is getting so messy. Strangely, I kind of love it. But I know for this weekend to work, we need to at least be civil, so I speak up again.

"I'm not trying to cut your part down, but it's hard for me to see a killer getting more character development than the people she hurt."

Willow is about to say something, but Hugh cuts her off. "I think you should calm down. Noa has a point."

I was not expecting that.

Clearly, neither was Willow, as she stops dead in her tracks and, somehow, turns an even brighter red. "You know what? Fine. Cut my part down if you want, but there's no way I'm doing it." She stands up from the table and walks away,

CHAPTER ELEVEN

leaving her half-empty Aperol still on the table. She is about to disappear up the stairs, but she walks back to us. "Oh, and I'm not staying here. I'm going to bed, and tomorrow one of you is driving me home!"

"Willow, don't be like this." Hugh tries to reason with her. It's too late for that.

"You know what else, Hugh? Find somewhere else to sleep because you're not stepping foot in *my* room tonight!"

And that was that. She's gone. The witch is dead. I have unintentionally done what everyone else in our class has been trying to do for years. Knock Willow off her pedestal.

"It's okay. You can sleep in my room if you want, Hugh," Caleb offers, to which Hugh accepts, and then ... he blushes?

Willow has pretty much ruined the vibe, and there's nothing more for us to do than call it a night. One by one, each of us leaves the table and heads to bed. Evelyn, Riley, and I all leave at the same time, leaving Kaya and Caleb the only ones at the table. While I head into my room, I say goodnight to the other two. Evelyn looks as lively as ever as she bids me goodnight, especially after all of those glasses of wine, but Riley seems off. She has ever since we stepped into the van.

"Riley are you okay?" I ask her but I guess it's too late, as she has already vanished into her bedroom. I'll ask her in the morning.

It's a struggle to get to sleep after that. All I can think about is Willow and her outburst, but mainly how she tried to relate to me with her dad. People say insensitive things all the time, but this is something entirely different. I'm sick of her always trying to shove herself into the center of attention.

As I roll around in bed, trying to get comfortable, I notice a noise coming from outside my window. It sounds like footsteps. As they continue, they freak me out more and more until I must look out the window. I pull open the curtain, and the moon illuminates a deer crossing the snowy plain before disappearing into the trees.

Chapter Twelve

The Groundskeeper - 12:00 AM - Saturday 29th January 2022

The forecast had predicted a snowstorm, and I want to be prepared, but I think the oversize wood pile will get me through the weekend with some left over. I have been keeping an eye on the lodge all night, watching the kids sing karaoke, have some drinks, and play what looks to be a drinking game of sorts, which ended badly, with one of the girls storming off. It happens to the best of us. What I keep thinking about is one of the girls. She was one of the girls building the snowman. She looks so familiar, but I can't pinpoint where I've seen her.

I hadn't met the owner's son before. I didn't even know he existed, but he seemed lovely. I tried to give the owners a call to double check it was okay, but I couldn't get through to them. It's not unusual. Phone calls don't always go through up here. Though, I'm sure they allowed all of it. I figured tomorrow I would let them know a snowstorm is coming, and if they want to be able to get home, they might have to cut their trip short. I hate to be the bad guy, but I'm sure they'll appreciate it. Nobody wants to be stuck on a mountain with no way down.

I curl up in my bed and try to get some sleep, seeing as I'm going to need to be up early if I want to clear some of that snow and make it back into town before the storm hits.

My tranquility is interrupted by what sounds like taps on the window. I slowly sit up in bed, looking at the window which is currently covered with a curtain. The taps continue in a slow, irregular pattern. Could it be one of the kids needing help? Surely not. I didn't let them know where I lived. I doubt they know a guest cabin is hidden in the trees. I open the curtains to see nothing. But the moonlight does illuminate the outside just enough to see a branch has been, and still is, tapping my window and creating the sound I heard earlier.

I take a moment longer at the window when I notice something behind one of the pine trees. At first glance, I assume they're branches. But they're different from the rest. Then they start moving. They're antlers. I guess it's a deer. Its body must be hidden by the trunk. I pull on my boots and walk outside in my pajamas. The icy air chills my skin almost instantly. I should have put on a jacket. It's a common occurrence this, having nosy deer, but I like to shoo them away as soon as possible, so they don't get comfortable and decide to stick around. Truthfully, they have always scared me a little. It's silly. I used to have a pet snake.

I approach the deer but as I near the tree, I stop dead in my tracks because it seems so unnatural. There is no body yet, just the antlers. Then, they start to move, and the head of a deer peeks out from behind the tree. But it's not a deer. It's a mask. It's a person wearing a deer mask with antlers. It's somebody luring me outside.

By the looks of it, I am a much bigger person than whoever that deer is and probably could overpower them easily. But

CHAPTER TWELVE

for some reason, my body is filled with terror. A normal, sane person wouldn't pretend to be a deer. This person is unhinged, and I can tell they aren't scared of me or my size.

Then, everything makes sense. Why this person terrifies me so much. Where I recognize that girl from. Noa Ortiz. The only survivor of the serial killer in Telluride. A killer that is standing a few feet in front of me. I feel my heart shrivel. What is he doing here? Has he come back for her?

Just then, the person breaks into a run directly at me. I sprint towards my cabin, but as I get on the porch, I slip on the ice and fall face first, half in the door and half outside.

I claw at the frozen wooden boards and drag myself inside, successfully managing to close the door behind me. I twist the lock and lean against the wood. I wait for the sounds of somebody trying to kick my door down, but it never comes. It's silent, except for the occasional creek of the floorboard on my porch, indicating somebody is still here. He's waiting for me, I know it. So, I don't move, I don't even breathe. Why is he here? What does he want with me?

After a few minutes of waiting, I slowly stand up from the floor and walk to the window, cautious not to make a sound. The closed curtains stare at me menacingly as I know very well there could be someone on the other side, waiting for me.

I slowly peek through the gap to find the porch completely empty. I see no antlers peeking out from behind the trees. I see nobody lurking on my porch. They left. But where have they gone? A pain rips throughout my stomach. Has this clearly violent person headed for the lodge because he couldn't hurt me? If he has, he's headed towards a group of however many defenseless kids. He's headed for Noa. Now, I *need* to warn them.

I reach for the lock and as soon as it clicks open, there is a thud from the closet. I freeze. My body goes cold, and I am immediately one hundred times more aware of my breathing. When I locked the person outside, did I in turn lock somebody else inside?

My fears are justified because after a minute of silence, somebody speaks from the closet. It's not a person's voice, it sounds mechanical. They hiss one word.

"Leave."

I race toward the closet, not allowing them to terrorize me any longer. I swing the doors open and there it is again. A person in the same deer mask is hunched mere inches from my face.

I scream out of fright, before grabbing the masked psycho by the throat. They weren't expecting it because they thrash around but are unable to free themselves. I drag them out of the closet and scream, "What are you doing here?"

They don't say anything. They can't. They swing at me, trying to push me away. It doesn't work. They're much weaker than me. Sure, they look menacing but it's all show. I'm not going to kill them; I just want them out of my house. I am about to drag them to the front door when suddenly, there is a sharp pain in my lower back.

I scream and let go of the maniac. I put my hand over the pained area and when I look at it, it's covered entirely with my own blood. I stumble backwards and out the door. I barely make it five steps into the snow when I am stabbed again. Higher up my back this time and then, everything goes numb.

I can't move. I can't fight. I can't make a sound. I'm paralyzed. I drop to floor like a dead weight and see two pairs of feet step close to me. I slip in and out of consciousness. I can't hear what they're saying, but they argue with each other. One of them even pushes the other. Then, I pass out.

Chapter Thirteen

1:00 AM – Saturday, 29th January 2022

Red snow is something you don't see very often, but it sure is beautiful. The contrast is striking. And it's very easy to clean. I shovel the red snow inside the cabin, leaving the outside a spotless white. The poor groundskeeper didn't do anything wrong except be in the wrong place at the wrong time. He had to go. I genuinely hate killing someone who didn't deserve it, but he could have stopped me. With him here, nothing would go to plan. I wonder if he had a family. Who knows. There is no point in dwelling on that now. I give the man a kiss on the top of his head, a farewell, before placing it on the bed, leaving the rest of his body sprawled out on the floor below.

IV

THE CREDO

Chapter Fourteen

Caleb - 9:00 AM - Saturday, 29th January 2022

I wake to the sunrise peeking through the curtains in the primary bedroom. I take a quick glance at the alarm clock on the bedside table—nine a.m. I roll over to see Hugh still fast asleep on his back. I drag myself toward him and lay my head on his chest, placing my arm on his stomach, careful not to wake him up. Last night was incredible. After Willow had caused a scene, which was quite entertaining, Hugh came to sleep in my room. He took it upon himself to lock the door, but I wasn't complaining.

When we got into bed, we talked deeply about life. More specifically about Willow. He told me how suffocating it is always having to please her and how he feels he's never good enough. I told him how I felt Willow was trying to take my best friend away from me.

He told me that would never happen.

Then, he kissed me.

And I kissed him back. Slowly at first, and then it got more and more passionate. It felt so refreshing not to have to suppress these feelings I know we both have. Hugh was raised in a highly religious household with an overpowering mother and a father who would cut Hugh out of their lives in an instant if they knew their son was gay. We've been posing as "best friends" for years, which has been an effective cover-up, but I can't help but hope for more. Well, we are best friends, but in truth, we're so much more. We promised each other that when we finished school and moved out, we could take our relationship to the next level. I always tell him "Every playwright is gay. You'll fit right in." Hugh objects to that, but we don't know what Shakespeare was doing in his free time and don't even get me started on Oscar Wilde.

A small part of me feels for Willow. Yes, she's insufferable, and I like the personal gratification of knowing her boyfriend loves me more, but technically *I'm* the other woman. I've talked to Hugh about breaking up with her, but he feels terrible. He doesn't want to be cruel and hurt her. That's what he says, anyway.

However, I think it's more like he's scared of his family abandoning him and what Willow will do when she realizes he's been lying and cheating on her. Willow is not the forgiving type. It's frustrating knowing *I* can't do anything or let her know what's been going on. I would never even *dream* of outing him but sometimes I wish he would hurry up and do it himself. Even though I love spending time with him, every time we're together it feels like I'm sneaking around. I feel this overwhelming guilt and fear that somebody will find out and he'll resent me for it.

But then again, through all that anxiety and stress, I see my life with him. When we move out together and share a bedroom like we are now. When we introduce ourselves to people as a couple instead of "best friends" and finally get to be free. It's so close, yet it feels so far. Only one more year, I keep telling myself. But it's not one more year until all of that comes true; it's one more year until Hugh even considers it. And I don't know what his decision will be.

I snuggle my head closer to Hugh's and rub his chest. For a theater kid, Hugh does have an incredible body. I slide my hand along his chest, then gradually move it down his abs until my hand goes under the covers and I meet the hem of his boxers. I stop moving when I feel Hugh's hand on top of mine. I angle my head to look at him. He stares down at me, directly into my soul, with an oh-so-comforting smile.

"Hey," he mumbles cheekily.

"Hi," I reply, with a smile so wide it physically hurts. He grips me harder, and I move my hand to his stomach and grip him into a hug.

"Last night was fun," I tell him. "We should do that more often."

"We absolutely should," he agrees enthusiastically. But we don't do it more often. Why don't we? Last night was the first time we'd ever done it, but I've wanted to do it for a while. We hang out all the time, usually alone, so does he just not want to? Is his family getting in his way? I wish he would tell me.

I suppose he can read my face because, after a while of silence, he turns and whispers, "Caleb, I'm sorry I can't be a real partner for you at the moment. There is so much pressure for me to be the person everyone expects me to be."

This breaks my heart. I want him—*us*—to be happy, but I know that we can't. Not yet. He grips me tight and pulls me closer.

"But trust me, when this high school and family shit is over, I want to spend the rest of my life with you. I-I love you, Caleb."

I jump at the phrase. It's something so unexpected but

something I've been waiting for. I think for a moment that he's moving too quickly, until I remember we've been in a 'relationship' for years. I stare at him and he stares back. My cheeks burn up. We've said "Love you" before but it has always been in a platonic sense. But right here, right now, the words pierce through my skin and implant themselves directly in my heart. This is something completely different to what either of us has ever said to each other, and he says it with such sincerity and honesty that I am on the verge of tears. I've always felt close to Hugh, but honestly, I had never fully considered the fact that I was in *love* with him until now. I love him so much.

"I love you too, Hugh," I respond, my voice slightly cracking.

He smiles as he pushes my hair behind my ears. Then, he brings his lips to mine for a prolonged kiss, full of face touching and morning breath. We kiss as Hugh slowly pushes my hand back towards his boxers. We make contact. While still kissing, I roll myself onto him, putting my legs on either side of his hips, and I rest on his groin. Every worry fades away into oblivion, every doubt that Hugh isn't ready vanishes.

I sit up and look at him. "Round two?"

Hugh responds with an extraordinarily enthusiastic nod.

Before I can remove his boxers, there is a loud banging from the bedroom door. In fright, I jump off Hugh and cover myself with the bed covers, to his disappointment.

Luckily, I do, though, because Willow's shrill voice bores through the door.

"Hugh? I need to talk to you!"

Chapter Fifteen

Willow - 9:00 AM - Saturday, 29th January 2022

My hand brushes over the empty side of the bed where Hugh should have been.

I open my eyes too soon, and they begin to sting. On days like these, I enjoy sleeping with the curtains open as it lets me wake up with the sun. I squint, giving them time to adjust to the daylight flowing into the room. I roll out of bed and walk towards the window. It really is beautiful.

Looking for myself, and not having Hugh yapping in my ear about how amazing it is, makes me appreciate it more. It seems to have snowed a lot overnight, judging by the pine trees on the perimeter of the yard being thick with snow and the half-submerged snowman I can spot from my bedroom.

I really wish I hadn't flown off the handle, but I felt so disrespected. I hated that my boyfriend, the person I *love*, didn't come to my defense. It doesn't matter what he thought was right. His loyalty should be with me. But then again, when I think about it, mine is definitely not always with him. But it's different. They were attacking *me*. The excitement I had felt for this trip, to finally let loose and have fun with these people I have tolerated for four years, had vanished in the span of a night. I was right, I have been right for the past four years. These people are not my friends. They have some sort of personal vendetta against me that cannot be ignored. I suppose it's back to being a lone wolf.

But, my god, I'm bored.

I mean, Fergus is the only one who isn't pissing me off. Maybe I should see what he's up to? Actually, scratch that. On second thought, that's a terrible idea. Unexpectedly, however, looking at the snowman makes me feel slightly left out. Even a bit jealous that all these people are so close, and I'm the odd one out. I keep telling myself that it wasn't my choice. They left *me* out.

I wonder how I am going to handle seeing everybody downstairs. Apologizing is out of the question. I could just blame it on the alcohol, but I don't think that would work after only having half an Aperol Spritz. Hugh did make it quite strong, though. Maybe I can simply stay upstairs. I can say I don't feel well. You know what? No. I don't have to explain myself to anyone. I just won't bring it up and let them initiate the apology.

I pull on a pair of American Apparel sweatpants and the sweater I wore yesterday and take out my fuchsia toiletry bag. In the bathroom, I brush my teeth and begin my skincare regimen. I peel off my pimple patches from the night before, apply my SPF 50+ moisturizer and use tea tree oil on any problem spots while doing a siren lip buzz. When I'm ready, I muster all the courage I can to open the door and make my way downstairs towards the great room. Voices echo around the vaulted room as I enter. Kaya and Evelyn on the couch together, talking about something so funny that they rock back and forth in laughter. Riley is on the armchair across from them, looking just as nervous as she was in the van. I

CHAPTER FIFTEEN

would ask if she's okay if I weren't on my silent mission.

She catches my stare, quickly puts down the hand she is gnawing at, gives me a slight smile, and then drops her head. She is typically a more reserved girl, so maybe she simply doesn't like being surrounded by this type of people for longer than a rehearsal or a school period. Me too, girl. Me too. As I walk past Kaya and Evelyn to get to the kitchen, they stop their conversation and look up at me, but I ignore them and continue my stride. They giggle. Stuck up bitches. When I enter the kitchen, I see Noa. I stop. She has her back towards me as she makes a cup of coffee. She hasn't seen me. I think about turning around quietly and walking out, but just as I'm about to, Noa turns around and spots me. She gives me a smile, which I do not reciprocate. I walk past her, heading directly to the Keurig. As the machine begins rumbling, I glance over my shoulder to see that Noa is still in the kitchen, looking at the ground. My skin crawls out of embarrassment. I hold my breath because, for some reason, I think if I make a sound, she will speak to me.

"Willow, I want to say I'm sorry about last night," she says anyway. Huh, I didn't expect my plan to work this quickly. "I think things took a turn, and more people got involved when they shouldn't have, but I want you to know I wasn't trying to cut down your part to hurt you."

I don't particularly know what to say at this moment. I'm good at many things, but having a heart-to-heart is not one of them. I used to be good at that with Noa but not anymore. The only thing I can muster up is, "Yeah, well. You did."

"I know. I'm sorry. But I want you to know that my issues with the play have nothing to do with you," she says. She doesn't sound angry or like she's trying to avoid a fight, she genuinely does sound sorry. I don't know how to act. I can't really remember the last time somebody apologized to me without me pressuring them into doing it. I finally turn to face her, insinuating for her to continue.

"Willow, I just lost my whole family. It happened three months ago, and I've been doing everything possible to avoid facing reality. I mean, I'm at an isolated lodge in the mountains with my theater class, for fuck's sake." She cuts herself off, and I see tears forming in her eyes. "I don't know if I'll ever get over this pain, but all I want to do is live my life. When I read Hugh's script, and I saw the murderer being the favored character, it reminded me that the person who killed my family is walking free while my family rots in the ground, and it makes me so fucking angry." Tears fall down her cheeks. "All I want is justice. I want that person to burn and suffer. And I thought this play could help me fulfill that need, even if it isn't real. Maybe someday I can separate art from real life, but not yet."

I stand there, completely lost for words. My plan is falling through my fingers. I can't be mad at her. Why am I mad at her? Looking at her now feels like I'm looking at the Noa from middle school. The Noa I would stay up till three a.m. with on the phone, talking about boys. I haven't seen that Noa in a very long time. I'm overwhelmed with guilt. It feels strange. It feels unfamiliar. I feel remorse for abandoning her. For being an awful person. All I can do is walk up to her and embrace her.

Tears roll down my face, and we stand in the middle of the kitchen together in silence. Unbeknownst to me, I had been missing Noa. I have been so lonely these past few years, and I have tricked myself into believing I was alright. I had Hugh but even he has been flaking on me lately. Why does he do

CHAPTER FIFTEEN

that? I feel even more guilt rush through me. Why is this happening? Have I been pushing him away unknowingly?

I seem to be in a forgiving mood, and he is next on the list. There must be something to apologize for, I'm unsure what it is though. I think about making amends with Kaya but when I see her stupid snickering face, I decide against it. With her, my plan is still in action. After walking out of the kitchen, I glance toward the front door and see Arthur and Samuel leaving. I make eye contact with them as Samuel takes a large puff on his vape, before walking outside. They're both in their snow jacket, pants, and boots. Perhaps they just want to look around the property, but I don't have time to ask. I'm on a mission.

I walk up to Kaya and Evelyn and ask if they have seen Hugh.

"I think he and Caleb are still asleep," Evelyn answers whilst Kaya looks down at her phone, not making any effort to answer.

Perfect. I'll go to their room and break up "bro time." I bet that will go swimmingly. I walk down the hall, up the stairs and stop in front of a double door. I lift my hand to knock, but I pause. I don't even know what I want to say to him. What am I apologizing for? Maybe I can subtly get him to tell me, sort of like improv. I put my ear against the door and hear muffled voices. At least I know they're awake.

I knock on the door three times and call out, "Hugh? I need to talk to you!"

Chapter Sixteen

Hugh - 9:45 AM - Saturday, 29th January 2022

Caleb and I race out of bed, rushing to find anything we can wear to make us look presentable for Willow. Anything that doesn't make it look like we were about to have sex. After sliding on a t-shirt that is sitting on the top of my bag, I twist the handle and open the door. She looks at me, probably confused as to why I look so out of breath, and then she glances over my shoulder to see Caleb sliding on his pants, and a look of confusion spreads across her face.

"Didn't I buy you that shirt?" she asks, pointing to Caleb's shirt. Damn. Yes, she did. She said Ben Platt wore it; therefore, she needed to get it for me when she saw it at a store.

"Uh, yeah, um. I let him wear it. It's okay." I rush her out of the room and into the hallway and shut the door behind me. I fear I may have opened the door prematurely, as she continuously looks over my shoulder towards Caleb.

"What's up?" I ask, still slightly out of breath. I remember our conversation from the night before. I mean, it wasn't really a conversation. It was more like we all sat and listened while Willow screamed at us. "Do you want me to take you home—"

CHAPTER SIXTEEN

"No," she cuts me off. "I wanted to apologize."

Woah. This is a shock. Never, in our two years of dating, has Willow apologized. Apologized properly, that is. I've received the odd "I'm sorry that *you felt* a certain type of way," which I accepted as the best I would get. I feel so uncomfortable. Listening to her willingly admit fault for anything is so unsettling.

"Who are you? And what have you done with Willow?" I say with a chuckle, to which she smacks my arm.

"Shut up," she tells me with a smile on her face. I like this, Willow. If I'm being honest, I haven't enjoyed Willow's company for about a year. I've forgotten why I even started dating her in the first place. But I'm ready for her to change. It will make this trip and the rest of this year a little more pleasant. But I shouldn't get my hopes up; there's still plenty of time on this trip for her to turn it all around.

"I feel like I've been caught up in my own shit for so long that I've ruined the two relationships that mean the most to me. All I want is to fix them before I lose them. I just-I just don't want to end up like my father."

Oh no. We're going deep, which reminds me of Caleb. Not entirely in a sexual way, but because I start to feel awful about cheating on this girl who is now pouring her heart out to me because she loves me. Willow has only told me about her father a few times and each time they have been different. She told me he was nice when we started dating, and the one time I saw him outside of school he seemed lovely. But then he started drinking and became abusive. Then he went missing, or left, or was killed by the maniac. That part is unclear. All I know is that Willow would call me in tears because her dad was getting aggressive.

"Willow, you are nothing like your father," I say as I caress her right cheek. She blushes, nesting her face into my palm.

"I love you, Hugh," she whispers.

The obvious response would be to say it back. I should say it back. But something is stopping me. Is it the fact that Caleb waits on the other side of the door, most definitely listening to this conversation? Maybe it's because, deep down, I know I don't love her. Not like that, anyway. I think there was a point in time when I did love her, or I thought I loved her, but that moment is long gone.

"Willow. I-It's just—" The sound of the door opening cuts me off. Thank God. Caleb looks at us, slightly embarrassed, squeezes between us, and walks downstairs. I look at Willow to find she stares blankly at Caleb until he walks out of sight. However, she continues staring directly towards the bottom of the stairs even after he's gone. Not moving. Not blinking.

"Willow?" I say, trying to cut her out of her trance. She looks at me. Directly into my eyes and into my soul. She looks numb. Does she know about Caleb and me?

"Do you not love me anymore?" she asks, with so much hurt in her voice it makes me want to lie. And I do.

"Willow, I love you. I do. I love you so much." This appears to lift her spirits, but it twists and turns my insides. All she wants is to be loved, and I can tell by how she acts and treats people that she doesn't feel loved. And here I am, lying to her face, knowing that one day I will have to tell her the truth. Dwelling on this will make me vomit, so I change the subject with the first thing that comes to mind.

"Have you eaten?" I ask her, and she responds with a shake of her head. "Come on, let's go downstairs. I'll make you something."

CHAPTER SIXTEEN

She smiles, and I lead her down to the kitchen.

Chapter Seventeen

Caleb - 1:00 PM - Saturday, 29th January 2022

Hugh airdrops us the revised versions of the script. He handled it the best way he could. Rather than cut down all of Willow's scenes, he added more 'townsperson' scenes and gave our characters actual names. I mean, everybody except Fergus, who remains the executioner. Poor Fergus. We talk about Willow being bitchy, but dear lord, can Hugh hold a grudge.

If it were up to me, I would have cut down her scenes, but I know if he did that it would cause an even bigger scene. Sometimes my rational mind can be clouded by my hatred for Willow. I know she's rude and annoying, among many other things, but strangely I think the reason I hate her so much has to do with Hugh. In my mind, I think she's trapping him when in reality, he's trapping himself. I understand he has many factors keeping him from being his true self; parents, religion, etc., but sometimes it's hard not to think he just doesn't love me enough. Even right now, he's sitting with her.

Willow actually seems to be in a good mood this afternoon. It's shocking to realize how much of our morale is held down by her negativity because now the energy is the best it has ever been. It's not enough for me to like her, but I don't think anything will ever be, especially not after the last few weeks. However, it's enough for me to tolerate her, at least just for the weekend.

We read through the script as a group, excluding Arthur and Samuel, who went outside at around 9:30 a.m., according to Willow, and haven't been seen since. Evelyn mentioned they were filming content for their TikTok-duo-comedy-motivational account. Yes, it's as bad as it sounds. The idea of them outside in the freezing cold either making a skit or giving life advice to strangers on the internet makes me cringe, even though I know that's not what they're doing.

As we go through the script, I am pleasantly surprised to find out it isn't too bad. Once Hugh added the extended townspeople scenes, the play really shot up in quality. His whole idea of the "empowerment of a scared group" is finally prevalent, and I can tell Noa is actually happy with it. She might even be finding comfort in the story.

We all sit together for the first time without a fight. Willow and Noa oversee the making of lunch; by the looks of it, they're laughing and having fun. That is not something I'd expect to see. I guess Willow is full of surprises today. So is Noa. They make an industrial-sized serving of vodka pasta, which is absolutely delicious, and the whole dish is gone within half an hour. We didn't leave Samuel and Arthur any. If they don't want to join us to eat, that's on them. I went to their room to check on them when Willow asked me to, but of course, they weren't there. We sit at the table well after we finish eating. I actually lose track of time, and when I look at my phone, it turns out we've been sitting down for an hour and a half, telling jokes, sharing stories and engaging in genuine conversation.

"Oh my god, it's 3:30 p.m. already!" I exclaim.

A few people gasp as they take out their phones and realize how long we've been sitting here. Nobody was complaining. It was nice just to sit and chat. It would have been nicer if Hugh sat next to me. I have to admit, most of the time we have been chatting, I've been intensely observing Willow and Hugh. Every time he put his arm around her I wanted to gag. I genuinely don't understand how he can feel so comfortable pretending to love her. When you think about it, it's a little sick.

We all stand up and clear the table. We wash the plates in the sink, but the conversation still doesn't end. When I look back towards Hugh, though, Willow is not with him. For a second, I'm relieved, but then I notice her looking worriedly through one of the many great room windows.

"Willow? Are you okay?" I ask, walking up to her.

"The wind looks like it's getting stronger, like ... a lot stronger," she says. I follow her gaze. She's right. The trees surrounding the plain look like they're about to topple over.

"Guys, can someone check the weather forecast?" Willow asks the group.

A few of them open their phones, and Noa looks shocked. "Uh oh," she says, not scared, but like she's been inconvenienced.

"What?" Willow asks, sounding concerned.

"Apparently, there's a huge snowstorm rolling in," Noa says calmly. "It should only last through the night, but it means we're probably stuck inside for today."

"Ugh, that's annoying," Willow groans. I almost giggle. If this news had been given last night, all hell would have broken loose. But today, I think everyone's relaxed nature, especially

CHAPTER SEVENTEEN

Willow's, puts all of us at ease. Then Willow speaks again, looking concerned, ruining the serenity.

"Wait, aren't Arthur and Samuel still outside?" she says.

"Oh, god," Noa replies, still sounding calm. "Yes, they are. I'll just call them and tell them to come back."

Noa pulls out her phone and dials Arthur's number. She presses her phone against her ear and waits for him to answer. But he doesn't. She looks back down at her phone with a puzzled stare.

"What's wrong?" Hugh asks, but Noa doesn't respond. Instead, she calls him again, pressing the phone against her ear. We stand in silence for another twenty seconds until she pulls the phone away from her ear.

"He's not answering," she says, almost confused. "Let me try Samuel."

She does, but there's still no answer.

"Maybe they don't have service out there", Kaya suggests. "It's been spotty all over the mountain so I'm sure it would be non-existent wherever they are."

Noa considers it, but it doesn't satisfy her. "But the call is going through. They're just not answering."

"Should we call the police?" Willow says, aggressively scratching her forearm, to which all of us look at her like she's crazy.

"Woah! I don't think we're there yet" Evelyn responds. "It's only been a few hours."

She points to the window. "Exactly! It's been a few hours *outside* in a *snowstorm!*"

We all look outside. She's right. The storm is getting stronger, rattling the windows and bending trees what seems to be all the way back. The snow is getting heavier. And the temperature is getting colder.

"Okay, calm down. I'm sure they're fine," I say trying to quell the nerves. I know it's freezing outside, but we've all grown up in the snow. We know how dangerous it can be. They wouldn't do anything stupid. I know they'll be okay.

Willow proposes a new idea. "Maybe we should go look for them, then. Maybe one of them is hurt."

It's a reasonable plan, one that everyone seems to agree to by nodding their heads, so I respond. "Okay, some of us will go outside and look for them. They can't have gone far."

I don't think it's entirely necessary, but for some reason, I find myself wanting to keep Willow happy. I think I'm starting to understand Hugh a lot more.

Hugh, Fergus, Evelyn, Kaya, and I put on our snow gear to go outside in search of the boys, whilst Noa, Willow, and Riley stay inside, just in case they return by themselves. I think it's a little funny that after all the fuss Willow made about trying to help them, she elected to stay inside in the warmth, safe from the unforgiving winter.

The five of us going outside split up into three groups, with Hugh and I together, Kaya and Evelyn together, and Fergus going out on his own. The group staying in the house sits down on the couches, each of them looking on edge, but Willow and Noa appear to be remaining calm. Riley, on the other hand, is as white as a ghost. She *has* to get her shit together.

"Riley, are you okay?" Willow asks, sounding extremely concerned.

Riley jumps at the sound of her name. She tries to play it off, "Yeah, I'm all good," she says unconvincingly.

"Are you sure?" Willow asks again, clearly not believing her.

CHAPTER SEVENTEEN

I don't believe her either. From the moment she walked into class yesterday, she's looked like she's been on the verge of fainting. Even today, when everyone was being all *Kumbaya*, she still appeared jittery.

"Willow, I'm fine!" Riley snaps back, and then she looks into my eyes with an apologetic expression. Why is she acting like this? It makes her look like she knows something.

Then, the five of us leave the lodge through the back door and begin our search. Hugh and I trudge through the heavy snow and the longer I'm out here, the more nervous I become. It's cold. *Hypothermic* cold. Even through my ski gear, my skin is tingling from the wind, but as the gale continues picking up, it only gets worse. I had believed Arthur and Samuel were fine, but now I'm not so sure. What if something really has gone wrong? We call their names but receive no response. We shout non-stop for what feels like half an hour before we decide to turn around.

When we reenter through the back door, everyone else is already inside and there is no sign of either of the boys. That's when we start to panic.

Willow suggests we contact the police, to which Noa rejects her by saying, "They won't be able to get here in all this snow. We should give them a few more minutes."

On the surface level, Noa sounds practical and strong, but a hint of fear is mixed in. No matter what we tell ourselves, we all know that if someone has been outside for this long in this weather, something is definitely wrong. The thought of losing someone else is clearly making her spiral, but she hides it well. We wait in the lodge as the weather outside becomes more ferocious. The longer we wait, the harder it is to make anybody believe that Arthur and Samuel are okay. Eventually, the sun begins to set, and we decide as a group that the search is over. It's not up to us.

Willow stands up. "This is ridiculous," she says, sounding irritated, "I'm over this. I'm calling the police. It's worth a shot."

And she does. Well, she tries. She grabs her phone and dials 911, but the phone doesn't ring. She lifts the phone high into the air as she walks directly to the living room.

"What is going on?" she mutters to herself. "It's not ringing."

"Maybe the storm is messing with the lines?" Hugh suggests. "Isn't phone service from space or something?"

"No, they're from cell towers. It must be down."

This was inevitable. On a good day, the service is awful. But with the addition of a snowstorm rolling through the mountain, we may as well kiss our chances of calling for help goodbye.

"Try outside," Noa suggests.

Willow nods in acknowledgement and walks out the back door. She returns a minute later shaking her head. She hurries toward the front door and swings it open. But this time, she doesn't make it outside. Instead, she stands in the doorway as she lets out the most blood-curdling scream.

It sends shivers down my spine and almost makes my heart burst from my chest. Hugh is the first one to jump to his feet and race toward her. We all follow close behind him. When we all reach the door, there a multiple screams and gasps. Riley looks like she's about to vomit, which isn't saying much. She's looked like that the whole trip. Noa's face goes blank, and she turns and walks back to the great room. Hugh's knees buckle and he collapses into an almost praying position. I don't know what good that is going to do right now.

CHAPTER SEVENTEEN

Arthur and Samuel are both hanging from the porch roof. Dead.

V

THE COMMUNIO

Chapter Eighteen

Willow - 8:00 PM - Saturday, 29th January 2022

I slam the door, both unable to look at the bodies anymore, and horrified that whoever did this is still outside. We need to leave. We need to get off this mountain immediately. But judging by the piling snow and the bitter cold, that is unlikely. The Sprinter van is not made for that kind of travel, and we physically can't make it down the mountain on foot. We couldn't even if it wasn't snowing.

I turn to face the group, and they all look back in a state of pure horror, especially Noa, who is sitting on the couch staring blankly at the floor. This is no pleasant surprise for any of us but for her, it must be awful.

Should we help them inside? I guess there's no point, they're clearly dead. They were as stiff as boards. But is it disrespectful to ignore the dead? I don't know. Besides, walking outside would only put ourselves in danger.

"What the fuck!" Kaya yells. "Is this some sick fucking joke?"

I don't think it is. I have a nauseating feeling that not only is it not a joke, but it's far from over.

"What happened?" Hugh finally asks. "Why did they do that?"

I look at him strangely. My mind jumped to homicide so

quickly that I hadn't considered the possibility it was suicide. Maybe it was. But why? Sure, I didn't really talk to them, but I didn't think they were sad. They seemed normal. They seemed exactly the same as they have been for the past four years. But maybe they were good at hiding it. Or maybe they weren't even hiding it, I wouldn't know. I suppose when they walked outside this morning, they had planned on never coming back.

"They didn't do anything," Kaya barks at Hugh. I understand it's a stressful situation but there's no need to be rude. "They didn't kill themselves!"

My ears perk up. Okay, I knew I wasn't the only person to have thought that. I feel vindicated even though Kaya agreeing with me makes me want to believe I'm wrong.

"What, so somebody killed them?" Hugh replies, terror trickling into his voice. "Oh my god, we have to call the police!"

I roll my eyes. I mean, come on Hugh. Has he not been present for the entire conversation leading up to this? "I just tried, there's no service."

"Dammit, then we have to—" He fumbles for the right words. "Lock ourselves inside."

"No shit, numbnuts," Evelyn scoffs. "Doors are already locked."

"Who are we even locking the doors for?" I ask. "Who did this? There's nobody else up here."

"It has to be that groundskeeper!" Hugh says. "There's something about that man that doesn't seem right. I saw his footprints when we arrived. He's been watching us!"

My skin prickles and I find myself turning and whispering to Kaya. "What groundskeeper?"

CHAPTER EIGHTEEN

"We met him when you were inside sulking", Kaya responds, leaving me slightly embarrassed.

"Hugh, calm down!" Caleb interjects. "He's just a normal—"

"You've never even met the guy," Hugh shouts. "He could be lying about being the groundskeeper for all you know!"

There's a silence among us. This is the first I'm hearing of any groundskeeper. I'm surprised it's taken this long to come up. I thought we were alone but turns out there's a strange man on our property. A man who apparently works for Caleb's parents, but Caleb has never met. Of course it's him, it has to be. Unless,

"Either someone is out there, and they're taunting us, or …" Noa pauses. She sits on the couch and is on the verge of hyperventilation. "Or it could be one of us."

The room somehow becomes even quieter. "You think … one of us killed Samuel and Arthur?" Fergus asks. Everybody looks at him in shock because he hasn't spoken yet, but then we all realize there are more important things to focus on.

"I don't know," Noa says as tears drip down her cheeks and into her mouth.

"No. Wh-when would any of us have had time to do that?" Hugh protests. But it does get me thinking. The timing seems nearly impossible. *Nearly*.

"I saw the two of them leave at 9:30 a.m. through the back door, and they never came back in," I begin. "They weren't answering the phone at around 3:30 p.m. So, sometime between those hours they must have been killed. Any one of us had time during the day to sneak outside and kill them!"

"How would any of us have been able to string two bodies up on the porch?" Caleb asks.

"I'm not sure" I retort. "I don't know the details of your

fitness status. All I know is there was more than enough time to do so."

"Okay, so where were you, Willow?" Riley asks.

"I was talking with Hugh, and I was with Noa *all* day. I never went outside once! Noa can vouch for me."

Noa gives a nod of approval.

"Riley, where were you?" I turn the conversation back onto her, which is something she clearly doesn't like. "And why have you been so fucking nervous the second we got here? What's going on?"

"That is none of your business," she spits.

"Oh, it isn't?" I ask. "I think considering recent events, it is entirely all our businesses! Maybe you're nervous about the fact that you could be found out for being a *fucking murderer!*" I can't even contain my rage and suspicion. Any person here could have done it.

"My dad is sick, Willow!" Riley shouts back, stopping my train of thought. "He could die any day now, and I chose to come on a bullshit weekend 'getaway' with my *fucking* theater class! So, forgive me for not enjoying myself!"

"Fucking hell, Willow," Kaya says as she shakes her head. "Seriously?"

The group looks at me like I'm the bad guy. My cheeks turn red.

"What? It's not like I knew her dad was sick. I had to put it out there to give her a chance to explain. If anything, I did her a favor!"

I'm also keeping in mind that her dad might not even be sick. Don't get me wrong, I would never say that to her face just in case she's *not* lying. The Willow from one day ago would have, but these are different circumstances, and I feel like I will need people on my side.

"Kaya? Where were you?" Hugh asks, coming to my side.

"Evelyn and I were together," she says, and Evelyn quickly comes to her defense.

"That's convenient," I scoff. "You expect us to believe it's not you because you were together? But nobody saw where you guys were. You didn't help with lunch, you spent a lot of time by yourselves, for all we know, you could've been *together* while you murdered them!"

"Oh, fuck off, Willow. I'm sick of your high and mighty bullshit! Before today, nobody liked you, and just because you've mended *one* relationship doesn't mean it will last. It's only a matter of time before you ruin it again!"

Ouch. That hurt, and it was uncalled for. It almost sounded like she was upset I didn't apologize or try to make peace with her, but I have never been friendly with Kaya. She's obnoxious and has few redeeming qualities. I don't know why she would expect an apology from me. I've learned in situations like these, where somebody hurts you, you have to hurt them back.

"You're deflecting and digging yourself a hole, and you're making it harder for me to believe you're not the killer. I mean, look at you. You look like the type of person who would viciously murder someone because they disagreed with your chronically online take. No, Kaya, having 'ADHD' is not a debilitating mental illness, and it certainly isn't an excuse to be a massive *bitch*. I mean, *fuck*, you'd kill someone if you got *BLACKPINK* tickets out of it." It all comes out like word vomit, and I can't stop. "And I know you think you're the protector of Noa, and that she's too fragile and couldn't possibly handle being friends with me, but I've known her for a lot longer than you have—"

"And she hates you!" She cuts in. "One day of apologizing doesn't make up for years of your shitty behavior—"

"*Enough!*" We both stop and look at Noa, who is now standing, looking much livelier than before. "This has absolutely nothing to do with what's going on, and right now, you're both embarrassing yourselves so stop!"

As Kaya desperately and pathetically tries to explain herself, I notice something on her hand, and I physically can't stop myself from grabbing it and holding it in place. Kaya viciously tries to pull her hand away. I take a closer look and realize her hands have been stained red, and there has been a clear attempt to wash it away. Blood.

"What's this, Kaya?" I say as I shove her hand in her own face. "Is this their blood? Huh? ANSWER ME!"

"Get the fuck off me!" Kaya screams, and some of the group does try to get me off her, but I don't let go.

"Whose blood is this, Kaya?" I taunt.

"It's mine!"

Lying bitch, I think.

"It's my period blood!"

I don't believe her, but I drop her hand just in case. "Ew! Why the fuck do you have period blood all over your hands? How does that even happen?"

"I think tampons are overpriced. They're a necessity, not a luxury. Also, they cause serious damage to the environment, so I free bleed. Okay?"

"What, into your fucking hands?!" I shout back. I was not expecting this.

"No, Willow! But sometimes it just gets places it's not supposed to!" She claps back.

CHAPTER EIGHTEEN

"Wait, don't you wash your hands?" Evelyn asks, sounding genuinely concerned, seeing as she was up close and personal with Kaya all day.

"Yes, Evelyn. I clearly wash my hands!" Kaya shouts back while holding up her hand. "IT STAINS!"

"You're lying!" I point at her. I don't actually believe that, but if this were a lie, I'd be genuinely impressed because What. The. Fuck.

"I'm not! Besides, they were hung! There's no blood in that," Kaya looks *livid,* but it's also clear she wants to take the blame off herself as quickly as possible, so she points towards Fergus, who has been standing in the corner of the room for the entirety of this interaction, not saying a word. "What about Fergus? What's he been doing this whole day? He was in the living room for about five minutes! He could have easily snuck out of his window and killed him!"

Ignoring Kaya's 'bloodless death' comment, even though she could have stabbed them first, I turn my head towards Fergus when I notice everybody else already has. For the first time since I met Fergus, he is showing emotion. He is panicked. I had never considered Fergus a suspect, which is strange because he is the perfect candidate. If I'm being honest, it's probably because I forgot he existed.

"Yeah, Fergus! What were you doing today?" Hugh yells at him.

"I-I was in my room," Fergus explains. He sounds so scared that I almost feel bad for him. *Almost.* I try to remember that he very well could have just murdered Arthur and Samuel.

"All by yourself?" Caleb says, joining in on Hugh's line of questioning.

"Well, none of you came to check on me!" He shouts,

sounding disappointed.

"You could have come to us", Hugh remarks.

"I get nervous around people!" Fergus yells. He's clearly feeling threatened, and he changes the subject like many before him. "Maybe this was a suicide pact. Or maybe it's a prank!" Fergus suggests.

"I'm sorry, Fergus, but that is the dumbest shit I have ever heard! Why would Arthur and Samuel want to do this? For an elaborate joke? They are literally the most chill guys on the planet. That's a pathetic attempt to get the attention off you! We literally saw their bodies!" Caleb retorts.

"You know what, Caleb? Where have you been?" Fergus asks, "You've been on the attack quite a lot tonight."

"That's true, Caleb," Evelyn says as she turns towards Caleb.

"I was in my room a lot of the day," Caleb yells defensively.

"All by yourself?" Fergus asks sarcastically, mimicking Caleb.

"Not all day, but my room is on the top floor. I can't just climb out the window!"

"I wouldn't put it past you!" I shout. "Who were you with, anyway?"

"I was with Hugh!" he exclaims. It seems a little suspicious because Hugh was with Noa and me for the majority of the day.

"Bullshit," I say. This earns me an incredibly dirty look from Caleb.

"It's not bullshit. He was not with you *all* day," he retorts. "Ask him!"

I turn to look at Hugh. I raise my eyebrows, telepathically asking him if it's true. He pauses, and I know he's about to tell me something I don't like.

CHAPTER EIGHTEEN

"He's telling the truth," Hugh admits. "When I would leave you, I would go see Caleb."

"And what would you do" asks Kaya, "When you would '*go see Caleb.*'"

"We-we would, just ... you know." Hugh gives me a concerned look.

My stomach drops.

"What? Kill people," Kaya pushes.

"Just hang out! I don't know!"

Evelyn scoffs, which for some reason, catches everybody's attention, and we all turn to look at her. I feel sick. I feel like I know where this is going, but I don't want it to be true. Hugh has told me numerous times that he and Caleb are just friends. That's it. I always saw them spending so much time together as a way to vilify Caleb, and for some stupid reason, I had never even considered the part Hugh plays in it.

"What did you do?" I ask.

"Willow, we didn't kill anybody," Hugh says.

"I know," I say. "But what else did you do? With Caleb?" I can barely conceal the heartbreak in my voice. I know I haven't been the best girlfriend to Hugh, but I never cheated on him.

Caleb's head drops and Hugh stays silent.

"Hugh, what did you do?" I pressure, with the intensity of my voice gradually rising.

"Willow, can we not do this right now?" he pleads, but I can't handle that right now. I feel my heart I didn't even know I had start splitting in two.

"No, Hugh! What the fuck did you do with him?"

Hugh's eyes glass over. He tries to hold my hand, but I immediately pull it away.

"You're a liar," I tell him. "You don't love me." My heartbreak is quickly replaced with rage and betrayal. Hugh comes for my hand again. This time, I am not quick enough to avoid it.

"Willow, no! I love you. I love you so much." He honestly sounds pathetic.

"Hugh, stop," Caleb says, looking disappointed.

"Willow, please!"

"Stop lying to her."

But Hugh doesn't stop telling me he loves me. Tears fall from his eyes, and his face turns red.

"I asked you so many times, and you always lied," I say. I don't look at him. I'm scared if I look at him, I'll cry. Or hurt him.

"I never lied," he assures me, but he doesn't seem too convinced. He's fiddling with his necklace again. "He's my best friend!"

I look toward Caleb, and he looks just as hurt as I do.

"Hugh, you're g—"

Caleb begins, but Hugh swings towards Caleb. "I am not fucking gay, Caleb! Stop pushing that shit onto me!"

The room goes dead silent. I look at Caleb. Now he looks more than hurt. He looks broken. He looks scared of Hugh, which I've never seen him be.

Hugh turns around to me once again. "Willow, I love you—"

"Don't fucking touch me," I tell him matter-of-factly. I am so repulsed by Hugh at the moment. I've never seen Hugh this mad over anything, so I know what Caleb is saying is true. Everybody looks at Hugh with pure disgust. Caleb sits down on the couch, on the verge of a breakdown. Noa sits with him, wrapping her arm around his shoulders. I walk to the couches and join them, followed by everybody else except

Hugh. And Fergus, but that is expected. Hugh buries his head in his hands and sits on the floor.

For the first time in ... well, ever, Caleb and I are on the same side. We have both been used and played by Hugh. I never really saw it coming. I didn't think Hugh had that in him. He's the common problem. I thought he was my only ally, but he never was. How long have they been doing this?

"Willow, I'm so sorry," Hugh sobs silently.

I can't look at him. He disgusts me too much. Even being in the same room as him is suffocating. It's like his sad, silent cries block out every other sound. I can't be around it.

"Fuck this," I scoff as I turn around and walk towards the staircase to my room.

"Willow, where are you going?" Hugh shouts.

"To pack!" I scream.

"We can't leave," Hugh explains, "Let me explain, please!"

How can he not understand that I don't want to be around him? Yet, he follows me upstairs and toward my room, whining the whole way there. I shut and lock the door, but he fiddles with the handle.

"Willow, please let me in," he pleads.

"No, go away," I yell through the door. I grab handfuls of essential clothes and shove them messily into my suitcase, leaving the heavy things behind. I zip it up, leaving a few articles of clothing peeking out the top.

"I'm sorry," he cries. "Just let me in."

Oh my god, is he for real? I barge to the door and swing it open.

"What about 'go away' do you not understand?" I yell in his face. I go to slam the door, but he stops it with his foot.

"Willow, please listen to me," he begs. "I didn't do anything.

Caleb is obsessed with me, okay? I have turned him down so many times, please believe me! I've never done this before. We were drunk. It was a one-time thing!"

I stare into his eyes. I know he's not telling the truth and, on some level, I understand why. His parents are assholes and would most definitely shun him for being gay. But that doesn't mean he has to condemn Caleb and accuse him of 'forcing' something. That's when he lost my respect.

"I don't believe you," I tell him before grabbing my suitcase and pushing past him. I walk back down the stairs to find the rest of the group has moved. Noa and Caleb are still sitting on the couch with Fergus standing next to them, but Evelyn and Kaya and peering through the windows. Riley is sitting on the dining table with her back to me. Still not coping I see. They all turn to look my way because Hugh is causing a commotion behind me.

"Caleb, get the keys," I order. "We're leaving!"

"Have you looked outside?" he responds. "There's no way we can drive through this."

"I don't care. We can try."

I walk straight for the front door and when I swing it open, I audibly gasp. The bodies of Samuel and Arthur are gone. It doesn't make sense. All of us were inside. How did they move? I guess it has to be the groundskeeper. Or was Fergus on to something when he suggested it was a prank.

I don't dwell on it. I need to move. I walk down the porch steps and trudge through the snow to the van. I throw my suitcase inside and climb into the passenger seat. The snow is whipping through the air, searing my cheek as singular snowflakes grip me, unwilling to let go. The temperature has already dropped significantly, and the windshield has frosted over. Caleb and the rest of the group follow me outside. Caleb climbs inside whilst the others get in the back. As soon as the door clicks shut, I press the lock button. But the van doesn't start.

"What are you doing?" I ask Caleb.

"I don't know," he says, his breathing getting heavier. "It's not working—"

As he says this, the van roars to life and I exhale a sigh of relief. But then, the beeping starts.

"No!" Caleb shouts. "Fuck!"

"What is it?" Noa calls from the back.

"It says there's a loss of pressure in all four tires."

My heart sinks. That relief did not last long at all.

"What does that mean?" Noa asks.

"The tires are flat."

"What? How?"

I roll my eyes. "Somebody slashed them!"

"But we can still drive on them, right?", Noa suggests, not allowing her hope to be destroyed just yet.

Caleb sighs and drops his head. "Not on the ice. We'd lose control and drive off the edge."

Then, out of the blue, the window right next to my head shatters and a brick flies past my face. I scream and jolt my head towards the window. I see the person, and I can't believe my eyes. The only thing I notice before shit hits the fan is the silhouette of antlers stretching outwards. In a frenzy, everyone climbs out of the van from the whichever door is furthest from the person. I scramble over to Caleb's seat and throw myself out. I don't look behind me, I don't want to waste time. I get to my feet and follow the group inside. I am the last one, so I slam the door shut and lock it. I collapse to the floor, my back against the door, hyperventilating.

We don't know what to say, so we say nothing. The whole group is clearly terrified, but Noa stands frozen. Her face is too pale, too still, but tears pool in her eyes. The first words she can get out send shivers down my spine.

"That-that was the Telluride Maniac."

Chapter Nineteen

Willow - 8:30 PM - Saturday, 29th January 2022

Everyone in the lodge turns slowly towards her.

"Noa, what the fuck do you mean *'that was the maniac?'*" Kaya asks.

Noa stands against the back wall, unmoving. She's in shock. I don't know what to say. She takes a deep breath and looks towards us. "That was the same mask he wore the night he killed my family. I think he's come back for me."

The silence that fills the room dissipates as everybody once again breaks into panic. Evelyn puts her hand over her mouth and grabs the couch arm rest to keep her balance. Riley falls apart. Tears stream down her cheeks, and she lets out small, staggered wails. I have no idea how to act at this moment because I know this whole situation doesn't make sense.

"I don't think that was the maniac," I chime in, which receives an outpouring of backlash.

"How do you know that, Willow?" Kaya shouts.

"Because why would he be back?" I yell in frustration. "You're telling me he stops killing for what … three months? Just to follow us up a mountain and start killing a random group of teenagers? That doesn't make any fucking sense!"

"We're not just a random group of teenagers, Willow!" Noa

pipes up. "He would have killed me if I hadn't left my house when I did. Maybe he's been watching me!"

"Noa, he hasn't been watching you!" My voice and temper continue to rise. "This isn't him!"

"Then who is it, Willow? Why is he wearing the mask?" Evelyn asks.

"I don't know," I say with a hint of defeat in my voice. "I thought we said the groundskeeper. He's the only one who makes sense."

"He doesn't seem like the type," Caleb says.

"You don't know him, Caleb," I remind him.

"But maybe it's someone completely different. What if someone did follow us up here?"

It's possible, but for some reason it doesn't sit right with me. It's a possible solution but it doesn't feel conclusive. Why would anybody feel the need to follow us?

I finally suggest, "Maybe it *was* a prank." Fergus lifts his arms up in a way to say *what have I been saying?* "The bodies are gone. Maybe this is a skit for their TikTok."

"They wouldn't do that, would they?" Kaya asks. "Not with them knowing what happened to Noa."

Noa tenses at the mention of her trauma. Why does Kaya always have to speak for people? But it makes sense. I don't think Arthur and Samuel would be that cruel. Even if they were, they'd be smart enough to know it's a terrible business move and would definitely get them cancelled. Tormenting the survivor of the Telluride Maniac by making her believe he's come back for her. The mob of empaths would grab their pitchforks within seconds.

"What if we found the groundskeeper?" Kaya suggests.

"What do you mean," Riley asks her.

CHAPTER NINETEEN

"I mean, he has to be around here somewhere, right? What if he's not the killer—"

Just as Kaya is speaking, the lights flicker and then the room is plunged into darkness. I try to stay rational. I know there is a storm going on outside and power can sometimes go on and off but knowing that two of our friends have been murdered and put on display, it's hard to think it can be anything but intentional. Especially, when I feel someone brush past me and slip something into my hands.

"Who is that?" I shout into the darkness.

Nobody responds but a second later, the lights turn back on, and everybody is where they were when they went off. I know I wasn't imagining things, and I have proof. It's just not proof I want to share with the group.

"I think we should find him," Kaya finishes.

I look at her in shock. She wants us to go outside when there is a snowstorm occurring and a murderer stalking us. I think she notices a few of our stares.

"I know it sounds crazy, but if we find him and he's not the killer, he could help us. He might have weapons or a truck to take us home."

She's right. This mystery man in the woods could be the difference between life and death. He could have everything we need to escape.

"And what if it is him?" Hugh asks from the corner.

"Just hope he doesn't catch you," Kaya responds dryly. It actually makes me want to laugh. Maybe we could have been friends in another life.

Our conversation has turned from screaming and hurling accusations and abuse to sounding very worn out. At least we're all agreeing on something for once. We all understand that finding the groundskeeper is essential. It's a risk, but if it pays off, it could mean survival. Besides, I can't tolerate being in this house anymore, so going outside, where a killer potentially lurks, sounds far more appealing.

I make my way to my room. I grab my warmest snow boots, along with my ski gear, come back to the great room. I'm grateful I left my bulkiest items behind, otherwise I would have had to brave the cold in my sweats and walked to the van. I pull them on and take the largest kitchen knife I can find.

Hugh offers to come with me, to which I immediately decline, deciding to go alone instead. Noa and Caleb and Kaya and Evelyn pair up. Riley goes with Hugh, and she looks as uncomfortable as ever. And, of course, Fergus will go alone. I know it would make sense for us to pair up, but I can't trust anybody. Besides, I don't want to go with him.

I step outside into the snow, turn my phone flashlight on, and begin making my way toward the tree line. What if he has them? What if it is him? And we've left the house, and I've gone alone. However, what should be scary feels comforting, because deep down, I know going outside is much better than staying inside. Leaving the house, and going alone, is the only way I can ensure I'm not walking with a killer. I pull out the slip of paper from my back pocket that reads, *"I know what you did."*

In the dark, someone in the lodge slipped that to me. Somebody knows what I've done. And now I know that whoever was standing at the van window, whoever killed Arthur and Samuel, is working with someone inside. One of us is not telling the truth. One of us is putting on a damn good performance.

CHAPTER NINETEEN

Somebody knows.
And somebody wants me dead.

Chapter Twenty

Noa - 10:00 PM - Saturday, 29th January 2022

I 've been walking with Caleb through the woods for about half an hour. We stand side by side, our flashlights shining in front of us, trying not to trip over any tree root or be pushed over by the strong wind. I am wearing a full snow suit, gloves, boots, along with a ski mask that covers most of my face, and still the cold is making my fingers, nose, and toes tingle. We haven't spoken to each other since we left the house. I'm not sure if it's because we don't want to waste our energy on chatter, or because it's too uncomfortable to speak after what just happened.

What Hugh did was cruel, and I can tell Caleb is hurt. No, he's more than hurt. He's *shattered.* When I looked over at him, his eyes were glossy and his cheeks were wet, but that could have been from the cold. I've always thought something was going on between Hugh and Caleb, but Caleb would never admit it. He didn't want any rumors to start about Hugh. Caleb knows those rumors all too well.

When we were sophomores, gossip about Caleb spread around the school. Even though he was in theater, and it was probably expected, he was still popular enough that it made people talk. Many of the guys were awful to him and

CHAPTER TWENTY

stopped inviting him to things. They didn't want him "falling in love with them." As if he didn't have standards. Most of the girls started treating him like a pet. I don't know which of them is worse.

Hugh and Caleb had been best friends for a few years at that point, and Caleb's biggest fear was that Hugh would desert him, but he never did. Hugh was sweet, and understanding, never treated him differently, and really helped Caleb through a lot of shit. He would stand up to the other guys when they would shout *that* awful word at him.

Caleb eventually came out officially, turned down all the "Gay BFF" offers from girls he'd never spoken to before, and became close with our theater class. He also became even *closer* to Hugh. Sometimes if they were alone together and you walked in on them, they would look flustered and blushing, almost as if they had just abruptly finished doing *something*. Caleb said they had grown closer because of how kind Hugh was to him through everything and that they were still very platonic, but I think it was pretty obvious what they were doing behind closed doors.

We all agreed not to bring it up to them and, instead, let them tell people when *they* felt comfortable. Caleb's face when Hugh yelled at him reflected all the hurt, embarrassment and loneliness from sophomore year. Yet, another person had deserted him when he needed them the most, and it was Hugh of all people. The one boy who had defended him.

I know Hugh was technically cheating on Willow with Caleb, but I always felt like Willow was just holding Hugh back. It made me hate Willow even more, but now the tables have turned. I've sort of revived my friendliness toward Willow, and now Hugh makes me feel sick. He has been stringing along both Willow and Caleb. He used Caleb for his own pleasure but the second it became uncomfortable, he dropped him. He used Willow to keep up the image of a good Christian boy even though it's clear he feels nothing for her.

We continue walking, not finding anything that could be helpful to us. I can't take his silence anymore. "Are you alright, Caleb?" I shout over the wind, "Do you want to talk about it?"

He subtly shakes his head and stays silent. I'm not going to force him to speak, but I'm going to need him to hold himself together for the night, unlike Riley and, now, most of the group. I'm about to let it go when Caleb finally speaks up.

"He really scared me," he yells, "I've never seen him so angry. He looked like he wanted to hurt me."

Nothing I could say would make him feel better, and I think deep down, Caleb still has feelings for Hugh, which makes this even sadder. However, it's something I think I could use.

"Hugh was cruel and awful, but tension was high before. I'm sure he didn't mean everything he was saying. He probably just panicked. He's been brought up believing being gay is wrong. And he was just being accused of murder," I say.

"Yeah, maybe," Caleb says. He waits a little longer. "But maybe it's better this way. Being somebody's secret doesn't feel good, even if being alone with him made me the happiest I had been in a long time. If he thinks being gay is 'wrong,' that's fine. I'm just not going to satisfy his fantasies anymore."

Thank God. I'm glad I finally have rational Caleb back with me.

"Just give him time, and maybe when he's out and comfortable in his own skin, you can rekindle whatever you had."

Caleb gives an uplifting smile, and he nods his head. Considering what has been happening tonight, I realize this conversation is ridiculous, but it puts me at ease knowing Caleb will be okay moving forward.

We finally decide to turn around and head back to the lodge. We've been aimlessly walking around in the freezing cold for nothing. However, when we turn around, we realize we're not sure which direction the lodge was. The trees seem so dense, and every direction looks the same. The wind blows my hair into my face, and the snow flies around us, creating a grey fog that lingers all throughout the woods. So, even if I did remember the right way, I wouldn't be able to see it. I can't see more than ten feet in front of me.

Caleb grabs my arm and begins walking me in a certain direction. *I'm* not certain if *he's* certain he's going the right way, but I save my voice the trouble, seeing as I don't have any better ideas. My nose is streaming and water gushes from my eyes. This elevation mixed with this level of cold is not something to mess with. I feel like I could turn into an ice cube any second.

We walk for a while, which I guess is our fault, seeing as we decided to walk that far in the first place. Nothing changes. Every direction we turn looks the exact same. I grab his arm and lead him to the right but still nothing changes. The snow gets deeper under my boots as Caleb turns us around. I follow him until I finally see a light ahead.

"Let's go!" I shout.

Caleb nods and grabs my hand, leading me toward the lights. We pick up the pace and run through the trees until suddenly, the trees stop, and we stand in the snowy plain, facing the cabin. We pause to take a breath, as I don't think the two of us had run that much since gym class two years ago. We race towards the lodge, but as we approach the front door, we see that is has been left ajar. Caleb and I were the last ones to leave, and I know for a fact I shut the door.

  We push it open enough to squeeze through. We creep along the hallway, but something catches my ear. As I get closer to the stairs leading to Willow and Hugh's bedroom, I hear faint classical music coming from upstairs.

Chapter Twenty-One

Willow - 10:45 PM - Saturday, 29th January 2022

The snowstorm has been getting stronger and I'm finding it nearly impossible to see, hear, or feel anything.

My eyes sting so much from the cold that tears roll down my cheeks. I regret my decision to come out here alone. I am still sticking with the decision that it's someone from our group, but what if they're working with the groundskeeper? Then none of us are safe anywhere we go. Maybe I should have gone with Hugh. I was so in shock at the lodge that I couldn't even look at him, but now I really wish I wasn't alone, especially with that groundskeeper running around snatching people and hanging them.

I ponder the possible outcomes of the night. Most likely, the groundskeeper is not actually the groundskeeper. He's probably a psycho and is working with one of us. Because whoever slipped me that piece was inside. Whoever slipped me that note is lying to everybody in that lodge. But I guess so am I. How are they connected to the groundskeeper? What if they're not? What if they just slipped me the note, and it's completely unrelated to whatever happened to Arthur and Samuel.

Something is not right here. It feels like I'm missing a piece of the puzzle and for some reason, the longer I walk, the more I think looking for the groundskeeper is a waste of time. In fact, it might be a detriment. Whoever is behind this has successfully split us all up. We are vulnerable and no longer have strength in numbers. At least, I'm alone. Usually, that's not a good thing, but right now, I'd take it over not being able to trust who I was with.

Everything looks the same. I don't think I'm making any progress. All I'm discovering is how incredibly cold I am. I can't even hear myself think through all the wind. I begin to turn around, but as I do, the blizzard slows. The wind stops briefly, and I can see clearly in front of me for the first time since I left. It's a subtle relief to my skin but it's one that feels so incredible. I look around, searching for a hint of light to guide me towards the lodge. I see something in the distance, light trailing through the cracks in the trees. I race towards it, petrified that the wind will pick back up and I will lose sight of it. Scared that I will be stuck in the woods, and if I get stuck, I'm as good as dead. I run, expecting to see the lodge, but I don't. Instead, I see a different cabin. Much smaller. More like a hut. Trickles of smoke rising from the chimney beckon me over. I crouch behind a tree, looking through the cabin window.

I grab my phone, thinking that maybe I could call for the others, but of course, there is still no service. I don't even know who I'd call, though. I don't have any of their numbers except Hugh's, and I don't really want to talk to him right now.

The crackling embers that remain from a fire illuminate the room, but I don't see any movement. This has to be the

CHAPTER TWENTY-ONE

groundskeeper's house. Is this where he's set up shop as he picks us all off one by one? I want to stand out here and wait for movement from inside or wait for someone to return, but I can't. It is so cold. I'm trying to grip the handle of my knife, but it keeps slipping from my fingers. They feel like they're going to snap, and my nose feels as if it's going to fall off. I've heard of kids back home who weren't dressed properly getting hypothermia being out in the snow for less than an hour. That's the last thing I need right now. I need to be in my prime body and mind if I want to survive.

I watch the hut for a few more minutes until I am confident nobody is inside. Nobody walks past the window, and nobody has returned from the woods. It should be safe.

I squeeze my knife as tight as I can and cautiously walk to the hut.

I step onto the porch, and it makes a deafening creak. I freeze and stand there with gritted teeth. Nobody moves inside. I move over to the window but still can't see anyone. The wind picks up again, my teeth clatter and my eyes stream, so I decide to enter the hut for warmth.

I open the door and a strange scent stops me completely. Why does it smell familiar? I swipe my eyes and look around the room. I take a step forward, but my shoe is briefly caught on something sticky. A thick red substance pools around my boot. Blood.

It's not just around my feet. It's covering the entire floor. Oh shit. Who's is this? It has to be Arthur and Samuels, right? But they were hanged. There's not usually any blood when you're hanged. Maybe whoever killed them stabbed them first, I didn't get a good enough look at their bodies. But it's already drying. They died too recently for it to already be dried. Maybe they have been dead longer than we think? Maybe the groundskeeper made quick work of them. But where are their bodies?

Then, I look at the bed, and it takes me a second to notice the decapitated head of an older man tucked between the pillows. I gag but manage to pull myself together before any liquid escapes my lips. Is that the groundskeeper? Oh no. This is not good. My main suspect is dead. Extremely dead. If it's not him, then who killed him? Who else is up here with us? Whoever was by the van could still be out there and may be coming to this hut. It's a great place to stay out of the cold and remain hidden in between attacks.

My brain is cloudy. Nothing is making sense. It's frustrating. I just want to scream. Who is doing this? Who knows about me?

What was that? I turn my head, thinking I can hear someone walking around outside. I need to get out of here. This cabin may be their haven and they might want it back.

I stumble backwards towards the door. The bottoms of my shoes are icy, so before I walk out the door, I slip landing on my back. I roll onto stomach and try to push myself up onto my feet, but I catch a glimpse further beneath the bed, and that is where is see the headless body of the groundskeeper. By now, rigor mortis has set in which means his open neck is no longer gushing blood. Instead, the blood has solidified, just like the body.

I grip the knife tighter, thinking that anybody could be lurking around here. Someone is not joking around. They murdered a poor old man for being in the wrong place at the wrong time. I can only imagine what they have in store for me.

CHAPTER TWENTY-ONE

As all this races through my mind, I hear a creak from the wooden floorboards on the porch. I swing around and plummet my knife into Fergus's neck.

VI

THE SANCTUS

Chapter Twenty-Two

Willow - 11:00 PM - Saturday, 29th January 2022

Fergus's blood spews from the wound, down the knife and onto my arm, trickling towards my elbow. Unlike the blood on the floor, this is warm. I stand there in shock while Fergus desperately reaches out to me for help as he slowly falls to the floor. In a panic, I pull out the knife and his blood squirts onto my face, mixing with the groundskeepers. There's steam coming from his blood when it meets the freezing air. Fergus falls forward, and I catch him in my arms.

"Fergus, I'm sorry. You're going to be okay. It's okay."

I know he won't, but I'm saying it more to keep *myself* at ease. I lower him to the ground, and he slumps, face down in the blood, his hand making small twitching movements until finally, he stops. Blood drains from his wound, a slightly different shade from the groundskeepers until they finally blend together and become indistinguishable.

"No, no, no, no, no!" I mumble as I flip over Fergus's body. I know he's dead, but I can't help tapping his face in a last-ditch effort to wake him up. It doesn't work, obviously. He has a gaping hole the side of his neck. Acceptance finally washes over me. What do I do? What's everybody going to think? I just murdered Fergus. I mean, yes, nobody was close to him or anything, but they're going to look at me like I'm the killer. I'm not. Well, technically I am *a* killer, but I'm not *the* killer.

I scramble for ideas. What am I going to tell them? I could pretend it didn't happen, and say I couldn't find anything, but I'm covered in blood. That will make me look even more guilty. Besides, I need to announce to the group that the groundskeeper is dead, and he is innocent. I can just tell them I found Fergus here along with him. But whichever one of us killed the groundskeeper will know I'm lying. Although they can't really say anything without incriminating themselves, so I guess it's a safe bet.

Then I think about Fergus. What was he doing here? Was he following me? Was *he* the killer? I wouldn't be surprised. Did I just end this possible nightmare? Or did he stumble upon this shack as I did? Maybe he saw the light too. What have I done?

I remember my initial goal; to look for help. Even though the groundskeeper can no longer help us, maybe he has something in here that can. I don't know what I'm searching for. A radio, maybe? I could call for help. Although, that won't do any good. I don't think anybody can get here in this weather. I see the pile of logs stacked against the back wall. He must have chopped them with something, but I don't see an axe or a chainsaw.

This is useless. I need to get back to the lodge. I gather myself, and when I'm about to leave, I notice my knife on the ground amidst the blood. I can't just leave that here, and I certainly can't go back to the lodge with it in my hands while I'm covered in blood.

I grab the knife, turn my phone flashlight back on, and walk out the shack door. I stand on the porch and look around, making sure none of the group has also stumbled across the hut. I hold the knife in my hand, walk into the snow and throw it as far as possible. It lands about forty feet away and burrows into the snow. Then, I run.

The snowstorm has picked up again, and my vision is so terrible I may as well have my eyes closed, so I don't notice the tree branch until I run directly into it. I land hard on my back, gasping for air. I lie there, limbs stiffening, hidden by the snow. I attempt to get up, but I'm too winded. I'm just about to try again when I hear something in the distance. I strain my ears, trying to discern the sound from the wind. Footsteps. Not from someone walking. From someone running. They sound like they're coming directly towards me, but I can't move. My best course of action is to hold still, and maybe they won't see me. The footsteps approach, closer and closer. But to my relief, they fade in the other direction just like they came. I manage to pull myself up into a sitting position and look in the direction they're running, and I catch a glimpse of a shadowy figure disappearing into the storm.

"Who is that?" I ask myself.

Why are they alone? The only people that were alone were Fergus and me, and I know it isn't Fergus. It has to be the killer. The one standing at the van window. The one who followed us up here.

I don't know why, but I pull myself to my feet and start walking in the direction they went. Where are they going? I pick up my pace, cautious of any tree branches in my way. It feels like I'm walking forever until finally I come to a clearing and realize what the killer was running to.

The lodge.

Nervous, I run towards the front door. I hear voices from inside, and all my caution vanishes. I barge through the door. I run into the living room where our group stands around the couches, deep in conversation, looking stressed. I'm the last one back. As I walk towards them, they stop talking and look at me.

"Willow?" Noa says.

"Who just came in?" I demand.

I was wrong. The person running in the woods was not the person who through a brick at the van, wearing the deer mask, it was someone from our group. They have just reentered the lodge, and somebody knows it.

"Willow, why are you covered in blood?" Hugh asks.

"The groundskeeper is dead. It wasn't him. He's not the killer. Who came in the house just now?"

"Willow, we've all been inside for ages. We were getting worried about you," Evelyn claims.

"Shut up, Evelyn. No, you weren't," I snap. "Who was the last person in the lodge?"

"The groundskeeper is dead?" Riley asks, ignoring my question. She looks genuinely shocked, and her face goes white.

"I saw someone running alone in the woods. They ran straight past me and directly for the lodge," I shout, my temper rising.

"Could it have been Fergus?" Kaya asks.

"No! Fergus is dead, for fuck's sake!" I shout. Oh no. I shouldn't have said that. The room goes quiet. Everybody's eyes are on me.

"What do you mean he's dead?" Caleb asks, almost sounding angry. Riley starts to cry. Softly at first, and then it turns into

CHAPTER TWENTY-TWO

a sob.

Shit. This is it. I have to lie. Okay, Willow. You can do this. This is what you decided to do. Blame the masked killer. Blame the maniac.

"I found both of them in a shack in the woods. I think it was the groundskeeper's cabin." I look around the room, hoping to see a look of confusion on somebody's face that could lead me to who the killer is. Whoever it is has an incredible poker face. Ugh, this is so much harder than I thought it would be. None of them show any confusion whatsoever. But Riley runs to her room, holding her mouth, and slamming the door behind her.

"I think whoever ran past me in the woods is the killer," I say. "I need to know who came back here last."

"Hugh did," Noa says, which earns her a betrayed stare from Hugh. "Riley came back early, and Hugh came back ten minutes later."

I glare at him. Of course, it was Hugh. He is not doing himself any favors.

"Why were you alone?" I probe.

"Riley wanted to go back to the lodge because she was scared," Hugh explains. "I wanted to look around more. I didn't want to give up if we were close to finding him, but I couldn't find anything, so I came back. I swear to you, Willow, I was not at that cabin."

It might be unwise to put my trust in him, but I believe him.

"Where is this cabin?" Kaya asks me.

"It's, um," and it occurs to me that I actually have no idea where it is, "Somewhere in the woods."

"How do you not know?" she barks at me.

"I don't know, Kaya. It was dark, and I could barely see

through the snow!" I explain.

"We have to get out of here," Hugh states.

"We can't," Caleb says, sounding irritated. Hugh always seems to forget that if it were possible for us to leave, we would have hours ago. "We're snowed in."

Even though Hugh and Caleb have moved the conversation along, Kaya is still glaring at me. I have a terrible feeling she is not buying what I'm selling.

"We have to try!" Hugh shouts back.

"How can we try, Hugh?" Caleb screams. I can tell this anger isn't isolated to this situation. He's still hurt by what Hugh said.

"I don't fucking—" Hugh cuts himself short, clearly trying not to start any more fights. "Can we walk?"

Caleb stares at him and then laughs. "Walk? Are you stupid? We're too far from anything, and we'd freeze to death before we even made it to the road."

"Can we call for help?" I suggest.

"With what, Willow?"

He's right. We've got nothing and nobody could make it here anyway. We're completely trapped here with no way to call for help, which is exactly what the killer wanted.

Then, everything goes black. Evelyn and Noa scream, and my breathing becomes more rapid and heavy. We each turn on our phone flashlights, and together, they provide enough light to brighten the room.

"What happened?" Noa asks with a quivering voice.

"The power went out again," Caleb states blankly.

"Yeah, no shit," Evelyn says. "How?"

Caleb answers mockingly. "I don't know. The ginormous fucking storm outside might have something to do with it. It

CHAPTER TWENTY-TWO

already took out the service."

"What if it was cut?" I ask.

"What do you mean?" Caleb asks.

"What if the killer did this?" I elaborate.

This question sends a larger wave of panic throughout the room.

"We can't just stay here like sitting ducks. I won't do it," Hugh states.

"And how are you going to help us, Hugh?" Kaya asks with a hint of sarcasm. Hugh ponders for a second, desperately trying to come up with some sort of solution that doesn't involve walking home or calling the police.

"Wait," Hugh pipes up. We all listen intently, hoping that something he says will make the tiniest ounce of sense. "When we were at the gate, I saw a fire tower in the distance. It didn't look that far. I think I have a good chance of making it."

Thank God. A small relief washes over me. Finally, some hope.

"Are you sure?" Caleb asks. Please don't ruin this, Caleb, I think. "It could take a while."

"I don't care. We have to do something," he says.

"Okay, but I'm not letting you go alone," I tell Hugh. "I'll come with you."

I see a faint smile come across his face.

"No," Kaya says. "You're helping me find this cabin."

I want to slap her. I don't want to spend time alone with her. I would rather be taken out by the killer. Which is probably what will happen if I'm alone with her.

"Why would we go back there? The killer could be there for all we know," I tell her.

"Exactly," she says. "Maybe we can stop him before he kills

anyone else. I don't want to wait here until help comes. I'm sick of waiting," she pauses. "And I also want to know if you're telling the truth."

Is she serious? Why would I lie about this? I mean, I am lying, but I'm not lying about what she's saying I'm lying about. She just doesn't like me. Then I realize that if Kaya came into the lodge covered in blood, claiming she just found two bodies, I'd be skeptical too.

"Noa, do you know how to use a backup generator?" Caleb asks to which Noa responds with a blank stare.

"I do," Evelyn declares.

"Perfect," Caleb says. "It's around the back. While we're gone, try to get it going."

Evelyn gives him a sharp military nod.

"So, Caleb," Hugh begins, which already earns him a nasty look from pretty much everyone, "are you with me?"

Caleb looks around, realizing everybody is partnered up. Everybody except Riley, who's still locked in her room.

"I guess so," he says in a disappointed tone.

"Is Riley going to be okay here by herself?" Noa asks.

"She should be fine," Hugh assures her. "We'll let her know what's happening and tell her just to stay in her room."

The group gets ready to leave, but I catch my reflection in the window and finally see what I look like. I'm covered head to toe in blood. My hair is soaked, it's smeared all over my face and hands, and my clothes are drenched. Then, as the shock fades away, I realize I'm freezing. The wet blood and snow that covers my jacket are icy and are making me shiver. I tell Kaya that I'm going to change jackets before we leave, and she tells me she'll wait in the living room.

I walk towards my bedroom and open the door. I pause,

CHAPTER TWENTY-TWO

looking at my bed. It's hard to imagine that it was only this morning I was lying here, alone, without a care in the world. Well, that isn't true. I was angry with everyone for how they treated me and at myself for how I acted the night before, but that is nothing compared to what we're going through now. It makes me wonder why I have been so uptight. It was never really that serious.

It's a shame I won't get to spend the night with Hugh. I'm immensely angry and disappointed in him for cheating on me, and I'm ashamed of how he treated Caleb, but I still love him and know he loves me. He was just stressed and confused. That's all. Caleb should know better.

I pick up a different jacket from the pile of clothes, throwing my old one on the floor. I go to leave the room but my eye catches something on the bathroom door. More blood. I'm confused as I hadn't gone over there, and there was no way I had gotten any on the door, but I realize it isn't mine. I shine the light on the carpet below and see there is a small trail of blood leading into the bathroom from the hallway. I approach the door cautiously and warily push it open. I almost faint at the sight. In the sink lies the kitchen knife I used to kill Fergus and written in blood on the mirror is one word.

Killer.

Chapter Twenty-Three

Caleb - 12:00 AM - Sunday, 30th January 2022

We stand in silence in the living room, waiting for Willow to come downstairs. Honestly, I hope she takes as long as she can because I'm dreading the thought of walking to a tower miles away with Hugh. A day ago, I would have jumped at the opportunity, and I thought Hugh would have as well, but now I'm not so sure. I'm realizing now that every time Hugh was excited to be alone with me, it wasn't because he was excited to see *me*, he just wanted to get off.

Everything he said to me this morning made me really believe we had a chance, that we could put the rumors and the secrets behind us and just be together. Only us. But now I have no idea if that's even what he wants. I thought he wouldn't be afraid for people to know about us finally, but it seems like he's ashamed of me. It made me look so stupid. Like I was some creep forcing him to do things he didn't want to do. Now I have to be alone with him, making small talk, ignoring all of our history. It would be easier for both of us if we ignored each other.

The silence in the room is deafening. We all stand, unmoving, with the only sound being Willow's footsteps from

CHAPTER TWENTY-THREE

upstairs. When we finally hear her coming downstairs, we all recognize each other's existence for the first time and begin getting ready to go. Willow's face is red, and she looks distressed, but she doesn't acknowledge it and walks towards us.

"Alright, let's go," she says, clapping her hands together.

Noa and Evelyn walk out the front door, and I watch as the light from their phones disappear around the side of the house. Then Willow and Kaya gather the things they need to make their way to the cabin. It comforts me that I'm not the only person who cannot stand their partner, but as the two disappear into the night, and I am left alone in the lodge with Hugh, all the comfort fades away. I would rather go with Willow at this point. I can sense Hugh is looking at me, but I just stare at the front door, pretending to watch Kaya and Willow for a little longer. I know forcing us to stand in silence is making the situation more awkward, but I don't care. I cannot bear to have a conversation with that boy.

"Are you ready to go?" he asks me.

"Yep," I say flatly, to which he gives a brief nod.

I walk past him to the counter, grab a knife, and walk towards the front door. He hasn't moved. He's just standing in the same spot, looking at me.

"Caleb, can we please t—" he begins, but I can't stomach it. Willow already rejected his apology, so now he's come to me. Typical. I'm an afterthought. A backup plan.

"Hugh, just grab your things and let's go."

He does. He quickly picks up his flashlight and walks towards me. I am standing by the open door, implying that he goes first. He is about to walk past me, but he stops and turns to me, looking into my eyes. He looks sorrowful, but I keep my face void of emotions. He finally understands that he won't be getting anything out of me, so he just drops his head and walks out the door. Part of me wants to slam the door and barricade it, leaving him locked outside but instead, I follow him. He points in the direction of the fire tower, but it's too snowy to see. However, as I focus my eyes, I realize there's a blinking red light far in the distance. Without saying anything to him, I walk in the direction of the tower. He follows, walking a few feet behind me, but every time I hear him getting closer, I pick up my pace to keep a comfortable distance away from him.

"Caleb?" Hugh calls. I don't respond. "Caleb? I know you can hear me."

"What?" I reply drearily.

"Can we talk?" he asks nervously.

"About what?" I bark.

He pauses. I want him to say what he did was fucked up. Not that I'd care, but it would be nice to know that he at least feels bad.

"About what happened between us earlier," he states flatly. I stop and turn around to him, which makes him stop, also.

"Us? No, what *you* said," I tell him. "There was no 'us' in that situation."

"Look, Caleb, I'm sorry, but—"

"No, don't say 'but,'" I interrupt. "Anything you say after 'I'm sorry' completely erases your apology."

He takes a deep breath in and speaks again. "I wasn't ready to tell people about ... us. And you were about to tell everybody."

I want to scream. In his deluded brain, he has somehow convinced himself that I pushed him to that point. I am the one to blame for his outburst, because of course I am. Hugh

CHAPTER TWENTY-THREE

would never do anything like that on his own. *Eye roll.*

"So, this is my fault?"

"No that's not what I'm saying."

Is it not? Because it's exactly what it sounds like. He was ready to condemn me to keep up appearances and save his relationship with Willow. A relationship he doesn't care about, by the way.

"How long will you keep lying to Willow?"

"It's not that easy. I feel bad for her!" he exclaims.

"And what? You don't feel bad *lying* and *cheating* on her?"

"You're the one who I was cheating on her with! You should feel bad, too!" he yells.

"I'm not the one pretending to be in love with her!" I shout. "You should feel bad for using me, too!"

"I wasn't using you!"

"Yes, you were, Hugh! You were stringing me along, promising me a life together with your pretty words, but when it actually came time for actions, you made me look fucking stupid. Look, I understand you're confused, I've been there, but you have been completely selfish!"

"I'm sorry but I'm not trying to be!"

"DON'T SAY 'BUT'!"

My screaming silences us. I sigh. I know screaming won't get us anywhere, but I can't stand to hear him making excuses.

"You have been staying with Willow because it's comfortable for you. It's easier. I'm sure you realize it hurts me, but don't give a shit."

We pause for another minute, not saying anything to each other. Then, I finally get the courage to speak up. "Were you pretending to be in love with me?"

"No. Caleb, no. I *love* you. I do!" he insists.

I can't help but laugh. First, out of pure second-hand embarrassment, and then it quickly turns to anger.

"Really? Do you love me? You have a really fucking terrible way of showing it! Because, if I remember correctly, you just confessed your love to *Willow* and told me to "stop pushing that gay shit" onto you!" I scream at him.

"Caleb, I do! I'm just so confused! I don't know who I am!" This catches me off guard. I really don't want to show him sympathy right now. "I've never felt more alive when I'm with you, and I want to spend the rest of my life with you, but I don't know how to express that to people yet."

I take a moment to think about what I'm going to say, and I know I have to stick to my guns. "I get it. Really, I do, but you just humiliated me in front of everybody just to cover up your own insecurities." I say it with more sincerity in my voice than I had planned.

"I know, and I'm sorry. Truly I am," he says as he grabs my hand. "I know I will never be able to express that enough. But we could just start again. Right now?"

I ponder his suggestion. Part of me really wants to accept, but my rational side knows what I have to do, so I pull my hand away from his. "I can't keep doing this. Everything you've said to me right now, you said to Willow. You keep lying to protect yourself and don't care who it affects. I'm so sick of getting hurt because I'm somebody's secret. All I ever see are my friends being in happy, *public* relationships. That's all I want, and I feel like I deserve it. So, until you're ready, ready to be with me, *really* be with me, that means no Willow, no excuses, no 'best friends.' I just can't keep getting into shit like this. I can't take it."

As I say this, a tear burns across my nose. Matching

tears form in Hugh's eyes. I think he understands and even agrees with me. He is battling his internal conflict, which I sympathize with, but I can't be with him until he wins it.

Strangely, this feels relieving. I got my feelings across to him the best way I could. The ball is in his court. I kind of wanted him to push further, I wanted him to fight for me, but that's childish and completely inappropriate considering the situation we're in.

"Okay," he says, the tears finally escaping from his eyes.

"Okay," I copy. That's that. It's over. We stare at each other for a few seconds before remembering we have a long way to walk to the radio tower and start moving again, now walking side by side. The walk feels like an eternity. Even though I've set my boundaries, there is so much sexual and romantic tension between us that ignoring him feels so unnatural. I really do love him, but I can't keep hurting myself.

At first, the path to the tower was a road with trees on either side of us. But after a while, the path becomes rougher and rockier. We take our time climbing over the rocks and logs, careful not to slip on the ice. We watch as the red blinking light becomes closer and closer until we can finally make out the tower through the haze. It sits on the top of a hill, but we stand on top of a small cliff, and below us lies a wide, frozen river we must cross.

Hugh goes first. He hands me his phone and asks me to shine it for him. He lowers himself onto the ledge and makes his way down, carefully stepping rock by rock until he makes it to the frozen riverbed. I toss down both of our phones and secure my knife in my belt. I manage to lower myself and make it to the first rock. I climb down the second and third but as I step down to the last one, I slip and fall forward. I close my eyes and put my arms out to shield my face but I don't feel an impact. As I slowly open my eyes, I realize Hugh caught me. He gives me a smile, and I can't help but reciprocate. We both give a little laugh, but soon the laughs fade, and like many times before, we are staring into each other's eyes. However, this isn't like any time before. I can't keep letting this happen. I know what he's trying to do. I get my feet on the ground and stand up without Hugh's help. I don't even say thank you.

We stand on the riverbed at the base of the cliff, looking across the river. It's not a *huge* way across, but it's long enough to feel uneasy about. It's completely frozen over, but I'm not sure how thick the ice is. There's only one way to find out.

This time I go first, taking each step incredibly slowly. Falling through the ice is deadly. I can't tell how forceful the river current is but I'm guessing it's strong. Going under even for one second could pull me far past the opening, leaving me to drown.

There are subtle cracking sounds coming from the ice beneath me. But slowly, one step at a time, I manage to cross to the other side. Next is Hugh, which is worrying as he does have a bigger build than I do and is a lot heavier. He doesn't cross as slowly or carefully as me.

"Hugh! Slow down!" I warn him.

The cracking under his feet is much louder. But instead of continuing slowly, he stops moving. I watch tiny fractures in the icy surface form, spreading out from his feet.

"Hugh," I tell him very firmly, but trying to stay as calm as I can. "You need to keep moving. Keep moving very, *very*, slowly."

He takes a step towards me, and another, and another. He's almost here, but the ice keeps cracking. I'm sure he's about to

CHAPTER TWENTY-THREE

go under, and there's nothing I'd be able to do. But somehow, against all odds, against his heavy footing, he makes it across the river. He stands shakily on the frozen riverbed, panting like crazy. I give him time to catch his breath and then we make our way up the hill and towards the fire tower.

We reach the base of the tower in about five minutes. Looking up, I see a rusty staircase that wraps around the tower's four sides and a ladder to enter the actual radio station, made of dilapidated wood. We begin our climb, making sure we hold onto the railings in fear of slipping through the cracks. Every step unleashes a series of creaks from the old metal bolts that barely hold this piece of junk together. We finally reach the landing under the station and begin our climb up the ladder. Hugh goes first, and I let him get to the top before I start climbing. He stops at the trap door and tries to push it open, but it won't budge.

"No!" Hugh screams, making me jump a little.

"What?" I call back.

"It's jammed."

Shit. I need him to be able to open this door. My entire body is aching from being outside, and I need a tiny bit of relief. He keeps banging and pushing until, finally, it snaps open. I let out a relieved breath, and he enters. I follow suit, quickly climbing up the ladder and making my way inside. I shut the door and feel only a slight liberation from the weather. The wind is gone, but there is no heat inside this rusty box. I breathe into my sleeves and my fingers regain a little bit of life.

We look around the room, trying to find the radio. We didn't consider the fact that we have no idea what a radio looks like, and there are various machines that could fit the description. As we look around the room, Hugh finds a map of the mountain, with the radio hut circled and a trail outline to what seems to be the lodge.

"Who are Shannon and Al?" Hugh asks me.

"Um, I don't know. Why?" I reply.

"Because this map says, 'Shannon and Al's Cabin,' but that isn't your mom and dad," he states.

I take a closer look at the map and realize he is telling the truth. The names 'Shannon' and 'Al' are written over the top of our cabin.

"Um, I don't know," I say. "This map looks pretty old. They're probably the people my parents bought it from."

"Hmm, weird," Hugh says monotonously.

I notice something on one of the many surfaces in this room. It's a machine with something long sitting next to it, tipped on its side. I go over to it, lift the object to sit upright and realize it's a microphone. So, *this* is a radio. I have no idea how to use it, so I call Hugh over. He clearly has no idea either, but he fiddles around with the buttons and dials. Somehow, he manages to turn it on. He turns the dial that changes the frequency while talking into the microphone.

"Hello? Hello? We need help. Hello?" Hugh repeats.

He turns it with no luck, just static noise. I am about to tell him to give it up until a voice comes through the speaker.

"Telluride Police. What is the problem?" it says.

"Hello?" Hugh says like he just won the lottery. "Hello! My name is Hugh, and we are stuck on a mountain with a murderer! 2312 Quinn Road! Please send help!"

There is more static noise from the other line until their voice finally comes back.

"Is anybody injured?"

CHAPTER TWENTY-THREE

"Yes! There are four people dead so far! Please send help!"

The voice doesn't come back straight away. We panic that we have lost them and we're stuck here for good. However, eventually, they respond, but I don't know if it's a good thing or not.

"I'm afraid we can't send anybody out there until the storm clears."

"What? How long is that going to be?" Hugh asks.

"According to the forecast, a few hours," the voice informs.

"Are you serious? We can't wait a few hours!" Hugh yells into the line.

"I'm sorry, sir. With this storm, we're unable to send an officer out to you. It's too dangerous. We could—"

The voice cuts out, and the static returns.

"No! Hello? Somebody?" Hugh screams, but nobody is there. I put my hand on his shoulder in an attempt to calm him down.

"It's okay. It's already one a.m. They'll be here by dawn," I tell him.

Hugh looks at me, defeated.

"If we're not all dead by then."

Chapter Twenty-Four

Willow - 12:20 AM - Sunday, 30th January 2022

Kaya and I walk side by side, making sure we don't lose each other in the snowy forest. We walk in silence, of course, and it couldn't be more awkward, even with the deafening storm in our ears. We were throwing childish insults at each other earlier in the night, but I think we both understand there are more important things to focus on.

After finding that message on my mirror and the knife in my sink, I almost passed out. I knew I couldn't leave it there and risk somebody finding it, so I grabbed a wet towel and wiped the blood off the mirror. I grabbed the knife and hid it under the sink. Somebody is messing with me, and they know what I've done. Not just about Fergus. What I've done before this trip. Why I'm really a *killer.* Something I've kept to myself for a while. Could it be Kaya? She hates me enough to do something like this.

We duck under branches and try our best not to fall on the ice. Yes, doing either of those things slows us down, but it's better than getting hurt. It also saves you the embarrassment. I'm so glad nobody saw me run into that tree.

"Are you sure you know where we're going?" Kaya asks in her usual tone, annoyed and judgmental.

CHAPTER TWENTY-FOUR

"I mean, no, not really, but I think it's this way," I reply, trying my best to sound as unfazed by that comment as I can. I already told her I don't know where the cabin is. Why is she now expecting me to act as a compass? I continue leading Kaya through the woods, trying my best to retrace my footsteps, but I can't. I try to stay as calm as possible, doing everything in my power to stop her knowing we are completely *fucking* lost.

"You're lying," Kaya tells me. "There is no shack."

"Oh, piss off, Kaya," I snap. "There is, I just have no idea where it is!" It doesn't help my case.

"How do I know you're not the killer?" Kaya asks.

"Seriously?" I ask disgustedly. "What is your problem with me?"

"Are you kidding? Everything, Willow!" she snaps back.

"What the fuck did I do?" I shout at her. We have stopped completely now. Somehow, I am able to ignore the cold just for this. "Seriously, what did I ever do to you?"

"What haven't you done?" she begins. "You're an awful friend! You're so completely ignorant and pretentious, and you barely have any talent to make up for it!"

Oh my god. Not this again.

"*I'm* ignorant and pretentious? That is so rich coming from you! And you don't know anything about me. How can I be a bad friend?"

"I know how you treated Noa!" she argues.

"Oh, for fucks sake! That has nothing to do with you!" I physically cannot help myself. There is something about Kaya that just makes me so irrationally angry. She has a perfect life. She is rich and has two loving parents but will always insist she has some sort of hardship affecting her. I mean, she *says* she's "bisexual", but she's dating a *guy* who graduated last year. She's a fraud. Her life is so boring that I'm not surprised she is inserting herself into mine just to keep herself entertained.

She is about to retort when I see something in the distance. I put my hand in front of her face, indicating for her to be quiet. I can see the light from the cabin creeping out into the forest. I start moving, and Kaya follows me, yelling about something I don't care to hear. I pick up the pace and then break out into a sprint, and I don't stop running until I come face to face with the groundskeeper's cabin.

"I fucking told you!" I yell at Kaya tauntingly.

Even through the haze, I can see that her face is scrunched up in a bitter expression. She clearly hates being wrong, especially about me. She walks to the door, and I follow her, but I stop in front of the porch. Kaya turns to me,

"You're not coming inside?" she asks.

"Absolutely not," I state, shivering. I'd rather freeze to death than go inside.

Kaya squints at me, then turns back around and places her hand on the doorknob.

"Wait, you're just going to barge in?"

"Yeah", she responds, almost as if I'm an idiot for asking.

"Okay, and what if there's somebody inside? What if the killer is inside?"

Kaya looks at me for a few seconds, then nonchalantly walks to the window and peers inside. She then looks back at me with a bored expression, walks to the door, twists the handle, and pushes it open. As the hinges creak and the room is revealed, I can see the blood all over the floor, and I wait for her reaction to finding the bodies, but it doesn't come.

"So, where are they?" she calls to me.

CHAPTER TWENTY-FOUR

I glare at the door, waiting for a "gotcha." But it's silent. I'm stunned. What does she mean? My legs move involuntarily up the porch steps and into the cabin door. I look around in shock. The blood is there, but Fergus and the Groundskeeper are gone. I look under the bed. Nothing.

"I … they were right here, I swear!" I shout, pleading for Kaya to believe me, and she does. But not in the way I wanted her to.

"What did you do to the bodies?"

"What? Kaya, I didn't do anything! You have to believe me!" I shout back.

She pauses, looking me up and down. "You're a *killer*."

I freeze. Killer. I feel my heart drop into my stomach. Killer. The writing on my mirror. The person slipping the piece of paper into my hands. Somebody in that cabin wants me dead. And nobody hates me more than Kaya.

"Oh my god," I say, staring at her in fear. "It's you."

"Wow, Willow, great defense," she says sarcastically.

"You're the one who wrote that on my mirror."

She looks at me, confused. "What the fuck are you talking about?" Kaya asks.

"You slipped me that note."

"What note?"

I'm about to run out the door when we hear a creak coming from the closet. We go silent, waiting for the sound again. The wind rages on outside but this sound was unmistakable. It was made by a person. Kaya takes a step towards it whilst I take a step towards the door. My heart feels like it could beat out of my chest.

Kaya reaches for the handle and as she grabs it, the doors burst open, and the person wearing the maniac's mask jumps out. We both scream and run out the front door as the killer trails behind us. I make it down the steps as Kaya reaches to door, but she slips and falls face-first onto the porch. She calls for my help, and I'm about to go back for her, but the deer grabs her leg and pulls her towards him.

"WILLOW! PLEASE! HELP!" Kaya screams.

I don't know what to do, and I don't know how I can help. I also don't know if I *want* to. Does she want me to fight the deer with my bare hands? I could maybe do it, but I'm not sure if I want to risk it. But when I see the deer pull out his knife and stab Kaya's back, I make my decision.

I turn around and run in the direction of the lodge, hearing Kaya's screams get fainter and fainter.

Chapter Twenty-Five

12:20 AM - Sunday, 30th January 2022

I stand alone in a dark, empty room with the door cracked open, providing a sliver of light that ever so slightly brightens the area. This lodge is magnificent. Since I arrived on Friday, I've been biding my time, and I'm so glad this night is finally upon us. I've had quite a bit of enjoyment already, but the night is still young, and there is still so much work that needs to be done.

All but one of the teenagers are outside, and I figure I might as well have some fun with her. It's been about twenty minutes since the group left the lodge, and the girl has not left her room. From where I stand, I am close enough to hear her occasional cries or frustrated scream. Something must be really eating away at her. I can tell the rest of the group thinks she's weak, and that makes her an easy target.

Finally, I hear movement from her room. The doorknob twists and the hinges squeak as she opens it and walks into the hallway. I watch through the crack of my door as the girl walks past. Her eyes are red and puffy, and she is breathing heavily. I chose this room specifically, as the door hinges seem to be well-oiled compared to the others. So, as she walks past, I silently open the door, ready to follow her. I'm so close that

I could reach out and touch her. I could grab her hair and pull back, hold a knife to her throat. I could give her the fright of her life.

But I won't.

I stop moving and watch as she walks into the kitchen, oblivious to my existence. She places her elbows on the counter and burrows her face into her hands.

"Oh my fucking god, Fergus," she cries.

She can't handle this. It would be kind of me to put her out of her misery. I just need to wait for the right time. Right now, she stands in the open-concept kitchen with easy access to the back door. To attack her now would be a mistake. I watch as she stands up straight and mutters to herself once again.

"I can't do this anymore."

She walks towards the basement door. Now is my chance. Her back is turned, and she has nowhere to run. I quickly creep towards her with my axe in hand. She opens the basement door and is about to walk down the stairs when a floorboard creaks under my foot. The room goes dead still, as if all the oxygen has been sucked out of the atmosphere. She knows.

She turns but it takes her a while to process what she's looking at. Then, she screams. Out of the goodness of my heart, I hit her directly in the temple with the handle of my axe, which sends her plummeting down the basement stairs.

VII

THE BENEDICTUS

Chapter Twenty-Six

Noa - 1:00 AM - Sunday, 30th January 2022

The longer the night progresses, the colder it gets. The storm continues, creating a heavy mist that makes completing any small task impossible. The snow becomes more and more difficult to walk through.

Finding the generator takes longer than I'd like to admit. The way Caleb described it, I thought it would be unmissable. In my defense, I can't focus on anything but how cold it is, my nose is going numb, and the lodge is enormous.

"Do you actually know how to use a generator?" I ask.

"Yeah," she responds. "My family used to have a beach house, and the power would often go out, so we were always starting up the generator."

At least one of us can be of use. Caleb never told us which side of the house it is on. I don't even think he knows. While we're walking, we notice a window slightly ajar. It's about six feet off the ground, higher than either of us can reach easily. From my angle, it just appears to be a dark room, but a sliver of light glares against the window. I guess someone left the door open. But I don't know why the window would be open, especially not in this weather, so I make Evelyn lift me up so I can shut it. She drops me prematurely and when I hit the ground, my feet are unstable, and I fall backwards into the thick snow. We laugh and it feels good. Yes, this night is no laughing matter I know, but I need to find little moments of joy in order to survive. I learnt that over the last few months.

We turn the corner, and to my delight, Evelyn makes out the generator. She races over to it, and I follow suit.

"Can you shine the flashlight over here?" she asks.

I hold the light in position while Evelyn fiddles with the generator. But soon, my arm gets tired, and I switch it to the other hand. Evelyn opens the panels to reveal a large array of wires, far too complicated for anybody to figure out. In my mind, I thought generators were just a wire you pull, and it starts. I guess not.

Evelyn kneels for better access and as she does this, my mind begins to wander. I ponder who could have opened the window. I know nobody needed cool air. Was it somebody sneaking out? Or was it somebody sneaking in?

"Hey, Noa?" Evelyn says, pulling me out of my head. "The light." Whilst I have been lost in thought, my hand has drifted off to the side, leaving Evelyn in the dark.

"Oh, sorry," I say. But before I move it back, I realize it is shining on the small glass pane that looks directly into the basement, and something catches my eye. Movement. Something shifts towards the back of the room, but the glass is too fogged up for the light to illuminate whatever it is clearly.

"Noa! Hey. Light," Evelyn reminds me.

"I-I think there is someone down there," I whisper nervously to Evelyn.

"Maybe it's Riley? I don't know."

"Yeah," I start. "That's why I'm worried."

"Can you please just shine the light over here?" she begs.

CHAPTER TWENTY-SIX

I do, but I make sure to keep an eye on the window. After a few minutes, Evelyn speaks up.

"Okay, this should do it."

She grabs a small lever and lifts it upwards, which creates a clicking noise, but nothing happens. The lights in the lodge remain off.

"Fucking hell," Evelyn exclaims.

"What happened?" I ask, "Did you do it wrong?"

"No, Noa, I didn't do it wrong!" she yells. Then she pauses and takes a deep breath. "Sorry."

I shrug. I don't care. I get it. I've never fixed a machine or anything. I tried to in the psych ward. They had cutesy little classes on engineering and carpentry. I got a few things out of that place, how to fix a generator or build a birdbath was not among them. Evelyn stands up. I hand her the phone back, and she walks to the side of the generator and opens a second, smaller panel. Her face goes white.

"What the hell," she mutters.

"What is it?" I ask, walking over to her. As I look at the panel, my stomach sinks too. The wires that power the generator have been cut, with no way to repair them.

"Who did this?" she asks me.

"I have no idea," I admit.

This was not supposed to happen. As we stand there in a mix of confusion and shock, I hear something. A faint buzz. It sounds as if it's behind us but far away. Then as the buzz gets closer, I understand what it is. An engine. We make out headlights piercing through the snow, shining on the distant trees, and realize a car is driving along the road. Now is our chance. The car is driving along the same mountain road we used on the way here. Right now, it's behind us but soon it will loop around and drive past the small dirt path leading to the gate. We need to go now if we want to meet it there. I dart towards the trees, heading directly for the fence. Evelyn follows me, yelling at me to stop, but I don't. We reach it relatively quickly. It's a wooden fence that isn't too high. I climb over first. Piece of cake. Then, Evelyn goes. And we're off. We run through the woods together, holding hands, making sure we don't get lost. The snow is thick, which makes running nearly impossible, but we push on. We leap as quickly as possible through the snow and forest until the trees thin. Eventually, there are only a few scattered around.

We are running so fast that we don't notice the steep slope that leads to the road. We slip and fall directly forward. I disappear beneath the snow, smacking the side of my face against the frozen ground beneath. I lift my hand to my cheekbone, and it stings. When I look at my fingers, I can see blood. Luckily, the snow prevents us from rolling any further. I stand up and see Evelyn a few feet in front of me. Her nose is bleeding.

Through the mist, we can make out the headlights as they turn the corner and begin heading our way. We've done it. Well, not quite yet. We're so close.

Evelyn and I leap down the slope, tromping through the drifts. The lights are getting closer and for a second, I'm horrified they will drive past. We approach the road. Closer and closer. Evelyn trips and falls back into the snow, but I don't have time to help her. I keep going. So does the car, which I can now tell is a large SUV. The perfect car for this type of weather. It's not a police car, but that's not important right now.

It doesn't matter what car it was. Everything happens so

CHAPTER TWENTY-SIX

quickly.

My feet meet the icy asphalt, and I wave my arms beckoning the car to stop. But they're too close. And they see me too late.

I make out the car speeding towards me, the horn blaring, and Evelyn's screams. In a last ditch effort to avoid me, the SUV swerves to the right but loses control and breaks through the side railing, flying off the side of the mountain.

Chapter Twenty-Seven

Willow - 1:00 AM - Sunday, 30th January 2022

I can no longer hear Kaya's screams. I haven't even looked back once. I feel terrible about it, but I had to get myself out of there. It was too late to help her. If I had gone back, the killer could have easily grabbed and killed me too. My body is pumping with so much adrenaline that I haven't stopped sprinting since I started, but I think I'm far enough away now that I take a moment to pause.

My head spins and my chest cramps, making it hard for me to breathe. My vision goes blurry and my knees buckle. Every step I take through the thick snow gets harder and harder and more painful until it's almost unbearable. I hold on to the nearest tree to keep myself upright, but that doesn't last long. I collapse, hunched over with my face mere inches from the snow. My stomach twists and turns, and before I know it, I gag and vomit all over the ground. I sit back against the tree, puffing and panting. After a few minutes, I can catch my breath, and my vision returns to me. I look down at the puddle of puke on the ground, and I think back to what Samuel had said when I vomited on the side of the road before all hell broke loose.

"Nah, man, that's green."

CHAPTER TWENTY-SEVEN

I let out a chuckle. When he said it initially, I did not find it funny. But now it all just seems so ridiculous. I took everything so seriously. Every joke was a dig at me. An insult. But they were just trying to have fun. I think about what my time at school could have been if I had just opened up a little more. If I took off my armor. Maybe I could have made some friends. Some real friends.

I realize that since this whole shitshow began, I haven't let the fear and craziness get to me. I haven't had time to let it all out, and I fear it's all finally catching up to me. Tears pour out of my eyes, and I let out uncontrollable sobs—a mix of grief and guilt. I haven't felt this way about anybody in a really long time. I've been numb for so long, and it's taken my friends being murdered to make me feel something. Well, not only that. It's more the fact that I don't think *they* would think of *me* as a friend. For some reason, that hurts more. I know deep down this is all my fault. Somehow, somebody knows what I've done, and they won't stop killing until they get to me.

I'm so lost in my own regrets that I don't even notice the footsteps that are quickly approaching me. When I look towards the sound, I rise to my feet, ready to run again, even if my body can't take it. I see the person in the maniac's mask standing twenty feet away from me, staring. They're on all fours, imitating a deer.

"What the fuck do you want?" I scream.

They don't answer but instead just crawl slowly towards me, taunting me. I slowly inch myself backwards, step by step, never breaking eye contact with them. As I scuttle away, the killer moves forward. I'm expecting the person to sprint towards me any second. They stop moving and then slowly stand up, still staring directly at me. It sluggishly lifts its hand toward me.

"Killer," it bellows in a deep, commanding voice.

I don't recognize it, but something about it doesn't sound real. There's a sort of metallic sound to it. I think maybe I'm just mishearing it through the wind, but then I notice a faint red light blinking on its collar. A voice changer. This is the person who wrote it on my mirror, but who is it? Why are they using a voice changer? They don't want me to recognize their voice, that's obvious. I'm so over running. Part of me wants to run towards them and rip that mask off. I want to know who it is and kill them before they do the same to me. Then, they reveal the hunting knife from their belt. I reach for mine but remember I don't have it. I found it in the sink and didn't have time to clean it off. I wiped the mirror and hid it in the cabinet. I did not grab another one. Ugh, what an idiot.

Then, out of nowhere, the killer breaks into a full sprint towards me. Instinctively, I turn around and race away once again.

I throw a terrified look over my shoulder every once in a while, to see if they're following me. They are. But then, I look back a fourth time and see they've stopped running and are now just standing in the trees, watching me. I don't stop. I keep running and running until I find myself at the clearing where the lodge sits.

"Help! Please, somebody!" I call as I sprint for the front door. I burst into the lodge, calling for help, but nobody answers. It's still pitch black. I'm guessing Noa and Evelyn couldn't start the backup generator. Maybe they never even tried.

I need to catch my breath and warm up. I am not used to this much physical exertion. I'm a triple threat, but dancing

CHAPTER TWENTY-SEVEN

has always been my weakest link. I'm a very strong mover.

I have my back against the door, but I remind myself that it's not safe. I know a knife could be driven through the wood any second. I lock it and run into the great room. It's empty.

"Hello? Riley?"

BANG.

I jump and turn back to the door. The door handle jiggles and then—

BANG.

There is another loud whack on the door. My heart drops. Is this the killer? Or is it somebody else that I've unintentionally locked out?

"Who is it?" I call to the door. Nobody responds. The lodge is completely silent. I don't even dare to breathe. I turn off my phone flashlight, hoping the person on the other side will just go away. But they don't. Instead, they slam their axe straight through the door.

They swing the axe again, making the hole a little bigger. They're making a hole big enough to reach the lock. I can't let that happen. I think on my feet. I turn my flashlight back on and notice the entryway table. I race towards it and begin pushing it closer to the door, all the while the person in the maniac mask strikes away.

As I drag it over, I notice there are no pictures on it. I didn't find it strange when I first got here. I just thought Caleb's family kept their pictures at home. But I realize now that the lodge is surprisingly void of any photos, even though there are empty spots on the wall that appear to be designed for a portrait.

After barricading the door, I return to the great room. I keep my eyes on the front door, listening to the incessant pounding sounds as the maniac tries to break in. What if he does? I'd be screwed. I'm all alone and defenseless, and he has an axe.

"Hello?", I scream throughout the house, hoping there is someone here who somehow hasn't heard the commotion.

Nobody emerges. I guess this time I'm the first one back. I know we left Riley on her own but when I call for her, she doesn't respond. I panic, immediately thinking the worst. I race to her bedroom and swing the door open. It's empty. Her window is shut. Where is she? I'm about to scavenge the entire house when I notice something. Silence. The house is completely silent. The maniac has stopped banging on the door. He's left. Or…

He got inside.

I grab a glass perfume bottle from Riley's dresser and hold it defensively in my grasp, as if the killer will be intimidated by it. I creep back to the great room, hoping to remain undetected by whoever may or may not be inside. I stand at the edge of the hallway, on the cusp of the room, concealed by the shadows. I slowly peek my head out towards the front door. My heart races. It becomes clear. I can see the front door is still shut tight, with the table placed directly in front of it.

He left.

Every muscle in my body relaxes and I sink to the floor. I don't know where Riley is, but at least I know I'm safe for now. Inside, away from the biting cold. The moment of stillness allows me to focus on how dreadfully tired I am. How do people in horror films fight the killer all night, and usually into the morning? I'm ready to tap out now. I need to sleep. Maybe we could reconvene tomorrow night. I'm sure the killer is tired too.

CHAPTER TWENTY-SEVEN

My eyes snap open and I spring to me feet when I hear a boom coming from outside. I shudder, thinking it's another bang at the door. But it's not. It's not that close, but it's *loud.* Then there's another sound which I immediately recognize. It's an explosion.

Without thinking, I race out of the back door. The cold immediately bites my skin as I was inside long enough to acclimate to the warmth. I know the sound came from the direction of the driveway, so I run towards it, using the moonlight to see where I'm going. I swear to God, if I survive this night, my quads better be huge. When I'm back in the woods, I run straight ahead. I hop over the fence and keep going until the trees stop. It's just a snowy, misty abyss in front of me, but when I look down, I see a steep decline to the main road and then nothing. I'm at the edge of the mountain. It takes me a while to make out two people on the road, looking over the railing at the sudden drop. I slowly walk down, trying to remain undetectable until I know whoever they are won't try to kill me. As I reach the road, I can make out Noa and Evelyn with their backs turned to me.

"What the fuck happened?" I shout at them, which makes them both jump.

They don't answer, so I walk over to the ledge, and when I look down, I realize what the explosion was. At the bottom of the mountain, I can make out a large fire through the haze. It's a car. Well, *was* a car.

"Holy shit! What did you guys do?" I question them.

"It was an accident!" Noa sobs. "I ran out to stop them, and they swerved to miss me, but they skidded on the ice and went over."

"What were they doing driving in the storm?" I ask them.

I'm mainly looking at Evelyn because Noa seems to be on the verge of a panic attack.

"How should I know?" Evelyn responds, not any calmer than Noa.

I want to yell back at her, but there's no point. She's in shock. They're both shivering, and Evelyn is as pale as a ghost. They have to get inside; they're freezing.

I walk back to the ledge when Noa stops me, "Wait. Willow. Where is Kaya?" she asks, sounding concerned.

I stop walking. I don't know how to break this to her. I mean, sure, we've already lost a few people tonight, but Noa and Kaya were best friends. I can't bear to face her.

"She's dead," I say flatly.

I don't hear anything. No audible gasps or sounds indicate shock, so I turn around to ensure the information is registered. I know it has. Evelyn has her hand over her mouth, and Noa stands there looking distraught.

"What?" Noa asks, her voice quivering.

"We were attacked at the cabin," I inform them. What I say next is completely untrue, and I honestly don't know why I even bother saying it. "I tried to help her, truly I did, but it was too late."

Evelyn and Noa both turn away, clearly struggling to comprehend it all.

"FUCK!" Noa screams into the void. She then turns back to me. "Why the fuck is this happening?" she asks feebly.

I know why, but I can't tell them. At least not here.

"I don't know," I lie. The look in Noa's eyes is so despondent. She has lost all hope. Evelyn still faces the other way, not saying a word.

"We can't stay here," I tell them. "We have to get back to the

CHAPTER TWENTY-SEVEN

lodge, or we'll freeze."

We trudge back up the slope, using all our might to cross the snow. I make it to the top first and help Noa and Evelyn; then, we begin the trek back. We have all given up on running, so we walk mournfully through the woods in silence. If the killer wants to say hello, we would be easy targets but honestly, I don't care. I'm exhausted and I'm cold.

Killer. It's the word that bounces around in my mind. That maniac asshole thinks I'm a killer. Not thinks. *Knows*. Is that why they're doing all of this? It seems like a lot of effort just to taunt one person. What is their goal? Do they want me to confess? If so, they've almost succeeded because it's getting harder and harder to keep all this shit to myself. What if the message on the mirror lines up with something one of the others knows? What if all of us have received similar messages? Maybe it could help us figure out who is doing this. But what if it doesn't? Then they'll all know what I've done and will never look at me the same.

I think about who could be behind that mask again. I've been by myself for the majority of the night, so I don't know if people really were where they say they were. It could have been Evelyn or Noa behind that mask. I know they didn't have enough time to get from the front door of the lodge to where the car crashed, but I know at least two people are in on it, so why couldn't there be more? Maybe Noa or Evelyn slipped me the note whilst their accomplice was outside. But why would Noa kill her best friend? Why would she do this after everything she's gone through?

Where are Hugh and Caleb? I ask myself. Are they really at the fire tower? Or did they just use that as a ruse? Could they be doing it together? That would make up for all the inconsistencies and contradictions. Why do they want me to confess? Do they want me to disappear so they can live their life together? Was Hugh lying to me? He has before. Does he *love* Caleb? But why kill everybody? That's the part I don't understand. It can't be all about me, which is something I've never said before. Because if it were, they would have picked me off straight away. They would have no reason to kill the others. Nothing is clicking into place. Nothing makes sense.

We finally arrive at the lodge and enter through the back door. We immediately turn on the gas fireplace and look around the house for candles and any other light source. After a while of searching, we gather enough to light the living room. It's a dim light, but it will do. We slump into the couches, defeated.

"Riley?" Noa calls.

"She's not here," I tell her.

"What do you mean she's not here?" she responds.

"Before I heard the explosion, I was here looking for her. Her room was empty. She's not here."

Noa sighs. "What the fuck is happening?"

"Where do you think the boys are?" Evelyn asks. "They've been gone a while."

"It's a pretty long walk," Noa says.

"Hmm. I guess," Evelyn responds, unconvinced. I can tell she's also aware of the very real possibility that the killer could be one of us. That means she must have seen something like I did. Did somebody slip her a note in the darkness too? Has someone been leaving her messages?

"I just want to know why," Noa says again with a sigh. "Why are they doing this?"

Shit. This is it. I know I have to be honest. I can't keep this

CHAPTER TWENTY-SEVEN

a secret anymore. I've barely recognized the weight that is on my shoulders. It's crushing. I need to tell them, but it's so hard to say it out loud. Maybe they'll be able to relate. Maybe they have secrets too. Finally, I muster up enough courage.

"I know why," I tell her. Evelyn and Noa share a confused glance.

"What do you mean?" Evelyn asks.

"The killer has been toying with me all night," I inform them. "I don't know why, but all of this comes back to me."

If they have gone through similar things, they don't show it. All they give me are looks that tell me to continue. It's too late to back out now. I take a deep breath.

"My dad didn't just leave ... I killed him."

Chapter Twenty-Eight

Hugh - 1:30 AM - Sunday, 30th January 2022

Once we had called for help, Caleb and I stayed in the tower. It seemed safer than braving the cold and possibly being slaughtered by a mass murderer, however, any tiny movement results in the deafening creak of the wooden boards that form the station. Somehow, they have lasted this long, so they should be able to last a little while longer. Although, I'm not counting on them to.

The storm rages outside, which unsettles me as every time the wind blows, the support beams shake and the metal clangs. It'll only get worse as the storm reaches its peak. Which I fear is happening now. I am worried that going outside could result in our deaths, whether that be from the cold or the killer, but I fear that being in here may not be any different. The metal is old and rusted, the wood is chipped and unstable. I'm not sure the last time it underwent a safety check, but considering the old map on the wall, and the way the trap door refused to open, I'm guessing it's been a while since somebody was up here. We're not safe anywhere, but still, I'd rather take my chances in here. That cold is unforgiving.

So is the person with the antlers.

I have been sitting in the chair that rests under the physical

CHAPTER TWENTY-EIGHT

radio while Caleb sits in the corner at the opposite side of the station. He's restless, constantly biting the skin around his fingernails and tapping his foot. Every time the tower unveils its imperfect foundation, he gets more uneasy until, finally, he stands up.

"Hugh, we have to go," he says, unable to take it anymore.

I know he's distressed, and believe me, I don't like being up here either, but looking out the window at the storm, I don't know how far we will get.

"Look outside," I advise him. "This is the worst it's looked. We'll freeze if we're lucky. There is a killer out there!"

"I'd rather take my chances out there than falling to my death in here."

"Caleb, we're not going to fall! These things are poured into cement."

"I don't care!"

"Can we just wait a little longer—"

As the words leave my mouth, the tower shakes again. This was not like the other times. This was stronger. The wind makes the windows shudder and I'm horrified they could implode any moment. If they do, then we may as well be outside.

Caleb lets out a whimper. He's always hated heights. One time, we were at the Telluride carnival and decided to go on the Ferris wheel. He didn't open his eyes once. Any time I laughed at him, he would hit me and tell me to shut up which, of course, only made me laugh harder. But I wasn't laughing now. Maybe he's right. It might be better to risk the outdoors and make it back to the lodge. To a room with a lock. Besides, when the police arrive, they'll go to the lodge.

We silently agree to stand up and run for the trap door. I

open the door and begin to climb down the ladder first. The second my body is no longer protected by the shelter, I feel the intense wind push me back. My arms fully extend, and I am certain I am about to be blown off the ladder. The metal is freezing and extremely difficult to cling to, but after a few minutes of grappling, and Caleb screaming at me to hold on, I manage to pull myself back toward the ladder. Then, I finish my descent to the landing.

Next is Caleb, but seeing as he is aware of the strength of the wind, he holds on a little tighter. After a brief struggle with the wind, he reaches the landing, and we head for the staircase.

I can feel the wind getting worse as the seconds go by. I believe that if I was wearing baggier clothes, I would take flight. I thought the ladder and the landing were bad, but as soon as I step onto the staircase, completely exposed to the elements, it's a different story. When moving against the wind, it's near impossible to even take a step forward, and when moving with it, you're at risk of being blown right off the edge.

Gripping the railings, we move down the stairs. We turn the first corner slowly. With each step we take, I can hear the entire tower creak. It makes my stomach churn, and I move a little faster, Caleb keeping up. I know the stairs are not sturdy, so I'm trying not to be heavy footed but it's hard when you're trying to keep your balance.

I turn the next corner. The wind is working with us. I descend a little quicker than anticipated and so does Caleb. But unlike me, Caleb doesn't stick the landing. He is pushed forward, flying down the last three steps, and when he lands, he yelps and falls forward. I catch him before he hits the ground, but he can't stand. He collapses onto the corner landing clutching at his ankle.

"What's wrong?" I yell through the wind. "What happened?"

He grits his teeth and lets out a pained grunt.

"I don't know!" he yells back. "It fucking hurts! I think it's rolled!"

"We need to get you back to the lodge! It's too cold. Can you walk?"

"I don't think so!"

"You need to try!"

He nods at me. He looks determined. I grab his arm and lift him to his feet. He squeals as soon as he puts pressure on it. Oh no, this is not good. He puts his arm over my shoulder, I take his body weight, and together we descend the tower. The metal creaks and I'm sure a section of the staircase is going to fall but miraculously, we make it to the bottom. Caleb and I hobble down the hill and arrive at the river. The frozen river.

God damn.

The river was hard enough to cross one at a time, so both of us going together is a recipe for disaster. We take the first step onto the ice and pause, waiting to hear anything. Nothing. We take another one and pause again. There's a little cracking sound. We stay still. I hold my breath. There are no more. We take a few more steps forward and as we reach the middle before there is another sound. Much louder. This time, it doesn't stop. Tiny fractures in the ice spread out in every direction, like a spider weaving its web. Because both of our weight is on me, the ice cracks directly below me and within a second, I feel the subzero water engulf my body. The last thing I hear before my head goes under is Caleb calling my name.

My body freezes and burns simultaneously, and my breath is instantly knocked out of me. I open my eyes for a second, but the temperature scalds them. Not that it matters, I can't see anything anyway. It's pitch black. I don't know which way is up or down. Is Caleb trying to find me? All I can feel is the cold. Is that all I'm going to feel forever?

Cold.

So cold.

Need out.

I swim up.

Or down.

I hit ice.

Caleb.

please help me

can't breathe

where is opening

so hard

sleep

drowsy

stiffening

hand.

arm.

hand on arm.

Hand on my arm.

I feel a hand on my arm.

Then another one.

My eyes shoot open.

The cold wind demolishes my skin but all I can do is gasp. I gasp for air as if it's my first-time breathing. It's so cold but I don't care. I can breathe. My vision is blurry, or is that the mist? Where is Caleb? My body is so numb I don't even feel

CHAPTER TWENTY-EIGHT

him grabbing my arm and dragging me off the ice. He gets my back to the frozen riverbed and drops my arm. Then, he kneels next to me and stares into my eyes. He says something but I can't understand him. My body isn't working properly.

He asks again but this time I can work it out. Mainly because he yells it this time.

"Are you okay?"

"Okay," I say with a pathetic thumbs up. I can't even move my fingers, so it's more like I just showed him the back of my hand. It's clear Caleb is not in the mood for my comedy attempts, so he grabs me and lifts me up.

"I need you to walk!" he tells me. He puts his arm back around me. I like it. It feels warm.

We climb up the rocks and make it back to the path leading towards the lodge. It's a long walk as is, but it's even longer in our conditions. We have to be getting close. We *need* to be. I don't want to be taken out by the cold when the police are on their way. We're so close. Just a few more hours.

Then, I see lights ahead of me. The lodge. We're almost there. But I stop. No, something stops me. It's something to the left. Something in the trees. A voice.

"What was that?" I shout to him.

"I don't know! We have to keep going!"

But I keep listening and this time I'm able to make out the sound. It is somebody calling for help. A girl's voice. I don't know if it's Willow, Noa, Kaya, Riley, or Evelyn. It could be any of them. From here it doesn't *sound* like it's any of them.

"Help!" the voice shouts again. Caleb tries to drag me away but I can't abandon one of our friends. I'd be dead if Caleb abandoned me. A pit forms in my stomach when I understand that I abandoned him earlier tonight. I left him out in the cold.

I left him for dead. But that's not important right now, so I clear my mind and listen back for the noise. I can think about apologies later.

The voice continues calling, *"Help! Help me!"*

Caleb drags me back. "We need to go now!"

"We can't leave them!"

I look back at him to see a worried look on his face. "That's not our friends!"

I am completely perplexed until the voice calls one more time, and I freeze. Literally. Caleb is right. It isn't any of them. From here, I can tell that it's a man's voice imitating a woman. Raising their pitch. Then, through the mist, I see antlers emerge, walking towards us. Without wasting another minute, Caleb grabs my arm and pulls back onto the path and we limp towards the lodge.

Chapter Twenty-Nine

Willow - 2:30 AM - Sunday, 30th January 2022

Noa and Evelyn look at me with their eyes wide open. They don't say anything, and I know I have to explain further, but I feel physically sick. Whatever I say, it needs to give them a reason not to turn me over to the police. This is something I thought I would take to my grave. Perhaps that may be coming sooner than expected.

"Willow, what the fuck," Evelyn gasps.

"It wasn't on purpose," I tell them, trying to maintain the tiniest bit of respect they have for me. I don't think it's working. I need to delve deeper. I need them to have my back. I need them to keep their mouths shut. Noa sits on the couch, looking anywhere but my eyes. She looks so angry. I get it. The last few months, she's been grieving the loss of her family and here I am, telling her that I *killed* my own father. They just sit there in silence, and it makes me squirm.

"H-he started drinking," I tell them. "He would come home most nights hammered. It started with him just saying out-of-pocket things. Things we could just brush off and blame on him being drunk. Then, they started becoming more personal. *Mean.* He would say things that made mom and me feel like shit. He would start talking about her weight. And how he didn't marry the woman she was today, he married someone else. He told me that I was talentless, and I shouldn't expect to get accepted into any theater schools."

Noa has stopped avoiding eye contact and is now looking at me. She still doesn't look happy, but it's an improvement.

Evelyn takes a short breath. She looks apologetic. "Willow, I—"

"Don't," I cut her off. I know she was about to tell me he was wrong, and I know she would be lying. She agrees with him. "I knew he was right. I knew deep down I wasn't good enough. The only reason I would get all the roles in school was because of him. But it was the one thing I had, so I pushed it down and lived in blissful ignorance. If I acted like I was the best, then maybe everybody would believe it. Maybe I would believe it. Maybe I would forget everything he said to me. It was easier that way."

Evelyn goes quiet, and Noa has a guilty expression on her face. I could be safe from legal repercussions after all.

"Then, over time, he became physical. Every single night, I could hear mom and dad arguing from my bedroom. She would cry, he would scream, and they would always end with a smack, then a thud. And then quiet. Mom stopped crying after a while. She just took the punches. Never fought him. Then ..." Tears form in my eyes. "Then he would hit me. He would barge into my room and, he was big, I couldn't stop him, no matter how badly I wanted to. It was just months of this. We learned how to avoid it sometimes. Just be quiet ..."

I trail off, not knowing how to continue with my story. I know as soon as I say the next few sentences, there's no going back. This is a confession. I look at the girls, who are wide eyed, staring at me. They want me to continue but there's a

CHAPTER TWENTY-NINE

bubble in my throat and tears are threatening to flow out of my eyes.

"But one night, Mom had gone to stay with my aunt. She just left me there. Alone. With him. I was so confused. Why wouldn't she just take me with her?"

There was no hiding it anymore. Tears were pouring down my cheeks.

"He came into my room, drunk. Red-faced, slurring his words, and stumbling everywhere. He started screaming at me, telling me how much of a disappointment I am. I tried to leave the room and just ignore him, but he followed me. He wouldn't stop. I was just so angry."

A choked sob escapes my lips. The girls say nothing.

"I turned around to him and told him to leave me alone. That pissed him off more. I saw it in his eyes. I always could. Like a lightbulb. The moment he decided to hit. I tried to cover my face but I was too late. We were right next to the stairs when he did. It was so hard I spun around and hit the wall. He was standing with his back towards the steps. I couldn't take it anymore, and screamed at him, *'I fucking hate you!'* And I…"

Here we go. Their eyes are locked on me. I could stop speaking. I could pretend it didn't happen, but they already know too much.

"I pushed him. He fell down the stairs and when he hit the bottom …" I pause, choking on my words. "I heard a snap. And he didn't move. I tried to wake him up, but he wouldn't. He was dead. I never told anyone. My mom thinks he left her and she's drinking herself away, waiting for him to come back. I thought she would be relieved! But instead, it's like I killed two parents."

It's done. It's all out in the open. My future is all up to Noa and Evelyn.

"And now whoever is targeting us knows what I've done," I begin, trying to fill any and every silence. "They've been taunting me. Writing on my mirror in blood. The maniac talked to me in the woods, calling me a killer. Slipping me fucked up notes. This is all happening because of me."

Noa and Evelyn don't speak. Don't move. They sit there. Stunned. I don't know what to expect. Are they repulsed? I wouldn't blame them. A wave of panic rushes over me as I truly realize what I've done and how serious the consequences could be.

Just as I'm wondering, Noa stands up and moves towards me. I flinch a little as I'm so certain she's going to hit me or accuse me of being the killer. Maybe even scream at me. But she does something I wasn't expecting. She hugs me. She hugs me so tight I can barely breathe. But I don't want her to stop. I sit in her arms, bawling my eyes out.

"I'm so sorry, Willow," she says softly, making me cry harder.

Finally, I'm able to pull myself together, and she releases me. I feel relieved. That's the strangest part of all of this. I feel relieved Noa has forgiven me, but I feel relieved I have gotten it off my chest. I feel relieved I'm not as alone as I was when I arrived at the lodge, despite half of us being murdered.

"It's okay, Willow," Evelyn comforts. "It was an accident. You were defending yourself. It's not like you killed him for no reason."

I give an understanding nod. *Self-defense.* Evelyn relaxes onto the couch and looks around.

"We have your back," Noa reassures. "He got what he deserved."

CHAPTER TWENTY-NINE

I smile. Yeah, I suppose he did.

"Shouldn't the boys be back by now?" Evelyn asks, now looking at the barricaded front door.

She's right. They should be back already. What is taking them so long? I know it's a long walk, but I didn't think it was that long. I try not to think about the possibility of them 'rekindling.' If that happens, I'll lose a great deal of respect for Caleb.

"They'll be back any second," Noa says, but she sounds distant, like she's lost in thought.

Out of the blue, Evelyn stands up. "I'm sorry, I really have to pee. I was holding it in that whole story, but I didn't want to be rude." Unexpectedly, this makes me laugh. Quite hard. Evelyn waddles across the room and goes into her room while Noa and I stay seated on the couch. A few seconds of silence go by before I turn to her. It hasn't been us two alone for a while, and I feel safest bouncing theories off her.

"Noa," I say, snapping her out of her trance. "There are only five of us. Us three, and Hugh and Caleb. I can, pretty confidently, say that it's none of us three."

Noa looks confused and I realize that for everyone else, they haven't been suspecting each other. Why would they? The person who broke the van window was definitely none of us. But I was slipped a note. I know somebody is lying.

"When the lights went out," I tell her, "Somebody slipped a note into my hand."

She furrows her brows, genuinely having no idea what I'm talking about.

"It said *'I know what you did'*. Referring to my dad. But it was somebody *inside*."

Her eyes darken. I can see the betrayal sprawled across her

face. Somebody she considers a friend has been trying to kill us.

"So," she pauses, "it has to be Hugh or Caleb working with somebody else."

"Exactly. Or both."

"Wait, but why would they orchestrate this whole thing because you killed your father? It doesn't make sense. Why would they care? Are you sure that's what they meant with the note?"

"Positive."

Suddenly, there is the sound of glass shattering from the room next to us, causing both of us to jump.

"Oh my god!" Noa whispers in a panic. "Is it them?"

I am about to say no, but I am in a constant state of denial. Then I realize something, and my heart sinks. The shattering came from Evelyn's room. I leap up from the couch, and Noa quickly follows. I run down the hall, past the stairs, and barge through Evelyn's door. My hand immediately races towards my mouth. She's lying on the ground in front of the shattered window, an arrow sticking out of her heart. Blood covers her shirt and spurts out of her mouth. Noa screams, and I fall against the bedside table. I can't keep doing this. It never stops. How could Hugh and Caleb do this to me? To us? I want to survive this night but I'm just so exhausted. It's like the killer is always two steps ahead. No matter what we do, we always lose. It makes it harder and harder to believe I have any chance of making it. Do I just accept it?

Noa rushes to Evelyn's aid but she stops halfway across the room when another arrow flies through the window, brushes past her face, and burrows into the wall. I look out of the window into the black, snowy abyss. The cold is streaming in, and I can immediately feel the side effects. That's when the next arrow flies in, landing impressively close to the first one.

I grab Noa and drag her out of the room. She calls for me to help Evelyn but I ignore her. She's long past saving. We stumble through the living room and into the kitchen, ducking behind the counters.

We stay put for a few minutes. We hold our breath and blow out the candles lighting the kitchen until we decide it's safe to move, but when we walk back to the living room, we are greeted by Hugh and Caleb.

VIII

THE GLORIA

Chapter Thirty

Willow - 3:00 AM - Sunday, 30th January 2022

There are only four of us left. Ten of us came up to this mountain, excited to spend the weekend together, but now only four of us remain. And at least one of us is a murderer. I am certain it has to be either Caleb or Hugh but now that I'm looking at them, I'm confused. They don't seem to be in any condition to attack us. Caleb is limping and clutching to Hugh for dear life, while Hugh is soaking wet with blue lips and shivering.

Without saying anything to us, they move straight for the fire. Caleb is limping so it takes them a while, but when they do, Hugh practically leaps into it. He trembles so vigorously that I think he's on the brink of death. He may be.

"What happened?" Noa yells.

Hugh doesn't talk, he just stares blankly into the fire.

"He fell into the river," Caleb answers for him. "He's going into shock. He needs warmth."

I'm still suspicious of them, and I can tell Noa is too, but we put all of that aside for now as we help Caleb find things to cover Hugh. I grab two blankets from the couch and wrap them around him tightly. Caleb limps back into the room, now holding Noa for support, holding a duvet for Hugh.

"Where did this happen?" I ask skeptically.

"By the fire tower," Caleb responds, not taking his eyes off Hugh, who seems to have regained some sentience.

It doesn't make sense. If they really were at the fire tower, they couldn't possibly have attacked Evelyn. They could be lying but considering Hugh's wetness and frostbite, I suspect they aren't. However, I have already deduced this is not a lone wolf. There is somebody outside and somebody inside. Somebody who has done the killing, and somebody who slipped me the note. Therefore, they are not off the table.

"Did you get through to someone?" I ask them. Caleb is busy fiddling with the gas valve, trying desperately to make it warmer, and Hugh still shivers but at least he shows signs of acknowledging me. He raises his eyebrows and looks at me.

"Hugh?" I repeat, crouching down to him.

"Y-yes," he chokes out. I wait for further explanation, but it doesn't happen.

"And what did they say?"

"C-can't come. M-morning."

I have to think for a few seconds to understand what he's saying. They can't get here until morning when the storm clears. I stand and approach Noa, who is now sitting on the couch, looking distantly at the front door.

"What do you think?" I ask her, quiet enough so the boys can't hear.

She flinches a little at my words, clearly being so out of it that she didn't even see me coming.

"I don't know," she says numbly.

"Do you think they're telling the truth?"

"Look at them, they have to be."

"I know ..." I trail off. "But what if only one of them is?"

CHAPTER THIRTY

She thinks about this for a second, so I continue talking.

"There's nobody else it could be. I think it could be Caleb."

This gets her attention. "What? Why?"

"I mean, it's his house. He invited us all here and now people are dying and he's somehow managed to survive."

"It just doesn't seem like Caleb. He's so ... gentle. Why would he want us dead?"

I think about it. I'd be lying if I said I hadn't already. The first reason that pops into my head I know would normally make Noa roll her eyes, but I think now she trusts me a little more to hear me out.

"What if he's doing this to be with Hugh?"

Noa looks at me, and for a while, I think she is seriously considering it, then she smiles and giggles.

"Are you kidding? Willow, no offense, but I seriously doubt that whoever is behind this, is doing it for romantic reasons."

I'm a little offended she didn't take me seriously, but forgiveness is something I'm working on.

"That's usually how all the true crime stories end," I respond.

"Yeah, but I have a feeling that's not the case here."

We go silent again. When finally, she sits up straight, having a new drive, and suggests to me.

"Maybe we should ask them."

Immediately, I think it's a terrible idea, but she stands up and walks over to the fireplace. I want to stop her because confronting a killer is rarely the best course of action. But it's too late.

"So, you got through to the police?" Noa asks, very obviously taking the offense.

Caleb and Hugh look towards her, Hugh's pale skin and blue lips glowing from the flames.

"Yeah," Caleb says, sounding confused. "We already told you that …"

"Hm," Noa retorts smugly. "And what did they say again?"

Caleb and Hugh look blankly at her. But when I take a closer look at Caleb's face, I realize he's turned red. "They said they couldn't get here until the storm clears. So not for at least another four to five hours."

Noa nods, then mutters, "Very convenient."

"What was that?" Caleb asks as he stands up.

"I just said it's very convenient."

"W-What's so convenient?" Hugh asks.

"I mean, morning seems like more than enough time to finish the job."

Hugh's jaw drops, and Caleb looks offended.

"What do you m-mean *'finish the job'*?" Hugh asks her, sounding genuinely confused. "We know it's not any of us. They attacked us at the van."

"But somebody inside slipped Willow a note," Noa remarks.

For god's sake, Noa. Why would she tell them that?

"What?" Hugh gasps. "What did it s-say?"

There it is.

"It doesn't matter. But it was enough for me to know one of us is in on this," I say, trying to deter the conversation from going any further down that route.

"Why wouldn't you tell us sooner?" Hugh asks, growing more aggressive, the shiver in his voice vanishing. He gets up and stands next to Caleb. "If we knew that, we could have interrogated people!"

"What do you think we're doing now?" Noa yells.

"We could have interrogated *more* people!"

"News flash, Hugh. All of those people are dead!"

CHAPTER THIRTY

Caleb covers his mouth. "Wait, everyone is dead? What about Kaya and Evelyn? What about Riley?"

"Well, actually I don't know where Riley is," I say. "But Kaya was killed at the groundskeeper's cabin and Evelyn was shot through the window."

"She was shot with a gun?!" Caleb gasps.

"No, a bow and arrow," I tell him and watch a look of relief wash over him.

"Which you already knew," Noa murmurs.

"Oh my god, Noa. No, I didn't!" Caleb yells. "Look, I swear on my mother that I'm not doing this. It's not my fault there's a storm and the police can't come."

"But you invited us," I add. "You probably checked the forecast. You knew we wouldn't be able to leave."

"Anybody could have checked the forecast!" he yelps.

"You guys are crazy." Hugh laughs.

"Wow, Hugh! Gaslighting?" Noa retorts. "You know what I find funny, and can't believe I didn't realize sooner? You were writing a play about a town murderer for two years! That lines up with the Telluride Maniac pretty perfectly!"

"Are you fucking kidding me?" Hugh screams, looking genuinely offended. "You think I'm the town serial killer? You think I killed your parents? All because of a play?"

"I think you're more than capable of killing all of our friends. I bet you killed them to know how to write about it in your shitty little play! Sorry, Hugh, you failed! Because your play sucks ass!"

I can see that one cut deep, and I think it might have been a low blow. Hugh and Noa scream at each other, shouting accusations while Caleb and I stand awkwardly behind them. It's ridiculous. I know Hugh isn't the Telluride Maniac. I thought we were going to accuse Caleb. There's no possibility of calming Noa down, but she has a right to be angry. Well, we all do, but *especially* her. I have to be the rational one.

"Did you call again? Like, maybe try to call somebody else?" I ask Caleb as the others keep fighting.

"That's not really how a radio works, Willow," Caleb scoffs.

Okay, that was rude. I don't know how a radio works. It's not like I use one on the daily. I think about other possibilities. All I know is that one of us is lying. But then I remember the car. I don't know what the car looked like, but maybe they did send out two officers.

"Noa," I say but she doesn't hear me over the screaming.

"Noa!" I yell. This shuts them up. "What about the car? Do you think it was a police car? Maybe they're telling the truth."

As I say this, I realize Noa is shaking her head at me. But it's not in a way that answers my question, it's in a way that says *"Stop talking."*

"What car?" Caleb asks. "What car? Were people coming to help us?"

"No!" Noa says. "It wasn't a police car."

"Well, where are they? Could they help us?"

"They crashed," I tell him.

"What the fuck!" Hugh shouts, looking over at Noa, who, when I turn to look at her, has her eyes locked on the floor, looking incredibly guilty. Now I understand why she didn't want me to say any of this. But to be fair, she told them about my note.

"How did they crash?" Hugh asks her.

"I was standing in the road, trying to flag them down, and they swerved to avoid me," Noa says, not looking up from the floor. Hugh's scoff mirrors the one Noa gave him mere

CHAPTER THIRTY

minutes ago.

"Wait, they crashed? Could they still be alive?" Caleb asks naively. "Maybe—"

"They went off the mountain," I interrupt him, and he pauses, mouth still wide open. "The car exploded."

"Oh, okay," Caleb mutters. "Never mind."

"So," Hugh says laughing, looking at Noa, "you're sitting there, accusing me of being a murderer, when you literally *killed* a person that could have helped us!"

"It was an accident!" Noa screams defensively.

"It doesn't matter!" I scream, unable to bear the accusations. We've done enough of that for one night. Noa has tears in her eyes. Her breathing becomes heavier by the second as her eyes dart from me to the boys and back. Over and over. Noa's mental state has been plummeting, and I know we're past the point of taming her. She walks over to Hugh, still holding the knife. Hugh backs up.

"Noa?" he asks with a shake in his voice. "What are you doing?"

Noa stops a foot away from him.

"I know this is your fault. I don't know how yet, but I will."

"Noa, please put the knife down!"

I can see it in her eyes. Reliving the moment, she came home that night. Staring directly into the eyes of her family's killer. I'm sure she would do anything to have killed them then and there. Maybe she doesn't want to make that same mistake again. This time, they're not getting away.

Then, she turns around and heads for the couches. I was so confident Noa was about to kill him and judging by the look on Hugh's face, he thought so too.

"Hold up," Caleb says. "You said you didn't know where

205

Riley is?"

I don't understand his angle.

"Yeah," I say. "I came to the lodge before finding Evelyn and Noa, and she wasn't in her room. She wasn't anywhere!"

"See, now that's convenient, Willow," Caleb mocks.

What? I thought we were past this. I thought me and Caleb had created an unspoken truce whilst Noa and Hugh were fighting. I tilt my head to look at him, narrowing my eyes, waiting for him to continue.

"So, you've found *four* dead bodies while you were completely alone?"

I hadn't even realized how that must sound. Was that the killer's intention? To make me look more like a killer than I already am. Whatever the reason was, it looks terrible on my part.

"First, you supposedly just 'find' Fergus, along with the groundskeeper" he goes on. "Then, Kaya is apparently murdered, but nobody was there to see it. And now, Riley has vanished, and you've just admitted you were alone in the lodge before any of us came back."

Damn. He brought receipts. I don't know how to tell him it's not me. Well, I did kill Fergus, but not in that way. But how many *ways* can you kill someone? A lot, I guess.

I mutter my next words. "I mean, technically it's only *three* dead bodies."

"Are you fucking serious?", he screams.

"I don't know if Riley is dead! Caleb, trust me!" It's the only thing I can muster up, but as it leaves my lips, I hear how pathetic it sounds.

"It's not her," Noa says, rescuing me. "We were together when Evelyn was killed."

CHAPTER THIRTY

"But you just said two people were doing this!"

He does have a point. It is such a good point in fact, that Noa turns and looks at me. She looks suspicious.

"No," I say. "No, no, no. Don't you dare!"

"You've always hated us," Caleb says. "It makes sense you would want to kill us."

"Oh please! I don't hate you I'm just ... shy."

The second I say it, I know it's bullshit. So do they. I don't like them, that's true, but that doesn't mean I killed everyone. I don't like many people. Honestly, if I killed everyone I didn't like, there'd be no one in the world left.

"What about Riley?" Noa finally asks.

"Riley?" I repeat, almost shocked at the idea. I barely even knew her. "I just told you! I didn't kill Riley!"

"No, I'm not talking about that. She's the only one who's *vanished* and hasn't been confirmed dead. No body. No evidence. Where is she?"

It's true. Is this what she's been so nervous about? Why would she still be killing people if she clearly didn't want to do it? Is she being forced to? Noa's last words linger in the air. *Where is she?* While considering each possibility, we are interrupted by the back door swinging open and a deer runs inside.

Chapter Thirty-One

Hugh - 3:15 AM - Sunday, 30th January 2022

It takes me a few seconds to react. I just stand and watch while the masked individual runs towards me, pushing between Willow and Noa. I only start moving when Caleb grabs my arm and pulls me away. Just in time, too, because the person swings their axe down right where I was standing. As Caleb leads me to the front door, limping all the way, I look back and see the person struggling to unearth his axe from the floor, whilst Noa and Willow begin moving toward the back door. When we reach the front, the hulking side table is blocking it. I groan. When Caleb and I were running back from the tower, we tried to get in through the front door, but it wouldn't budge, so we had to come in through the back.

After seeing the antlers in the trees, we bolted, not looking back once. The whole way back to the lodge, I thought he was following us, calling for help in that creepy high-pitched voice, mimicking one of our friends. It took me a minute to realize what the mask reminded me of.

When researching for *Requiem*, I chose the Great Plains region as the setting. I read about some ancient folklore and came across a creature called a Wendigo. A Wendigo is a mythological creature or an evil spirit that possesses human-like features. In some representations, the Wendigo is described as a giant humanoid with a heart of ice. A foul stench or sudden chill might precede its approach, which is fitting because this whole mountain has been devoured by snow. Some pictures of them appear to have antlers, just like the killer's mask, and in some instances, they are known to mimic another person's voice. I thought it was so cool and had potential to make a really great story, but when I told Willow about it, she told me not to use it. Apparently, it was too scary. So, in order to keep her happy, I scrapped it and came up with the play we have today. A story about a town, with a monster even more terrifying than a Wendigo. A human. It's a shame nobody will ever see it. Maybe if I get out of here alive, I could still put it on. Maybe the media buzz that will undoubtedly surround tonight's events will give it a major boost in popularity. Maybe it could go to Broadway.

What am I thinking? How can I fantasize about taking a play to Broadway when I'm currently being chased by a killer? What I mean to say is that when I heard that voice in the woods, it sent a chill down my spine. Yes, because it was terribly creepy, but mostly because I had a thought. The killer isn't any of us, it's a Wendigo.

But I don't see why a Wendigo would use an axe and slip people notes, so that theory quickly goes down the drain. Also, when Noa said it was the same mask the Telluride Maniac used, I knew it had to be a person. But how are the two connected? Why would the maniac take a hiatus from killing just to follow us up a mountain? Maybe it *is* because of Noa.

Both of us begin to move the side table, but we're not quick enough. The Wendigo manages to get the axe out from the floorboards and is now running towards us. I push Caleb out of the way, and the axe burrows into the table. I realize I pushed Caleb a little too hard because he slams into the wall and falls onto the floor.

Now, the axe is stuck into the table, which is still blocking the door. I ram the person forcefully with my shoulder, trying to get them away from their weapon. They stumble backwards and hit the wall, but it doesn't stop them completely; it only slows them down. They turn their face to me, antlers almost hitting me as they swivel.

They immediately regain their composure, grab me by my neck, and push me up against a wall. I try my hardest to make them release me, but their grip doesn't loosen. I flail, trying to hit their face, but it hurts when my hand makes an impact. The mask isn't a bendable rubber or cheap plastic; it's a hard material, almost like a real animal skull. I start feeling lightheaded, and it becomes more difficult to fight back. I gasp for breath, but I can't inhale. The hands around my throat are too tight. Just as I feel I'm going to pass out, he releases me.

A miracle. I collapse to my knees, gasping for air and holding my neck. I look up to see that Caleb has struck the Wendigo in the back of the head with a drawer he pulled from the table.

It doesn't give us long, but it's enough. The Wendigo fumbles around, their hands on the back of their head, and then they fall to their hands and knees. I guess the back part of the mask isn't as durable. This is it; this is when everything can change. The axe is still in the table. It's up for grabs. This is when the night can end.

I walk over to the table, placing both hands on the handle.

CHAPTER THIRTY-ONE

But right as I'm about to unearth the axe, I am grabbed and pulled away by Caleb.

"What the hell are you doing?" I shout as he moves us towards the back door, still limping. He doesn't respond. Maybe he didn't know what I was doing and just wanted to get us out of there before they came to.

We near the back door and all I can think about is the cold and how much I really don't want to go back out there. The storm has progressed even more and by the looks of it, I don't think we'd last five minutes. But as we make it halfway through the great room, something steps through the door and into the room. Another Wendigo.

I scream. We both turn around and see the Wendigo by the front door is standing and has regained possession of the axe. There's nowhere to go. But where did Noa and Willow go? Did they make it outside? Mid thought, Caleb grabs my arm again and limps towards the staircase. Why would he take us upstairs? That's the number one rule in horror movies. Don't run upstairs. But in this case, both doors are being guarded by the killers. We're not swimming in options.

We climb the stairs until we reach the top. We move to the nearest door, which is mine and Willow's room, but when we go to push it open, it's locked. We hear the Wendigo's footsteps heading towards the stairs so we quickly move down to Arthur and Samuel's; luckily, the door is unlocked. We shut it and are completely engulfed by the darkness, the only light being the moon creeping in through the window. We go to lock the door, but there isn't one. Come to think of it, I don't think mine and Willow's room had a lock either. The moon provides enough light to illuminate the two beds that fill almost the entire room, and Arthur and Samuel's clothes cover every free inch of the floor. *God, this is small.*

The closet would only fit one of us and is undoubtedly the first place they would check. Hiding under the bed seems like a death trap too but seems like the best option out of the two.

"Get under the bed," Caleb orders, pointing to the bed furthest from the door.

"What are you going to do?" I ask him, concerned.

"Hugh, just shut up and hide!" he says in a rough whisper.

I don't waste any time. I run over to the bed, but before I get under, I look at Caleb. I watch as he slides the window open. For a minute, I think he's going to jump, but instead, he grabs a pair of boots from the ground and tosses them out the window, trying to create the illusion of us escaping. Then he gets under the other bed. I don't know how successful this diversion is going to be, but it's better than doing nothing. Caleb and I lay flat on the ground, looking at each other from the two beds. My heart is going to beat out of my chest, and my throat is sore from when the Wendigo choked me, making it almost impossible to quiet my breathing. Footsteps reach the top of the stairs and walk to the first door. It's locked. Then the steps come closer to our door. Caleb lifts one finger and holds it against his lips in a shushing motion. Then, the door creaks open.

One Wendigo walks into the room. I cover my mouth with my hand to stop the sound of my breathing. Instantly, they swing open the closet doors. When they find nothing, they turn around to face the beds. That's when they notice the window and hurry towards it. Their feet are still for a few seconds, indicating they're looking down. I watch as Caleb scrunches his eyes and does all he can to stay silent. His head is mere inches from the Wendigo's feet. He starts to go red as

CHAPTER THIRTY-ONE

he holds his breath. I hear a grunt of annoyance, and the feet walk away. It worked. When the Wendigo reaches the door, he is greeted with a second pair of feet.

Please go away, I think.

Who are they? Willow and Noa said it was one of us, someone in the house but I don't see how that's possible, as all four of us were inside when the Wendigo attacked us. But who is the second one? Then, I remember. I think back to earlier tonight at the fire tower.

Shannon and Al. The two names on the map. Who are they? Caleb looked like he had no idea who they were. The map was old, but it didn't look *that* old. What if–

The footsteps hadn't even made it to the stairs when Caleb moves his head and smacks it on the wooden slats of the bed, creating a noise loud enough the alert the attackers.

The footsteps stop, and then they turn around and run back into the room. It happens in a matter of seconds. One of the killers grabs Caleb's feet and drags him out from under the bed while Caleb lets out a shrill scream. The other Wendigo comes to my bed and tries to drag me out. He manages to drag me halfway across the room, but I kick his hands, and he lets me go. I jump to my feet while the two Wendigos stare at me, the one I kicked holding his hand in pain, the other is holding Caleb in a headlock. They're blocking the door. I'm trapped. My brain is fuzzy, and I can't decide what to do. I refuse to let these assholes take me. I do the only thing I can think of to get me out of here. I turn around and run to the window. I have to jump. I put my left leg out and begin squeezing through. The Wendigo grabs my arm and tries to pull me back. They're not as strong as the one that choked me, so I know it's the other one. After a few seconds of struggling,

I free myself, and I fall forward out the window, landing on my feet. But immediately after touchdown, I feel a sharp pain in my left ankle and fall to the ground. I look up at the window and see the antlers of one of the Wendigo's masks glowing in the moonlight until finally, they disappear back into the bedroom.

The last thing I hear before they slam the window is Caleb's deafening, blood-curdling scream.

Chapter Thirty-Two

Willow - 3:15 AM - Sunday, 30th January 2022

I watch in horror as the deer barges through the back door. At first, I thought it was running directly towards me, but when he pushed past me and went for the boys, I was relieved. Which is awful, I know, but I've survived this far; I'm not going out now. I take back everything I said about giving up. I'm not fucking dying.

The deer pushed me with such force that it knocked me to the ground. I sat on the floor, looking up at the deer with a mixture of anger and fear. I wanted to rip off that mask then and there, but I know that wouldn't be the brightest idea. The axe sticks in the floorboards, and he struggles to get it out. I slowly get to my feet, and Noa yells at me to hurry up, but the deer turns his head directly towards me, and I just stand there, looking at him as he lifts his hand and slowly points at me, just like he did in the woods. Then, he goes back to yanking his axe out of the ground. I use this as an opportunity to follow Noa.

Noa runs up the stairs that lead to my bedroom, but I stop at the bottom.

"What are you doing?" I say, gesturing towards the back

door. That's when I see it. Lurking outside, just in range of the fireplace light. Another killer.

I don't waste another second. I make it to the top step and look back, making sure he's not following us. He's not, but the killer already inside is going after Hugh and Caleb. I honestly feel cruel about leaving them to fend for themselves, but I'm in survival mode right now, so I'm okay with any diversions that give me time. As we make it to the pitch-black second floor, I hear the axe hitting the table, something hitting the wall with a loud thud, and people struggling. I grit my teeth, hoping I don't hear any screaming and race into mine and Hugh's bedroom. Well, I guess it's technically just *my* bedroom because Hugh never ended up staying with me.

Yet another person I drove away. If there was one thing I didn't expect to happen on this trip, it was to feel remorse. For *everything* I've done. Noa shuts the door and takes a look around the room.

"Holy shit," she whispers in amazement. "Your room is huge."

I take a look around, wondering if this is the most relevant conversation to be having right now. "Is it?" I ask.

"Are you kidding? Mine and Kaya's ..." she pauses. "Mine is the size of a broom closet."

"Oh," I say, trying my absolute best to sound interested, but I can't do it for long. "We need to keep the door shut," I tell her.

She reaches for the lock, but there isn't one. We both scavenge the room for something to block the door. I grab the chair and place it under the doorknob, slowing any potential entry. We stand in deafening silence together, with our eyes locked on the door. We hear the fight occurring downstairs

CHAPTER THIRTY-TWO

then two pairs of footsteps running up the stairs. We haven't talked about what we would do if someone managed to get in. There is a window, but it's a far drop and would probably cause an injury, which is not a great plan considering the weather. The cold would only make it worse. We can hide under the bed, which is the most obvious place. We could also hide in the tiny closet, but once again, that's an obvious spot. Now that I have the luxury of hindsight, I realize this was a terrible room to hide in.

No words are exchanged between the two of us as we hear the footsteps approaching our door and the door handle jiggles. I hold my breath, not knowing who it is. Is it Caleb and Hugh or the killers?

"Should we open it?" Noa whispers, clearly stressed and unable to make a rational decision.

"No," I tell her bluntly.

"But they need help!" Noa scolds me in a whisper, raising her voice, but I cup my hand over her mouth.

"If we open that door, we could be letting in a murderer," I tell her firmly. "Or two."

She takes a breath as if she's going to say something, but then she exhales and sits on the bed. I stay standing, watching the door. I look around the room for something to defend myself with. Then I remember the knife currently sitting under my bathroom sink. I hid it there after finding it in the basin. I hurry quietly into the bathroom and retrieve it, then walk back into the room and stand back at the door.

"What is that?" Noa asks worriedly. I never told her I was the one that killed Fergus. But hopefully, it's too dark to see the blood.

"Self-defense."

217

The lodge is silent. That is until I hear more footsteps walking up the stairs. These have to be the killers. I hold my breath as they walk over to our door and twist the handle. My heart is pounding so loud that I worry whoever is on the other side of the door can hear it too. But their footsteps move away from our door, and Noa and I let out a silent sigh of relief. The door to the next room opens, and the footsteps walk inside. I stand, paralyzed in fear, waiting for anything.

Hugh and Caleb must be hiding in there. I pray the killer doesn't find them. The closet door squeaks open. Surely, they weren't stupid enough to hide in there. But it's still silent. After a few seconds of complete and utter silence, I hear the footsteps walking away. They've done it. But how? Did they jump out of the window? I guess the vision in that mask is terrible, so they may not have seen them in the darkness.

But then I hear a loud thud and the footsteps pause, and then they turn around and hurry back into the room. Then, the screaming starts.

I hear Caleb scream so loud it sends shivers down my spine. And then I hear Hugh's, which creates a pit in my stomach. But Hugh eventually stops. What happened? Caleb is still screaming. Is Hugh dead? Oh my god! I have to help him.

No. I can't. I restrain myself from removing the chair barricade. He wouldn't do the same for me.

The footsteps stomp away as Caleb screams until they reach what seems to be the top of the staircase.

"Please don't!" I hear Caleb scream, and then, nothing.

Just the sound of someone stomping down the stairs, dragging something behind them. Caleb. After a few minutes of silence, I walk to the door and remove the chair.

"What are you doing?" Noa asks.

CHAPTER THIRTY-TWO

"We have to go," I tell her. "Before they know we're up here too."

After a brief internal conflict, she gets up and follows me out the door. We stand at the top of the stairs, trying to see the living room. There is no sign of the boys.

"Wait here," Noa tells me. "I'll get a better look."

I want to tell her not to, but we need to know if the coast is clear, so I don't stop her. Noa slowly walks down the stairs, careful to avoid any creaky floorboards. She gets halfway down and surveys the room, then turns to me, shaking her head and lifting her shoulders, indicating that she can't see anyone. She walks down a few more steps, but I notice something. On the floor, I see a shadow. A shadow of something hiding behind the wall next to the stairs. It's too late to warn Noa because the second she reaches the bottom of the stairs; the deer pops out from the wall and tackles her to the ground as she screams. I cover my mouth and duck behind the railings in an effort to remain unseen. What am I doing? I have a knife. I could help her. But I don't. There are two of them and only one of me.

After a while, Noa's screams die out and just like that, I'm the last one. I just sit on the floor, with my hand covering my mouth, covered in blood. How the fuck did this happen? Less than a day ago, all of us were laughing, enjoying our time together, without a care in the world. Now everyone is dead. Everyone except me.

My hand drops from my mouth, and I sit resting against the railing, staring blankly at the wall. For the first time in a while, the lodge is completely quiet. Uncomfortably quiet. But that's all interrupted when classical music begins blasting from downstairs.

I have to get out of here. Now. But I can't. I can't go outside and run. I'm too far away from anything and it's too cold. I can't stay upstairs all night until help arrives. It's too risky. I need to somehow get downstairs and find a place to hide out until the police arrive. Preferably some place with a convenient escape route. But getting downstairs may be dangerous, as just demonstrated by Noa.

Is the deer waiting for me down there? He's been tormenting me all night; now, I'm the only one left. So, now what? The game is over. All that's left to do is kill me. There is no more safety blanket.

The classical music is so eerily beautiful. I would love it in any other situation, but it sends chills down my arms and back right now. I creep back towards the stairs. From what I can tell, nobody is standing behind the wall. One step at a time, I move down the stairs. When I reach the bottom, I freeze. The room is not empty. I see the deer slowly dancing by himself in the middle of the living room. It's a horrifying sight. He sways left and right as if he were dancing with a partner, but it's just him. Where's the other one?

I don't know where to go. The back door is so close but being outside provides no safety. The garage is near the front door, but going there requires walking directly past the dancing deer. My eyes land on the kitchen. Then, my eyes land on the basement door. But it's ajar. A warm feeling rushes through my body. Hope. What if Noa, Caleb, and Hugh aren't dead at all. Is the basement where they've taken them? If it is, I don't know if I want to go down there, it could be a trap. Luring me to my inescapable murder. But I can't stay on the staircase. It's too visible.

He spins and when his back is towards me, I get on my hands

CHAPTER THIRTY-TWO

and knees and crawl towards the kitchen. I pause behind the couch to catch my breath for a few seconds. I peek out and look at him again to see he has turned back around to face me. I can't go yet. After a few minutes, he turns back around, and I finish the crawl.

I duck behind the counter and watch the deer continue dancing through the kitchen window reflection. The house is dark, but the basement looks like a void. A black hole. A perfect hiding place. I pull out my phone from my back pocket, ready to turn on the flashlight. Then, I slowly pull open the door.

I find myself at the top of the basement stairs, looking down into the black abyss. I don't want to turn on my light before the door is shut in case the deer sees me. I put two fingers under the door and begin pulling it shut. I have almost done it without making a sound, but as I pull it an inch or two more to close it, the music comes to an end, the lodge is silent, and the hinges let out a small creak.

The deer sharply turns his head towards me. I'm able to see him through the tiny crack in the door. He looks my way for about three seconds and before he decides to come over and check for the source of the sound, I quickly but quietly descend the stairs on my hands and feet. Now is the best time to turn on my flashlight and try to find a place to hide. I do, but shining it around the room, I see a nice, finished basement, which is odd because Caleb told us not to go down here because it was *unfinished*. The floors are carpeted, and there's a couch that would fit fifty people. There's nothing *dangerous* about it.

Nobody's here. Not in this room, at least. In this main area, there are three doors. Have Noa, Caleb, and Hugh been

221

shoved in one?

I am about to check them when the basement door swings open and the same metallic voice I heard in the wood taunts from the doorway. "I know you're down there."

In a panic, I turn off my flashlight, open one of the doors and rush into the room. Even in the darkness, I can see that *this* room is unfinished. It is just a large hallway with cement floors and loose bricks all over the place. I silently close the door behind me, but stand by it, trying to hear if the deer has made it downstairs. He has. The footsteps become muffled, indicating he's walking on the carpet. He's faintly humming the same melody from upstairs. I grip the bloody knife in my right hand, ready to attack when the door opens. But it doesn't. Instead, another metallic voice calls from upstairs.

"Hey, come here!" the other voice calls. "We need to set up."

Set up for what? What else have they got planned? The humming pauses and footsteps dart up the basement stairs. My body relaxes, and when I hear the door shut and the classical music restart, I let out a breath that has been trapped inside of me for what feels like hours. Then I notice the smell. It's so pungent. Is that... urine?

I turn my flashlight back on. And I have to cover my mouth to stop myself screaming.

I'm not alone in this room.

But the people joining me are not alive. Lying on the floor are the bodies of Arthur and Samuel. The ones that started it all. That's what the smell must be coming from. Their bladders might have relaxed. They lie still on the ground. So still. It makes sense, seeing as they're dead, but for some reason, they look *too* still. Arthur's arm is hovering above the ground, unmoving. He's stiff. Doll-like. Then my stomach

CHAPTER THIRTY-TWO

drops as I touch his leg. It's not a leg. The thing wearing his clothes is not even human.

It's a mannequin.

I do the same for Samuel. It's a mannequin, too.

Everything clicks into place. Now everything makes sense. How people were able to avoid suspicion. How everyone had an alibi. Because Arthur and Samuel were never dead. Arthur and Samuel are wearing the mask.

But it doesn't answer everything because when somebody slipped me the note, we had already found Arthur and Samuel's bodies. Then I think about Riley. As Noa said, she's the only other person to not be confirmed dead, and she was with us when the power went off. It has the be the three of them. It's the only option that makes sense. But why was she so nervous? She talked about her dad, but if her dad was really sick, why would she come here to kill people? What is so urgent about this? Why are any of them doing this? How do they know what I've done?

I'm interrupted by a noise on the other side of the room. I swing my flashlight over there in fright. My light doesn't illuminate to the other end but that's where the noise came from.

I don't know why I start moving toward the sound. It feels like a terrible decision as soon as I start, but I don't stop. I'm so curious. I need answers. I feel like I have everything I need to put the pieces together, but I just don't know where they go. I walk through a sticky object that I immediately know is a spider web. I gasp and flail around trying to get it off me. Eventually, I do and keep walking, careful not to walk through anymore. I'm looking up, so focused on spider webs and the strong stench of urine and body odor that I almost don't notice the hole in the floor. It appears to be a wine cellar but there's no ladder. Who would take that out? It's deep enough that if someone was stuck down there, they couldn't reach the opening.

Then I hear the faint crying.

It's a girl. My heart skips a beat, thinking that this is where Noa could be. I've found her. I was right, she's not dead. I shine my light inside.

"Hello?" It echoes in the hole, even though I was quiet to the point of being inaudible. Then, I hear the crying soften, as if she's trying to remain undetected.

"Is someone down there?"

Now it's dead silent. Maybe I was just hearing things. I am going to leave when someone steps into the light. It's not Noa. It's a woman I've never seen before. She is bloody and covered in dirt, all her clothes are stained and disheveled. Her hair is messy, and there are huge black circles around her eyes. She looks up in fear and lets out a whimper, but when she realizes it's me and not the deer, she slightly loosens.

"Please! Please help me!" the strange woman pleads.

I'm so confused. This was the last thing I expected from this night.

"Shh!" I say. "Who are you?"

The woman takes a minute to catch her breath.

"My-my name is Shannon. Shannon Miller," she stutters.

I have absolutely no idea who she is. So, I press her with more questions. "Are you alone?"

"No," she tells me. "My husband Al is here."

Then, a man steps into the light, looking just as worn down as her. He has a gash on his forehead, and dried blood all down the side of his face.

CHAPTER THIRTY-TWO

"Please help us," he whispers. It seems he is more aware of his volume than her.

I don't understand. Why are they down here? What's their relevance to everything that has happened?

"What are you doing here?" I ask her.

"Th-this is our cabin," she utters, tears rolling down her face.

This stops me. It doesn't make any sense. "No, it's not," I tell her. "This is my friend's cabin."

"No, it isn't!" she shouts up at me before Al shushes her and she returns to whispering. She needs to learn how to control her volume if she doesn't want the killer to find us. "We came up here a few days ago, but we were attacked by two people wearing antlers. They trapped us down here."

That's it. That's the last piece. The thing that makes it all fit. Caleb.

He's been lying to all of us this whole time. It all starts to make sense. Why there are no family pictures around. Why he didn't want us to go into the basement. Why the groundskeeper didn't recognize him. Why nobody even knew he had a fucking mountain lodge. He doesn't. He's been working with Arthur, Samuel, and potentially Riley. But who did they drag down the stairs? Is this all one big performance? It's fitting for this kind of group.

"Please! You have to help us!" Shannon begs.

I don't know what to do. There's nothing I can do. There's no ladder in sight and there's nobody to call. Then I think. Did Hugh and Caleb ever even call for help? Is Hugh involved in all of this too? Why does Caleb want to make me pay for what I did?

"People are coming," I tell her, doubting if that's actually true. "You just have to hang on."

I can't take it. I stumble away from the well, my head spinning. Shannon and Al beg me to stay with them. I feel sick. I rush towards the door. I swing it open and collapse on the carpet. Thankfully, nobody is here. At least, that's what I thought. There's a closet on one side of the room, and I hear rustling coming from inside. I'm sick of this. I'm sick of hiding. If the police aren't actually coming, I need to save myself. I grip my knife and open the doors.

I find Riley. I want to strike but I stop myself. Her mouth has been duct-taped shut, and her hands and feet are tied together. Her eyes are puffy, as tears still stream from them, and she has an unmissable lump on her forehead. Then, I notice the body of Fergus inside the closet with her. I cover my mouth, not wanting to scream. This is where he is. When I went to the cabin with Kaya, they made me look crazy, but he was here the whole time.

Riley looks up at me in shock. She grunts, trying to communicate, but I don't understand her, so I rip the tape off her mouth.

"Willow!" she shouts. I quickly put my hand against her mouth.

"What happened?" I ask her. "What's going on?"

"I'm so sorry," she cries. "Nobody was meant to die! They told me nobody was going to die!"

"Riley, what are you talking about?"

Before I can even process what she is saying, I realize the classical music upstairs has stopped again, which allows me to hear the footsteps behind me. I swivel and get out of the way as the deer swings an axe down and plants it directly into Riley's skull.

CHAPTER THIRTY-TWO

Blood splatters all over my face, and she slumps backwards, lying dead on the floor. The abruptness and brutality of the act completely stuns me. So much in fact that I forget to close my mouth, and the blood trickles in.

I slowly look up at the deer, his antlers towering over me. There's nothing I can do. I'm so tired. My time is up. Is this Caleb? I'll never know. I sit there as the deer raises his axe again and strikes me in the face with the handle.

Then, everything goes black.

IX

THE AGNUS DEI

Chapter Thirty-Three

Willow - 6:00 AM - Sunday, 30th January 2022

My head is spinning. Blood is dripping from my nose and into my mouth. Although my eyes are still closed, I'm conscious. I can hear muffled sounds, and light shines on my eyelids. I'm exhausted, but I slowly open my eyes, and a bright light blinds me. As my eyes adjust, I realize I am in the living room, tied to a chair. Golden light pours through the windows as the sun rises over the mountain. It's morning and help shouldn't be far away. That is if it's coming at all. I hear a groan from next to me, and when I look over, I see Noa tied to an identical chair. I guess this is what they needed to *set up*.

"Noa?" I whisper, but she doesn't respond. She just sits there, slumped over.

The lodge is in disarray. The dining room table is on its side, and the chairs are all over the room. The couch pillows have been cut open, and feathers cover the floor. I swing around as much as possible in my chair, trying to see if somebody else is in the room. But there is nobody. I turn back to Noa.

"Noa!" I say a little louder. "Please, Noa! Please, wake up."

Noa stirs in her chair. She's obviously not dead, but she doesn't seem too far from it. She has blood on her face, but I can't see a wound. I guess that's a good sign.

"Noa!" I shout hopelessly, not being able to contain my sobs.

I wanted to believe I knew why I was involved when I saw the word "killer" on my mirror, but now that the deer are targeting Noa too, I can't escape what this is *really* about. How would Caleb, Arthur, and Samuel know? Why did they go to these lengths? They killed our whole class just to get to me. It doesn't make any sense. What the fuck is going on?

I hear another sound from Noa. I look over at her and see her head bobbing up and down, and she groans.

"Noa?" I whisper, hopeful that she'll hear me. "Noa, you have to wake up!"

Her eyelids flutter for a few seconds until finally, they open, and she murmurs nonsense.

"Noa? Please talk to me!" I plead.

Noa lifts her head, and her eyes are squinted. A smile spreads across my face. I'm not as alone as I thought I was. I'm not lost in the darkness just yet because Noa is sitting here with a rope, somehow pulling me up to the surface. All hope is not lost. Together, we can escape.

"What's going on?" she asks with a groan. When she realizes that she is tied up, she begins to panic.

"Noa, please calm down! They'll hear you," I tell her.

She doesn't listen. She continues fighting the restraints. Our dynamic reminds me of Shannon and Al, the two poor people trapped in the basement. She needs to be quiet. I need to tell her what I know, but she's not listening to anything I'm saying. Finally, she gives up and sits back in her chair, accepting defeat. She begins to sob silently.

"Why does this keep happening to me?" she cries. Three months ago, her parents and siblings were murdered, and

CHAPTER THIRTY-THREE

now her entire class and potentially her. I feel awful, but I know it's about to get much worse.

"Noa," I begin. My voice is shaking. Knowing that Caleb is behind all of this will destroy her. She's already gone through enough. I know she was interrogating him, but desperate people do desperate things. It was in the heat of the moment. Knowing it's actually true is entirely something else.

"What?" she replies. I look into her eyes. She looks broken. I take a breath. "It's Caleb."

She looks confused. "What do you mean?"

I take my eyes off her and focus them on the ground. "Caleb is the killer."

A look of betrayal spreads across her face. "What? No."

"He's doing it with Arthur and Samuel."

She starts laughing, as it's the only thing stopping her from crying.

"No, Willow. That's crazy," she tells me. "They're dead. What are you—"

She trails off, her brain still foggy from whatever they did to her. I don't speak, all I do is look at her until she realizes that I am not at all joking. Then, she breaks out into cries.

"Fuck!" she screams.

"I'm so sorry," I tell her genuinely. But she's in no mood for niceties. Maybe I'm just trying to soften the blow I know is about to come.

The basement door opens behind us. I try to turn around, but I can't turn far enough. Noa and I sit in silence, listening to the footsteps approach us. Then, the person in the deer mask comes into view and walks in front of us, stopping in the middle of the seats. He walks exceptionally slowly, as if almost trying to cover up an injury. I feel physically sick looking at him. Is this Caleb? Or is it Arthur or Samuel? For a big reveal like this, you must start with a bang. The deer stares down at the two of us, and we stare back.

"Caleb?" I say. "I know it's you."

This makes his head turn sharply in my direction. The deer is now solely looking at me, ignoring Noa. He then lifts his hand and points at me, just like in the woods and in the lodge. I guess this is kind of our thing now.

"Killer!" he groans in the familiar metallic voice.

Noa looks at me, but I avoid her stare. I try to ignore his words, but he takes a step towards me and shoves his face mere inches from mine.

"Killer," he repeats.

"Okay?" I say as if it doesn't bother me. It does, but I refuse to give this prick the satisfaction of seeing it. If I die, I'm dying unbothered. "You think I don't know that?"

The deer doesn't move an inch. He continues staring at me. His beady eyes scanning my features.

"You have the nerve to call me a killer? What exactly have you been doing tonight?" I ask rhetorically. "You're no better than me. You know what? You're fucking worse!"

The deer slowly tilts his head at me. "Am I?" he questions.

Is he? Yes. He brutally murdered so many people, but didn't I too in a way? Then, finally, the deer lifts his mask, revealing his face, and confirming what I had thought.

Caleb.

He gives me a smile. I knew it was him, but seeing him dressed as the killer makes it all sink in. My face burns, and I'm full of rage. I feel my arms start twitching. I want to leap up and attack him, but I'm held in place by rope that makes my wrists itch like crazy. Noa's face drops, realizing I was

CHAPTER THIRTY-THREE

right. He grabs the voice changer connected to his mask and holds it to his mouth.

"Hi, Willow," he says metallically, with a smirk.

"Fuck off," I spit.

Caleb exaggerates an offended look. He never was a very good actor. "That's not very nice," he taunts.

I feel my blood pressure rising.

"Where are Arthur and Samuel?" I ask him.

This causes him to give me a shocked look and it's intensely satisfying. He doesn't know I know.

"They're dead," he says.

"Is that what you call those mannequins in the basement?"

He doesn't respond to me, but his face goes red. It's either rage or embarrassment. Most likely it's a mix of both. He wasn't expecting anybody to figure out his childlike ruse. But he's not admitting it and I'm not getting anywhere.

"Where's Hugh?" I ask him.

He lets out a chuckle. "Hugh? Aw." He takes a step towards me and kneels, so his eyes are level with mine. "Turns out you didn't know him as well as you thought," he jeers.

I know what he's implying. This is more than him being a killer. Caleb is gloating. He is still trying to prove something. This is about their relationship. I had always had an inkling about the two of them, and this trip simply confirmed it. I thought it was just a one-time thing. Maybe Hugh was merely confused. Now, I know it goes deeper, but I can't bear to admit it.

"You were a rebound, Caleb," I say coldly. "He doesn't care about you like he cares about me."

Caleb's smirk fades, and he lets out an authentic chuckle. "Okay," he says patronizingly.

Jealousy combines with my anger and fear, and my stomach turns as if I'm going to throw up. If I do, I want to do it all over him. I try desperately to free myself from the restraints. They're tight, but the knot is poor. Messy. The more I wiggle my hands around, the looser the rope becomes. But it hurts. I need to do it slowly. *Keep distracting him.* Caleb stands up and walks back towards the middle of the room.

"Is it Hugh?" I ask timidly. "Is he helping you?"

Caleb lets out a loud cackle. "God, no!"

Relief washes over my whole body. "Then where is he? Is he dead?"

"You know," Caleb says, interrupting my train of thought, "he was going to leave you as soon as high school ended. We were going to move out together. We *are.* He never loved you. You were just the easiest cover-up. He *loves* me." Oh my god, I fucking knew it. He sounds insane, but I believe every word. I wish I could rub it in Noa's face that she was wrong about "the killer not doing it for romantic reasons", but I think that would be slightly inappropriate.

Noa looks numb. She's given up on being scared. She's accepted her fate, but I cling on to any sliver of hope I can find.

"He won't love you when he finds out what you've done!" I shout.

This takes Caleb aback.

"What I've done?" he says, his face slowly morphing into a scared expression. "Willow, it's what *you've* done. How could you have killed all those people?" he wails dramatically. Then, his expression returns to normal, and another smile spreads across his face. "But luckily, he won't need to leave you. I'll take care of that for him."

CHAPTER THIRTY-THREE

"So, you've been doing all this to be with Hugh? Fuck, you can have him!" I shout.

"Oh no, Willow," Caleb says condescendingly. "I don't need to do all of this to have him. Besides, I'm not sure if I even want him anymore. I'm doing this because I know what you've done."

Noa looks at me.

"My dad," I assure her, but Caleb shakes his head.

"No. You and I both know that's not what I'm talking about," he sings.

Oh no. I was waiting for this. When I first read the note and the mirror message, I knew instantly what it meant, but I didn't think it was possible.

"What's he talking about?" Noa asks me. I can't tell her. She'll hate me.

"Confess," Caleb states.

"I already have," I lie.

"TELL THE TRUTH!" Caleb screams.

"Stop!" I yell.

"Why did your father start drinking, Willow?" he interrogates me.

"Willow, what did you do?" Noa asks me with tears in her eyes.

I feel my heart beating a hundred miles per hour. I can't say it. I won't. Tears burn in my eyes.

"Did he find something out about you?" Caleb pushes.

"Willow, what the fuck is he talking about?" Noa yells.

"I don't know!" I sob.

"The abuse story was sad and all, but it's a little problematic to lie about that stuff." Caleb mocks.

"Shut up!" I howl. How does he know about that?

"What. Did. You. Do?"

"Willow, fucking answer him!" Noa pleads.

They're both looking at me. Pressure builds and builds, and I feel as if I could explode. But I can't. She can't know. So, I swallow it down.

"I didn't do anything," I whimper.

Caleb stops questioning, and his face turns from intimidating to disappointed. He looks at Noa, whose face has changed from despair to irritation. And then, Noa stands up, revealing that her arms were never tied. Confusion floods through me. My eyes dart back and forth between Noa and Caleb. Somehow, my heart races faster than before. Noa walks over to Caleb and stares at me.

"You can come out, guys!" she calls. "She didn't admit it."

The basement door opens and I hear multiple sets of footsteps approach. Then, four deer step out in front of me. It doesn't make sense. The deer take off their masks, and the first faces I see are Arthur and Samuel. I was right and it feels strangely gratifying. I beat them to it. Then, Evelyn and Kaya reveal themselves. Arthur and Samuel didn't come as a shock, but now I feel as if I might throw up.

"What—" I stutter. "What the fuck."

All of them look at me, the lust for revenge on all of their faces. How is this possible? It feels like I've died and gone to hell. I watched Kaya and Evelyn die plain and simple. And Noa? How does she know?

"No. I saw you guys die!" I shout. I try harder than ever to free myself from the chair but the skin on my arms is raw and it burns every time the straw grinds across it.

"Did you?" Kaya asks.

Thinking back on it now, it seems so obvious. As I figured

CHAPTER THIRTY-THREE

out, Arthur and Samuel's bodies weren't real. I left Kaya in the woods. I saw the "Maniac" stab her from a distance. I guess a fake stabbing is extremely easy to produce. I don't even think I saw blood. Evelyn, however, stumps me. I saw an arrow through her chest. But that is quickly resolved when she pulls out a fake arrow and, this time, places it around her neck. It looks so real, but I recognize that it's just a prop she stole from our theater class. Evelyn sticks out her tongue and closes her eyes, imitating death. Then she and Kaya laugh. Noa walks over to me.

"This is your last chance," she says. "Tell us what you did."

She already knows. They all do. They have all been acting clueless this entire trip. Maybe even for months. They have been pretending to be my friends. They have been playing me. I have to hand it to them; their acting was good. For their standards. But I refuse to give them the satisfaction they so desperately desire, so I stay quiet.

"I'll help you, shall I?" Noa says. "I, Willow Montgomery, am the Telluride Maniac."

Chapter Thirty-Four

Noa - 5:00 PM - Wednesday, 15th December 2021

It's been just over a month since my parents died, and I still haven't learned how to live with my grief. Right now, it's harder than ever. It's my first Christmas without them. Walking down the snowy sidewalk, I see families putting up their Christmas lights together, laughing and having fun. Every single person reminds me of them. It reminds me of when my mom used to build snowmen with me in the front yard. It reminds me of when my dad used to lift me up so I could put the star on top of our Christmas tree. It reminds me of when my siblings and I used to wake up at three a.m. to see if Santa had come. All these people go about their day, their world still spinning, not caring that my world stopped a month ago.

I don't know where I'm walking. I don't care. I just needed to get out of the house. My aunt is comforting, as comforting as she can be, but it's so painful staying there. She looks so much like my mother that some days, I can't even look at her. She's trying her best to help me, but we're always getting into fights. It's my fault. Sometimes, I can't hold it in and start breaking down. I've trashed my room dozens of times already, but she never holds it against me. My cousins have

CHAPTER THIRTY-FOUR

been great too. We've always been close, so they provide me with a relationship that's almost like siblings, but every once in a while, I remember they're not, and I freak out at them. They know how much I miss my family.

Although they know it's not my fault, sometimes I can get scary. I don't even remember it. It's like I go into these blackout rages where it's only afterwards, when I see my wake of destruction, I realize what I've done. It's hard to describe, but the blackouts aren't completely black. I always see him. I always see those antlers.

I felt so guilty that the next time I had to take my anti-depressants, I swallowed the whole bottle. My youngest cousin found me and called my aunt. The ambulance showed up within five minutes and I was rushed to hospital.

That was the first time I was sent to the looney bin.

It was hard. Every time they tried to make me sleep, I could see him again. Each of those nurses wanted to kill me. Each of those nurses had antlers.

They gave me strategies to work through my anger. Half of them are bullshit, like "taking a deep breath" or "know you aren't alone", but some of them work. One of them is going on walks to "clear my head." I have to admit, although it's tranquil, sometimes all I want to do is break something. Throw, and smash, and destroy until I feel better. And sometimes I wish I had something extra to help numb the pain.

Without realizing it, I had made my way to my old house. I guess it was instinctive. I stand on the sidewalk, looking in through the living room window. It feels so empty. Obviously, it is empty, but it feels like a void. Sucking the life out of everything and everyone that comes near. The Telluride Maniac seems to have stopped killing people for the moment–how generous of him–so the town is opening up again. I get the slightest bit of pleasure that I am probably the reason he stopped. He was spooked. He was almost caught.

Hundreds of true crime podcasts have covered the murders, so tourists pour in to see if they can solve the mystery the police can't figure out. That's why there is tape covering the front door and side gate, most likely in an attempt to keep all of the true crime nuts away. It doesn't look too effective.

From here, I can see the family photo that usually hangs above the couch is gone. The whole house has been cleared out. Now it just sits there, a hollow shell of what it once was. A for sale sign on the lawn. I look towards the upstairs window my mom fell out of, but it's been fixed, like it was never broken. The front step is covered in snow but all I can think about is the blood that was there. All I can see is my mother's body laying twisted out of shape.

I walk towards the side gate, push it open and enter the backyard. The back door is unlocked, so I let myself in. Jesus, they're not taking the whole 'security' thing very seriously. The rug has been removed so each step echoes through the hollow hallway. The downstairs is completely spotless. It looks as if the house was simply vacant, only empty because it's for sale. But, as I walk up the stairs and look down the hallway, the simple emptiness feels more like a black hole that swallowed my mother, father, sister, brother, and me. All of their rooms are completely empty. No beds. No desks. No posters. The life has been thrown away. Just like theirs. I walk into my brothers room and slide down the wall and onto the floor.

Just being in this room fills me with so much dread that I don't even know why I entered the house. It wasn't planned,

CHAPTER THIRTY-FOUR

but I couldn't stop myself. I had lived here all my life with my parents, and my siblings came along over time. We were so happy. Sure, they were strict, and some days I couldn't bear them, but I still loved them. Through every fight and disappointment, I loved them. Then, in the span of one night out, my family was gone. The Telluride Maniac took everything from me and gets to walk away into a life of infamy.

It's not fair. That thought has consumed me. I cannot believe I have to grow up this way. My parents will never see me live my life. I'll never get the opportunity to make them proud. They won't meet my future partner. They won't get to know their grandchildren, and my kids will never know their grandparents. I won't see my siblings finish school, move out, and discover who they are. For every second that life goes on and I get older, my family stays the same. Frozen in time.

My eyes begin to well up. My sister's room is similar but for some reason the hollowness is extra present in here. I feel physically ill, but I can't help looking around. Part of me doesn't know if this is somehow helpful. Maybe seeing the house empty will provide me with enough closure to begin to move on. If it is, it's not feeling like it yet. Tears are already leaking out of my eyes, but when I open my parents' bedroom door, my sobs become uncontrollable. Hysterical cries tear out of me. I stumble towards the replaced window and look down at the spot where my mother fell. My feet give out, and I collapse onto the carpet. I sit there sobbing for over half an hour. My phone buzzes with texts from my aunt asking where I am. I ignore them. When I finish crying, I sit against the wall. Then I realize maybe I was right. It actually feels therapeutic to be back here one more time before it inevitably sells.

I message my aunt back, *'Coming home.'* Even though I'm already here.

I stand up and leave my parents room. I walk down the stairs and out the back door, telling myself this is the physical manifestation of me leaving them behind. Not fully, but maybe it's a step in the right direction.

I duck under the tape and head back to the footpath. I turn right and begin my walk. The sun is setting. I pass a few other pedestrians and smile at them, reassuringly not seeing my family's faces in theirs. But then I see *him*. I see those antlers. Not again. I can't keep seeing him everywhere I go. I squeeze my eyes shut but when I open them, the antlers are still there. He is standing on the pavement, looking in through the window of another house. Is this what he did with my house? Did he watch us like he's watching them? Then, the Maniac turns and looks at me.

The contentment I have been feeling vanishes. All I feel now is rage. But it's not blackout; it's driven. I need to stop him. I need to catch him. He just stares at me, and he seems shocked when I break into a sprint and chase directly after him.

He darts towards the house he has been stalking and disappears into the backyard. I follow him, jumping over their back fence and into the woods behind the house. I see footprints in the snow. A trail left by the person I know is the Telluride Maniac. The person who killed my parents. I follow the trail through the trees. I pick up the pace and break into a run. I can't see him. The trees are thick and can easily shield anybody from view. The sun has set, so the footprints become harder to follow, but I pull out my phone flashlight

CHAPTER THIRTY-FOUR

and keep running.

I'm running parallel to the highway based on the distant sounds of engines and car horns. I finally make it to the other side of town and see a row of houses, and the prints lead me to the one on the far left. It looks so familiar. As if I've been here before. It's not as nice as the other neighborhoods in Telluride. I turn off my flashlight as I approach the house. The tracks lead to a side window and then disappear. This is where they live. This is the house that contains and nurtures such evil. The lights are on. I stand a safe distance, but I'm close enough to make out pictures on the wall—pictures of Willow and Hugh.

I don't understand. Willow? She can't be the Telluride Maniac. But this is her house. I knew I'd been here before. Maybe it's not her. Maybe it's her dad. No, that makes no sense. I've met him through the theater department, and he's always been charming. I'm beginning to think I'd followed the wrong trail when Willow walks out of her bathroom, looking entirely out of breath and red-faced. My stomach drops and my heart shatters. I can't believe this. I try to poke holes in my story. I try to find any information to prove to myself that she is not the killer. But I can't. Because when she opens her closet, I see the deer mask I saw right before I found my parents dead. Directly after *she* had killed my parents. The same mask that has haunted me ever since.

Willow is the Telluride Maniac.

Any ounce of catharsis disintegrates. The only thing that could possibly make me feel content is justice. I don't need "closure". I don't need to "move on". I need to know the person who put my family in the ground suffers.

I need to see that bitch hang.

Chapter Thirty-Five

Noa - 6:30 AM - Sunday, 30th January 2022

"I, Willow Montgomery, am the Telluride Maniac."

The room goes silent. I watch as the information registers—her dirty little secret, one she believed she had gotten away with, is not much of a secret after all. We all know, and soon, *everybody* will know. Her pupils shrink, and she turns white. It's been two months since I followed her home from my house—two long, excruciating months of living with this information.

The second I got back to my aunt's house; I told her what had happened and where I'd been. I was shocked she didn't believe me. There I was, standing in front of her, saying I had uncovered who was behind the murder of my mother, of her sister. But she was too focused on the fact I went back to the house. She was convinced I was seeing things again. That I was too blinded by my own rage and guilt to be thinking clearly. Then, she called my psychiatrist, and I was back in that place. I was back with the screams echoing down the hallway. I was back with the nurses telling me what I went through was awful, but I have to *"let go."* I realized then and there that nobody would believe me no matter what I said.

No one was going to believe a seventeen-year-old girl could

CHAPTER THIRTY-FIVE

pull off a string of murders and remain undetected. But I know Willow. She's sociopathic in every sense of the word. In every theater class and conversation, it is clear she cares for nobody but herself. She is the most obvious candidate for a serial killer. When Hugh gave her the part of the killer in his shitty play, I actually had to hold in my laugh.

When I got out of the ward, I knew I had to keep my mouth shut. I couldn't risk going back there. It's so lonely. It's so cold. It was even worse because I knew I wasn't crazy, not like some of the other people in there. People who pissed on the ground. People who thought aliens were after them. Unlike them, I was justified. But just because I kept my mouth shut, doesn't mean I wasn't thinking about it constantly. I was plotting on how to catch her in the act for weeks, but the killings didn't resume. She knew it was too close, and I knew I had to get creative.

I finally opened up and told Kaya about Willow. I told her what I found, and she trusted me wholeheartedly. Unlike everybody else, Kaya wanted to believe Willow was a heartless monster. She told me we must gather evidence before turning her in.

"We need a confession," she had told me.

I had no idea how to get one. Confronting a serial killer like Willow would have been dangerous, as I had no idea what she'd do. I suggested we tell a few people about it and confront her in a public space. Somewhere she couldn't kill her way out. We could have told the police about the mask in her closet. It could have been quick. It could have been painless.

But Kaya had a different idea.

She wanted to make her feel exactly like the entire town of Telluride. Terror. Scared for their life. She wanted to break

Willow down enough so she would admit it herself. This was a perfect way to make her do exactly that. And that's how the plan was formed.

When we thought about it further, we told Caleb. He didn't believe us, but when we explained it, he jumped at the opportunity to traumatize her and make her pay. Then we told the class, excluding Hugh, Fergus, and of course, Willow. If we wanted this to work, everyone had to be involved. As it turns out, everybody's quiet disdain for Willow was exceptionally helpful. We didn't tell them the entire truth, just snippets. We said that we were going to play a prank on Willow. I told them how much it made me angry that she would lie about her dad being murdered to garner the same *sympathy* as me. I told them I wanted her to realize she couldn't piggyback off somebody else's trauma for attention. She needed to be taught a lesson. Riley thought it was cruel, even for Willow, but everyone else was instantly on board. Sure, I might have guilt-tripped her into eventually agreeing, and I felt bad about it, but I couldn't afford her ratting us out. But she still felt sick to her stomach with the prospect. I'm not sure whether or not her dad was sick, but most of that nervousness was our doing.

We didn't tell Hugh because he would never have let us do it and definitely would have tried to stop us, and Fergus, well, we just didn't *want* to tell him.

Truthfully, I thought the whole idea was a little insane. I knew if the entire class backed up my story, the cops would have to look into it, but Kaya and Caleb didn't want that. They were so hellbent on making her pay. They didn't want to sit by and watch justice be served, they wanted to be the servers.

And I understood it.

CHAPTER THIRTY-FIVE

They had their own reasons not to like Willow, and I was sure they wanted to enact this plan to satisfy their own personal vendettas rather than justice for my family, but it coincided with my needs. So that was that.

The plan was to fake our deaths and make Willow believe somebody knew her secret and was targeting her and it would only stop when she confessed, even though everyone thought it was to make her see the error of her ways. We all had to try our best to be pleasant with her, otherwise she wouldn't give two shits about anything that happened to us. I needed to soften her up so maybe she would grow a heart and do the right thing. Of course, that didn't happen.

Nobody was meant to die; Riley was telling the truth. However, we hadn't considered the fact that Willow was *actually* a serial killer and, when cornered, could kill any one of us. When cornering a rat, it will chew through you. The groundskeeper was entirely something else. That was an accident. Well, it was initially. It was self-defense. He was going to kill Caleb. But then Kaya interfered and saved him... then cut off his head. She said it was to make it look more real and that when Willow is tried for murder, it will make her look even worse. I didn't really understand it, seeing as Willow had already brutally murdered a dozen people in Telluride and the headless groundskeeper wasn't going to change that. It was overkill. Unnecessary violence; which is exactly what we were trying to stop.

When he winded up dead, the group freaked out, so we had to reveal the truth. We pinned it on Willow and told them that she is the Maniac, and we needed a confession. Surprisingly, that was all it took for them to believe us. I wish my aunt was that easily convinced. But even if they didn't, there wasn't much they could do about it because like Willow, they had nowhere to go and nobody to call.

And then when Fergus ended up dead, it was pretty obvious that was Willow. All of us had been in constant contact the entire night.

Caleb found this lodge and said he knew the owners would be gone for the week. It was the perfect location and when we found out a storm was rolling through this weekend, it was time to set the plan in action. Sure, there would have to be some explaining to do afterwards, about why we broke into a lodge, but I figured everything we did could be pinned on Willow. Things got way too out of hand, like the axe marks on the door, and the complete destruction of the living room, but my desperation and hatred for Willow were enough to keep me going. If this next part works, we should be in the clear.

So, right now, strapped to Caleb's chest is a microphone, and when Willow confesses, this weekend will have been a success. Months of suffering, begging for closure and revenge will come to an end. But right now, she stays silent.

"Is that it?" I ask her. "You're not going to say anything?"

Silence.

"You kill my entire family, and you stay silent!" I yell at her. Finally, she looks up at me. The Willow from twenty seconds ago is gone. There is nothing behind those eyes except hatred. Earlier this trip, I almost didn't believe she could be the killer. I thought my *'soften her up'* plan had worked too well. I thought maybe I had gotten it all wrong, but I fully believe the girl in front of me is a cold-hearted murderer.

"So, you were pretending to be my friend this whole weekend?" she growls.

CHAPTER THIRTY-FIVE

Is she serious? That's what she's worried about? Of course, I have been. I needed her to trust me. I needed her to like me, so she could feel the pain of losing me. I know there's no chance in hell I would ever be friends with this girl again, but it gives me great joy to know that she thought we had hope, and I got to crush it.

I lean towards her and whisper, "Abso-fucking-lutely." I stand back up. "Do you seriously think anybody would be your friend? Anybody would *ever* love you?"

Willow looks hurt. Good. She should be.

"Have fun in prison, bitch," Evelyn cheers.

"Nobody is going to believe you!" Willow shouts.

"Oh, yes, they will," Kaya laughs as she pulls out her phone and plays a video. It was taken from outside the groundskeeper's cabin. The footage shows Fergus walking through the door and getting a knife to the throat, and as he falls, Willow is revealed behind him. Her face drops.

"That—no, that's out of context!" Willow shouts, genuinely trying to convince us that *it isn't what it looks like.*

"Oh yeah?" Arthur says. "And what context is that?"

"I thought he was attacking me!" Willow cries.

"Good luck getting anybody to believe that," I say, chuckling.

"They will!" she shouts. "Was he involved in this sick plan of yours?" Willow asks.

A few of us laugh.

"No," I say flatly. "Nobody even wanted to invite him, but we felt kind of rude leaving him out."

"Oh," Willow says understandingly. "Well, what about Riley?"

"What *about* Riley?" Kaya responds.

"You killed her!" She yells.

"Yes, I did, Willow," Kaya says. "She was a problem. She would have said something. She could barely hold it in around you, imagine what she would have been like around police officers. They're going to question the shit out of us. She would have broke."

"I mean, you didn't have to be so aggressive," Caleb admits to Kaya. "An axe was a little much."

The rest of the group are still shaken from that. I think when Riley died, they all fully understood the trouble we could all be in. Samuel has turned white and I'm right there with him. At first, I bet he thought this whole weekend could be great content for his TikTok, but now that people are dead, he's realizing that this isn't a fun video concept. This is real. Actually, I'm surprised everyone else isn't feeling that way. They seemed to have moved on from Riley in a matter of minutes. Is this just a class of psychopaths?

"I didn't really have many options." Kaya explains. "Yes, it was cruel, and I'll miss her every day, blah blah blah, but all anybody needs to know is that *you* did it."

I guess it is. There's a pit in my stomach. It's almost like when I would wake up from a blackout and realize what I'd done. I've been in a blackout ever since I found out about Willow but hearing Kaya talk about taking another life so nonchalantly makes my skin crawl. I hate to admit that I had a part in creating a monster. I should have never agreed to this.

"And the groundskeeper?" Willow asks again.

Kaya looks guilty about that. That's a positive sign, I guess.

"Okay, that was an accident," she justifies. "Caleb forgot to mention there was a groundskeeper—"

"I didn't know," Caleb adds. "We just wanted to scare him

CHAPTER THIRTY-FIVE

off but then he attacked me, and Kaya had to do what she had to do."

Willow stares in disgust. I know they went a little far but she is the last person who can judge. However, I'm kind of with her. I'm starting to believe Kaya might enjoy this killing thing too much ...

Willow's breathing gets heavier.

"Hugh!" she says. "How do you think he'll react when he sees that all of you are alive? He won't believe any of you!"

"He's probably already dead," Kaya says. "Arthur let him jump out of that window. He most likely froze."

"What, and you're just okay with that?" Her head turns to Caleb. He's clearly struggling with that fact but doesn't want her to know it.

"You know what? Hugh sold me down the river. He doesn't care about me. Besides, he knows too much. His story won't line up with ours. He's a liability."

His voice is cold, and I can tell he doesn't mean what he's saying. Hugh *is* a liability, but Caleb is not okay with letting him die. They have too much history but when Caleb agreed to do this, he knew some things might go wrong.

"Besides," he continues, "even if he survives, when he sees the footage of you murdering Fergus, he'll never trust you again."

A tear rolls down Willow's face, and her head drops.

"How long have you known?" she asks.

It's so close to a confession. I need her to admit it.

"Known what, Willow?" I probe.

"Known," she pauses. "Known that I was the Telluride Maniac."

Done. I guess she realized there was no point in denying it

anymore. I look over to Caleb, and I give him a nod. He pulls the microphone out of his shirt and presses a button, turning the flashing red light off.

"Perfect," he says. "Thank you for your cooperation, Willow. We'll just have to trim it and then it's good to go."

Willow's face twists, and her sadness is replaced with resentment and a look of betrayal.

"Since December, when I found you staring into that house," I tell her. "I followed you home."

She looks up at me, shocked.

"That was you? Fuck, I could not see anything in that mask. Why not just turn me in?" she asks.

"I told my aunt. She sent me away. Trust me, you think I'd be doing all of this if I didn't think it was an absolute last resort? I can't fucking go back there!"

I realize I'm screaming at the end and everybody, including Willow, looks terrified. But she's right. This is ridiculous. We should have turned her over to the police. Now we're stuck in the eye of a shitstorm.

"But now you've confessed. People will believe me now. I still want to know, though, why did you do it?"

She pauses. "I don't know."

I look at her with so much hatred in my eyes. The microphone is off, and she is still lying.

"Answer me," I tell her threateningly.

"I don't have to tell you fucking anything!" she screams, and I slap her with so much force that it nearly makes the chair topple over.

"Do you know how painful it was? Knowing who killed my parents and not being able to tell anybody. I had to sit and listen to you *lie.* I had to listen to your sly jabs and put-downs

CHAPTER THIRTY-FIVE

and not say anything in order stay out of that institution. I had to play along as you tried to become my friend after killing my parents. I had to listen to you tell a bullshit story about how you 'pushed your dad down the stairs because he was abusive.' Bitch, you have a one-story house! He knew what you were, but he couldn't bear to be known as the father of a serial killer. I deserve to know the truth. Why did you kill them? Why the fuck did you kill my parents?" I find myself once again screaming so hysterically that I can barely understand myself. "Tell me! I *need* to know."

She pauses again. Then, she takes a deep breath and says, "I hated them. I hated you. I thought they were the reason you stopped being friends with me."

That's it? I feel my face burning more and more by the second.

"I hated you so much for deserting me." She continues. "I planned to kill you too, but you were out. When I think back on it now, though, I like the idea of you feeling as *alone* as I felt," she says with a quiver in her voice.

I don't know what to say. I look back towards the group and see they are as dumbfounded as I am.

"Do you seriously believe that what you did was justified?" I ask her. "You think that killing my entire family is equivalent to me unfriending you?"

"To me," she says flatly.

"You're sick!" Arthur pipes up from behind me.

"I know, but I've changed!" Willow shouts. Her persona changes so quickly. It's jarring. It's like she's testing which one works best, figuring out which one will grant her the most sympathy.

"Bullshit!" I scream. "You haven't changed. You don't

deserve to change. Not anymore."

Willow looks upset, but I know it's not because of what she did; it's because somebody found out.

"No, I can. You can help me change! Noa, I'm so sorry," she cries. There is a hint of remorse in her eyes. Another mask. Somehow even worse than the one with antlers.

"Shut the fuck up, Willow," Caleb says.

Willow looks towards Caleb. Then, any trace of remorse vanishes as she rolls her eyes and lets out a chuckle. She's finally dropping the act.

"I'm sorry, Caleb," she mocks.

"For what?" Caleb asks patronizingly. "It's not like you killed *my* family."

"I'm sorry for holding you and Hugh back all these years. That wasn't very nice of me," she says with a smile.

Caleb goes red. She knows she can't escape this situation, so she's trying her best to tear us apart.

"It's okay," Caleb says. "After finding out that his insufferable girlfriend is a serial killer, he won't want anything to do with you anyway."

Willow isn't listening. "Maybe it *was* my fault that he never gave you what you wanted."

"It was," Caleb mutters.

"Or maybe," Willow continues, "It was the fact that Hugh would never want to be with a pathetic, little *faggot* like you." She says it so calmly that what she said doesn't register with any of us at first.

"You're fucking evil!" I shout at her.

"Sure," she says indifferently. "You are too."

"I am nothing like you!" I scold her. "I'm not a killer!"

"Drop the shit, Noa," Willow snaps. "At least I can own

CHAPTER THIRTY-FIVE

what I've done. I know I'm a bad person, and it's so humiliating watching you delude yourself into thinking that you're not. You've stood by while your embarrassing vigilante friends murdered and abused innocent people. A poor groundskeeper, a harmless couple, and you're own fucking friend."

I feel sick. This has gone too far. I've been so focused on catching her that I have barely considered the repercussions of this whole weekend. This is a potential life sentence I brought upon myself in the name of revenge. Kaya and Caleb's sick lust for retribution made me think this was acceptable. I mean, they have absolutely no reason to be doing all of this. Sure, she's annoying and rude to them, but you can't kill people over it. The only person who has the right to be doing this is me. But even then, do I have the right? But I can't stop, especially now that we have everything we need. We have her confession; we just have to wait for help to arrive.

"You did that!" Evelyn shouts, clearly just wanting to be involved.

But something doesn't sit right with me. Well, many things don't, but it was something Willow said just before. "A harmless couple?" What is she talking about?

"Did I kill someone?" Willow asks. "I'm not sure I did. Because I talked to the couple in the basement. Shannon and Al. Right before *you* murdered Riley. She didn't recognize me, but she remembered two people dressed in Maniac masks." She looks at all of us. "Do the math. There's one of me. Suddenly, your whole story about me being the sole mastermind isn't too plausible."

My stomach drops. The couple in the basement? Fuck. I turn to Caleb.

"What the fuck is she talking about?"

He stutters and avoids eye contact. "We may have … kidnapped the couple who lives here."

"WHAT THE FUCK!"

"I'm sorry! It was an accident!"

Kaya chimes in. "We were here on Thursday, making sure everything was ready, and they came home. We panicked!"

"Just like you panicked with the groundskeeper?" I scream back.

I can't believe my ears. It seems every second that goes by, we are plunged deeper into this pile of shit we have created. Not only now do we have to play off breaking and entering, but we also have to play off *KIDNAPPING*! I feel like I could vomit any second. This harmless prank just keeps growing more harmful.

"Look, they're safe," Kaya says, trying to calm me down. "We can let them go now, we have her confession. With persuasion, we can get them on our side."

"They're not children," Willow interrupts. "They know what they saw."

She's right. Unless we find another scapegoat, it won't add up.

"You have two options," Willow continues. "You can let them go. Be the *good, lovely* people you claim to be. However, this would poke holes in your story and make the police question everything you say. Or," she pauses "you can kill them and be the *awful, hypocritical* pieces of *shit* you always have been. At least then you could blame it on me. Do you think they have kids? Do you think the groundskeeper did?"

She looks so proud. I want to fucking kill her.

"You know what?" I say as I walk over to her, holding a

knife. "Maybe I am a killer. But you turned me into one."

I hold my knife to her throat. Her smug face has been wiped away. She looks scared.

"You gifted me an anger that I don't think will ever go away. You turned me into somebody I don't recognize, and I hate that. All I wanted was for you to feel what I felt. I wanted you to feel alone. Rotting in prison for the rest of your life," I tell her. "But now, I want you to feel *everything* my family felt. I want you to be in pain. I want the last moments of your life to be *excruciating*."

Her eyes widen, but she is trying to conceal her fear. I even think she's trembling, but I realize she's just trying to free herself from the ropes. But then, she focuses on me.

"I will fucking kill you," she utters.

"I thought you only killed people while they slept. You're a coward."

I am about to lift the knife. I don't think I could do it. I've never killed anyone before. But when I look into her eyes, I can see the antlers. These were the last eyes my family ever saw. So, I raise the knife. I don't think it should be an issue.

Then, I hear a loud shattering sound coming from the basement. I turn my head sharply and walk towards the kitchen. Caleb follows me. Before we get the chance to go down, I hear a scream from the living room. I turn back to see that Willow has somehow freed herself from the chair. She kicks Arthur in the groin and in his pain, he drops the knife. That's such a cheap shot but hey, it's effective.

I immediately begin to run to her, as does everyone else. I can't let her get away with this, not after everything. Not when the police are almost here. But we stop dead in our tracks because when Samuel reaches her, she picks the knife up from the ground and stabs him square in the chest. Everyone screams as she stabs him again and he slumps to the floor. Then, she grabs Arthur by the hair and holds her blade to his throat.

"Don't come any fucking closer!" Willow orders Kaya and Evelyn as they are the closest to her. "Drop the knives!"

They do. But it was a trick. Willow laughs.

"Fucking idiots," she says as she plunges the knife deep into Arthur's eyeball, causing blood to squirt all over Kaya, Evelyn, and herself, then she runs out of the room.

I start to follow her, but Kaya yells. "Don't worry, I've got this!" she says gleefully as she and Evelyn trail close behind her.

I'll let them deal with her. Kaya could easily take her in a fight, so I'm not worried. Caleb and I have to deal with whatever is going on in the basement. We have to take care of Shannon and Al. We have to start building our alibis.

This is the pinnacle. It's time to give the best performances of our lives.

Chapter Thirty-Six

Shannon - 6:30 AM - Sunday, 30th January 2022

The cellar is malodorous. It's dank and pitch-black. I can't see anything. The only thing that grounds me and stops me from giving up is the warm embrace of my husband. I still don't understand why we're down here. It was a Thursday evening when they attacked us. We were staying with Al's parents in Telluride, and the plan was to stay with them over the weekend. But in-laws being in-laws, we grew sick of them quite quickly. We heard about the snowstorm rolling through the mountains and thought it could be a nice idea to head back to the lodge before we were truly stuck with them the entire weekend.

When we arrived, we found the front gate open. I grilled Al about leaving it open, but he was convinced he shut it. He's always been the forgetful type, so I didn't believe him. When I saw the front door was ajar also, I thought he must be losing his mind. But when he swore to me he shut and locked the door, and when I saw the rock that conceals the spare key had been moved, I believed him. I begged him to stay outside and call the police, but he told me I was being paranoid. I don't see how I was, seeing as someone was very clearly in the house, and very soon after, we both found out I was justified.

Al took a cautious step inside the lodge.

"Hello?" he called.

There was no response. There were no sounds. But the first thing I noticed was every single picture had been taken. I gasped. Why would they steal our photos? Photos of us and our children who have now moved out. Everything else seemed to be in place, like the ridiculously expensive vase on the mantle. If they were robbing us, why steal photos that were worthless to everybody else, but priceless to us?

Al shut and locked the door, thinking the people inside had already left. It didn't make me feel any safer, knowing these people still had our spare key. I was about to call a locksmith when a sound came from upstairs.

I didn't want to move any closer. I wanted to go outside and call the police, but Al didn't. Typical man. For some reason, he thought he could take on whoever was there. He thought he could do a better job than an officer with a gun. He started moving toward the staircase.

"Please don't go," I whispered to him aggressively.

"I'll be fine."

He wouldn't be fine.

I stayed in the living room as Al disappeared up the staircase leading to our bedroom. A few minutes of silence went by, which eased my nerves. Maybe nothing was up there and the people already left. That's when Al screamed.

"Hey!" he yelled.

Then, there were bangs as Al fought with whoever it was. I heard somebody hit the wall, so I ran towards the staircase, hoping to help him. That's when he fell backwards and tumbled down the stairs.

He hit each step, and I immediately thought he was dead.

CHAPTER THIRTY-SIX

I ran over to him, begging him to wake up. He was still breathing, and I was relieved for a few seconds, then I looked up and saw a figure wearing a mask. Then I saw the large antlers. My heart sank. The Telluride Maniac. He was back. And we were his next victims.

But then, someone else stepped out of the bedroom. Someone wearing an identical mask. There were two of them, and only one of me. I screamed as I got up and ran to the door. I didn't even think twice about staying with Al. That's not true, I felt terrible, but I wasn't going to stop. I thought I could get into the car and get help. I wasn't quick enough, though, because before I even got the chance to unlock the front door, something hit the back of my head and I fell to my knees. Then that expensive vase shattered around me.

I was going in and out of consciousness as one of them grabbed my legs and dragged me across the floor. They picked me up when we reached the kitchen and carried me down the basement stairs. I saw the other one had Al, but he was too heavy to carry, so he was dragged down the stairs. That's when they threw us down into the wine cellar and pulled up the ladder. Then, they left. We were trapped.

We've been without food for however long we've been down here. Every once in a while, someone in the mask has given us a bottle of water. I guess that's good but we're getting desperate for something to eat. I feel weak. My hands are shaky, and I can't stand up for too long at a time. There was a girl that found me. I should have asked her for something but it looked like she was dealing with her own predicament. Why was she in our house? She said help was on the way, but I can't wait much longer.

We've tried climbing out, but the opening is too far away

for us to reach. We also tried me sitting on Al's shoulders, but I couldn't pull myself up. I fear now it may be too late. I can't even stand up, how am I going to pull myself out of this hole? But we have to try. We have to do something.

"We need to get out of here," I tell Al.

He knows that, of course he does. But he's fading away like me. He's given up. But I can't let that happen.

I feel around for something to use. I try pulling one of the mahogany shelves to use as a ladder but they're fixed to the wall. Al is my only option.

"Get up," I tell him. "We're trying again."

He doesn't look too thrilled, but to be fair, he doesn't look like anything.

"There's no point."

"How could you say that? Get up. I'm not dying down here, Al."

I understand what he's thinking but when I think about our children, I feel a rush of energy. I'm not letting them lose both of their parents because we gave up. I'm getting out of here and I'm seeing them again.

"Get up," I order.

He does, reluctantly. I tell him to grab my foot with his hands and lift me toward to opening. On the first try, my fingers clasp the ledge and he keeps pushing me. My hands are now gripping it but I'm not strong enough to pull myself up. It's too hard.

But then I remember my kids. I think about my grandkids. It's enough for me to lift myself up onto the floor.

"Keep pushing!"

"I can't!"

He can't lift me anymore. It's up to me. I swing my leg up

to the opening, but I miss. I try again and this time, it works. Half of my body is out. And within seconds, I climb out of the cellar and roll onto my back, finally free.

I lean back in to help Al, but it's too difficult. He's too heavy. There's no chance I could pull him out without ending back down there.

"Go without me," he tells me. "Get help!"

I nod. I owe it to him. I'll do what I tried to do on that ill-fated Thursday evening. I make a promise to myself that I'll be back. I'm not leaving him down there to die. I pull myself to my feet. My head spins and my body sways side to side. I stumble down the dark hallway until I see the light coming from under the door. It's daytime. Help mustn't be far away. I rush towards it, so happy to be free. I swing the door open and run into the finished basement, taking my first of many breaths of fresh air.

My excitement is short-lived, as the second I step foot into the room, a boy slashes a knife into my neck.

My vision immediately goes spotty. Blood squirts from the wound, painting the white carpet red. I stumble forward, trying to find something to balance myself with. I can't, so I fall directly into the glass coffee table, causing it to shatter. Now, my vision starts going in and out. I can't breathe. Every gulp of air pours straight out the open hole in my throat. This can't be happening. I promised Al I'd be back. I promised my kids I would see them again. I wonder where they are. Are they having breakfast? Did they sleep in? Are they taking their kids to school? Is it a school day? What day is it? Did they wonder why I wasn't picking up the phone?

I look over at the basement window, knowing they're out there somewhere, and close my eyes.

Chapter Thirty-Seven

Hugh - 6:30 AM - Sunday, 30th January 2022

I can barely move my fingers. I've been stuck outside for nearly three hours. When I fell from the window, I couldn't move, but I heard footsteps bolting down the stairs, so I forced myself up and limped along the lodge's exterior, trying to ignore the excruciating pain in my ankle. The door opened, and one Wendigo came outside looking for me. I peered from behind a wall and watched as they scanned their surroundings. After a minute of holding my breath, they walked inside. I sat back against the side wall of the lodge and waited. I couldn't go inside; I had no idea where the Wendigos were lurking. Knowing there are two of them changes everything. They could be guarding multiple doors at once. What did they do to Caleb? Where are Noa and Willow? After about an hour of waiting, I thought about running into the woods, maybe even to the groundskeeper's cabin.

Still, I had no idea where that was, and I would never have made it on my ankle, so I stuck by the lodge, trying desperately to shield myself from the wind. It partially works. I'm not bearing the full brunt of the storm, but I know I can't stay out here much longer. I'm hoping an opportunity to go inside will

CHAPTER THIRTY-SEVEN

present itself. I pick myself up and limp, but the cold has made my ankle worse. I hop on one foot around the lodge. It takes me a while, as the snow is much deeper than before. I turn a corner and trip over what I assume is the backup generator. And when I fall, it's impossible to get back up. Maybe it's a sign. I can't go inside, or they'll kill me. But I can't stay outside, or the temperature will kill me. I roll onto my back and look up into the sky. Like a message from above, the mist appears to dissolve, revealing a golden, pink sunrise. It's so beautiful. Is it His way of sending me off in peace? Is it Him welcoming me home? It's comforting, definitely not the worst final view.

But the sunrise isn't His message. He's trying to illuminate my next move. Because when I turn my head to the left, I see the sun shining on a small window looking into the basement. In desperation, I crawl towards it and attempt to push it open, but it won't budge. I can't give up. It's my only escape from certain death. I reposition myself so my feet are directly over the window.

It takes three kicks, but finally, the window shatters. I use my sleeve to clear any glass fragments from the window. I go in feet first, careful still not to slice myself on the shards of glass. I drop down into the basement, careful not to land on my ankle, and once inside, I collapse to the floor, give the cross hanging around my neck a kiss, finally feeling relief from the cold. All I have to do is wait for help to arrive. Sounds simple enough. Wait for help, but also try not to get murdered. Directly in front of me is a glass coffee table, and a kitchen knife sits on top of it. Why is that down here? I don't think much about it at first, and I take the knife for protection. Then I wonder, why *is* that down here? Why is *anything* down here? There is a couch and a television, along with a fluffy gray

267

carpet. Caleb told us that the basement was unfinished. He said there were wires and that it was a safety hazard. What's going on? If he didn't want us down here, it begs the question, what is he hiding?

I hear muffled voices upstairs. It sounds like multiple people. Is it the police? Are they finally here? I get to my feet and hop towards the stairs. I get to the first step and realize that hopping creates too much noise. It might not be the police after all, but even if it is, I don't want to hurry over to them. I don't want to give them any reason to shoot me. I grit my teeth, place my left foot on the second step, and then quickly follow it with my right one. Putting weight on my foot is agonizing, but I don't stop. I continue up the stairs, somehow holding in any grunts of pain. I finally make it to the top of the stairs. I'm sweating profusely and can't catch my breath. The basement door is slightly ajar. I gently pull it towards me and poke my head through. My heart sinks.

It's not the police.

In the living room, I see Willow tied up. Standing in front of her are Noa, Kaya, Evelyn, Arthur, Samuel, and ... *Caleb*. I don't understand. How is this possible? They all died! Was it them this whole time? Where are Riley and Fergus? Are they dead for real? I stumble backwards in shock, but I can't catch myself before I hit the wall. Caleb has been lying to me this whole time. They all have. Everyone except Willow. Why are they targeting Willow? Is any of this real? Was it a prank gone wrong? My heart sputters frantically. I make my way down the stairs, enduring the pain once again. I don't know where I'm planning on going. I can't go back outside. I guess I just have to hide. When I reach the bottom, I turn around and watch the basement door. I'm terrified that one of them

CHAPTER THIRTY-SEVEN

heard me coming down the stairs. Then, my fears come true.

A door swings open. But it isn't the basement door. It's a door behind me. Is this Riley or Fergus? Have they come to finish the job? Reflexively, I swing around with my knife tightly gripped in my hand. I'm looking at a woman. One who is a complete stranger to me. I wish I could stop but it's too late. My blade has already sliced her throat open. I drop the weapon on the carpet and watch in horror as the woman stumbles across the room and eventually smashes into the glass coffee table. Holy fuck. What have I done? I'm a murderer, and somebody *definitely* heard that. Footsteps approach the basement door. Then, all hell breaks loose upstairs. There is heavy stomping and thuds as something big hits the floor—a body. The stomping moves quickly away, then, the footsteps continue to the basement door.

I have to get out of here. I limp to the basement window, avoiding the broken glass on the floor. I grab the frame and drag myself out. I do it just in time because as soon as I crawl out of view, I look back to see Noa and Caleb descending the stairs and into the basement.

Chapter Thirty-Eight

Willow - 7:00 AM - Sunday, 30th January 2022

I quickly run down the hallway and up a set of stairs. The front door is still barricaded and leaving through the back door would require me pushing through everybody to get to it. I find myself at the double doorway to Caleb's bedroom. I thought it was Caleb's, but now I know it was Shannon and Al's. I run through and shut the door, locking it behind me. I back up against the wall, my eyes fixed on the door. I hear Evelyn and Kaya's footsteps approaching. The handle turns, and they bang at the door.

"Open the door, Willow!" Kaya taunts.

"Yeah!" Evelyn repeats. Unlike Kaya, Evelyn doesn't sound like she's having fun. She sounds angry and horrified that she just watched two of her friends die. She is far more aware of how real things have gotten. "Don't get all shy on us now. You weren't shy with Noa's family!"

I don't know why I became a killer. It started with small animals. One time a bird flew straight into my bedroom window, and I went outside to see if it was okay. It couldn't move. I felt terrible that the bird had to live in this pain, so I picked it up, and in a moment of impulsivity, I snapped its neck. I didn't want it to suffer. I thought it would make me

CHAPTER THIRTY-EIGHT

sad, but it didn't. Strangely, it did the complete opposite. It made me feel powerful. I got to be the dictator of life and death, even if it was for something as small as that bird. As I got older, the animals got bigger. I found a stray cat in the woods and tried to pick it up. When it scratched me, I was offended. How dare this low-life cat disrespect me like that? It had to be punished. So, I twisted its head all the way around and dropped it to the ground. Dead.

I could never fully satisfy these urges inside of me. Animals were fun, but I always yearned for more. Something bigger. When Hugh started writing his play, the one thing he told me about was a Wendigo. I was immediately fascinated by them. Their look was so striking; a mix between monster and human. It was terrifying in the best way possible. Then the ideas started flooding into my brain. I wanted something more, but I didn't realize what that was until then. I wanted to kill people. I wanted to play God. Hugh had wanted to use the Wendigo in his play, but I told him not to. I said they scared me, but in reality, I didn't want anybody to be able to make a connection between my boyfriend's play and my mask.

The first person I killed was an older woman. She was widowed. Her children had moved away, and she was alone. She was miserable. After a week of watching her, I broke into her house wearing the Wendigo mask and killed her in her sleep. I did her a favor. That mask gave me the power to be who I really am. It's ironic, really. Every time I put that mask on, I feel more like myself. Killing her started the long string of murders in Telluride. Nobody suspected me. Why would they? I was a teenage girl who did theater. I guess the misogyny plaguing our society actually worked out well for me. Yay for the patriarchy.

Then, one night, my dad found the mask in my room and a collection of trinkets taken from my victims. I never admitted it, but he knew what I was. He couldn't live with the information. He started drinking, and sure, he got angry, but he wasn't as bad as I said. I never pushed him down the stairs. Noa was right, I live in a one-story house. He booked a weekend spa retreat for my mom because he was finally willing to turn me in and accept the shame. He didn't want her there to see it. I wasn't going to let that happen. So, I stabbed him fourteen times, smothered him in plastic wrap, and dumped his body in the woods. Dragging his fat ass to the car was the hardest thing I've ever done.

Every time I killed, I felt more alive. But it did come with a downside. I got cocky. I got away with it for so long, that I almost forgot getting caught was a possibility. That's when Noa saw me looking into that house. I hadn't known it was Noa until now, the vision in that mask is not the best. Noa nearly ruined my life that night. I could have gone to jail.

It shook me. For the first time since I started my spree, I felt mortal. Like I was just a teenager that was capable of being punished. So, I stopped killing. It was never going to be permanent, just a break until it was safe to continue. But now, that day may never come.

Kaya and Evelyn continue ramming the door until the lock tears out of the frame and the door swings open. They enter the room with their knives raised towards me.

"Aw, look at you now, Willow," Kaya says patronizingly. "You're not so scary anymore."

It's abundantly clear she thinks she sounds so cool. I want to watch the smug look on her face disappear.

"Are you just jealous that I chose to kill Noa's family instead

CHAPTER THIRTY-EIGHT

of yours?" I ask her. "Because if I didn't, you could finally have a *real* problem to complain about."

She loves to think she has issues and that her life is somehow more challenging than everyone else's, and she believes that if you have been dealt great cards in life, that's something to be ashamed of. She wants to be the underdog. That's why she is doing this. I wouldn't be surprised if she forced Noa into all of this. I've never done anything to her, I've barely ever spoken to her. She craves a sense of injustice.

She laughs. "Oh, I have plenty of things to complain about."

"Yeah? Name one thing," I tell her flatly.

She can't. She comes from a white, wealthy family and has more privilege in her pinkie than anybody else in the world.

"I don't owe you anything," she says, her knuckles turning white from gripping the knife.

"It's okay," I tell her. "I can give you one."

I run at them with my knife raised. I swing once and they both jump back. Then Evelyn swings at me. I dodge it and manage to slice her thigh. She falls to the ground, screaming as blood flows from the wound. Kaya kicks me in the chest, and I basically fly across the room, dropping my knife along the way. Damn, she's strong. She runs at me while Evelyn stays on the ground, still screaming. So overdramatic, I barely touched her. I grab a painting from the wall and use it as a shield. Kaya's knife pierces through the canvas and stops mere inches from my face. I push the frame away and knock Kaya over. I run to my knife and pick it up but am interrupted by Evelyn. She swings her knife at me, but I jump back. She is quick, though, and she leaps closer and punches me square in the jaw. It takes me by surprise, but I don't let it slow me down. I grab her hair and smash both of our heads together.

Ow.

That is nothing like the movies. A pain rips through my head, and I stumble around for a second, trying to regain my balance. Eventually, I do, and I do it before Evelyn. So, I grab my knife and approach her. She barely gets a chance to scream before I shove my knife straight into her mouth.

She coughs up blood as the blade rips through the back of her throat, and she topples to the ground. Then I stab her one more time just to be sure. One down.

Out of nowhere, Kaya tackles me to the floor, and my knife slides to the other side of the room. I'm lying on my back, and Kaya is on top of me. She pins my arms under her knees and holds her knife against my throat. She's much stronger than I am. She raises the knife.

"This is for Noa—" she says proudly.

"Shut the fuck up," I say, cutting her short.

I knee her in the ass with so much power that she drops her knife and leans forward. I use this moment of weakness to free my right arm and punch her in the throat. She gasps for air and holds her neck as she rolls off me onto the ground. I grab her knife and stab it straight into her stomach. She tries to scream but all that comes out is a raspy growl. But I don't stop. I stab her over and over in a fit of rage. I've always hated her. She's always been so self-righteous. She needed to be taken down a notch. I continue stabbing her long after she's dead. It feels good to be doing this again.

"Willow?" somebody whispers from behind me. I leap off Kaya and hold the knife towards the bedroom door, ready to attack, but it's just Hugh standing in the doorway, terrified.

"What did you do?"

X

THE REQUIEM AETERNAM

Chapter Thirty-Nine

Noa - 7:00 AM - Sunday, 30th January 2022

I creep down the basement stairs with Caleb close behind me. I don't know what the shattering sound was, but my best guess would be that it was Shannon or Al attempting to escape. I am still so angry at Caleb and Kaya for kidnapping them. The plan was never to harm anybody, and we've failed miserably.

All I wanted was to get back at Willow. I wanted to make her pay for what she did to my family and the rest of Telluride, but now I've become exactly like her. When Caleb and Kaya said everything was fine, I shouldn't have believed it. I should have gone with them. Maybe if I had, this wouldn't have happened.

"Why the fuck did you kidnap them?" I scold him. "Why wouldn't you just leave?"

"I know, I'm sorry," he says. "We both wanted to keep the plan going. For you. We wanted you to have closure."

"Bullshit!" I exclaim. They wanted to continue the plan because of their own selfish needs. Caleb wanted Hugh. Kaya thought she was protecting me. She hates Willow more than anyone. I don't know why, seeing as Kaya's interactions with her don't extend past theater class.

"It's not bullshit! Look, we made a mistake, I get that. But technically it was self-defense. Al attacked us first—"

"I don't think that holds up in court if *you* broke into *his* house."

"Whatever! He never saw our faces. Besides, we can let them go as soon as the police arrive. We could even let them go now; we have her confession."

It's good in theory, but as Willow pointed out, they were too stupid to realize that Shannon and Al would tell the police that there were two kidnappers and because we are trying to incriminate Willow *alone*, that won't work.

I grip my knife tight as I near the bottom of the stairs, though when we finally reach the basement floor, I realize there is no need for it. It's dark, as the only light source is the tiny basement window on the left wall. Arthur and Samuel killed the electricity. It was meant to be a simple *flick of a switch*, but they "couldn't find the switch", so they decided to cut through the generator wires, forcing us into darkness for the entire night. It was so difficult trying to tie Willow to a chair by candlelight.

I think I have discovered the source of the noise when I see the basement window is broken. But then I see the coffee table.

"Is that who you are going to release?" I ask Caleb as I point to the body of a woman, I assume is Shannon, lying face down in a pool of broken glass and blood.

"What the fuck," Caleb states. "How did she get out of the cellar?"

Caleb kneels closer to the body as I stay standing, massaging my temple. This is all too much. If I had planned this weekend myself, I think there would be far fewer casualties. I have more of a headache now than when I was kept up till four in the

CHAPTER THIRTY-NINE

morning hearing people scream in the psych ward.

"What happened to her? Did she trip?" he asks me. I shrug my shoulders.

If so, that's a really depressing way to go after escaping from a cellar in your own house and almost making it to freedom. I feel terrible about Shannon. I truly do. She didn't deserve this. Nobody deserved this. Not Riley, not Fergus, not the groundskeeper. I'm even sad I never learnt his name. I mean, if you're responsible for his "accidental" death, the least you can do is know what his parents named him.

"It had to have been an accident. Maybe she tried to open the window but fell backwards."

Maybe. But that accident wouldn't have taken place without us. We are to blame for everything. Besides, this night is too much of a disaster for anything to be a simple mistake. We were shocked when Evelyn and I saw the car lights in the distance. We had planned out the timing of this trip perfectly. The storm would ensure that nobody would be able to reach us, but there was someone. It could have been a police officer for all we knew. That was another thing Caleb screwed up. He wasn't meant to call for help. We were meant to have more time. Now, the police could be here any second and Willow is running loose upstairs.

Sending the car off the side of the mountain was a *mistake*. Deep down, I knew we had enough to convict Willow. We had video footage of her killing Fergus. *That* was enough. And that's all that matters. The whole point of this was to get Willow to confess; we didn't need to terrify her. Although it was satisfying, it was unnecessary, and it didn't matter to me. All I needed was my family's murderer put behind bars. That's all I care about. I don't care about Caleb and Kaya's petty grudges and psychopathic tendencies. I could have saved Arthur, Samuel and Riley. Their deaths will weigh on my conscience until the day I die.

When I ran towards the car, Evelyn wanted me to stop but I didn't listen to her. Maybe I knew how terrible this would all turn out. I could have ended the night then and there. But instead, the car went off the mountain, and the driver died a fiery death. Then, I was back at it. Running around, pretending to be scared, digging myself a deeper hole.

Although, getting that confession felt incredible, and who knows what Riley would have said. So, maybe I'm secretly grateful for that crash.

I slowly walk towards Shannon's body and roll her over.

"Holy shit," I say. "Her throat has been cut."

"What?" Caleb walks over to me and looks at her.

"Fuck!" he exclaims. "Who did this?"

I think about it. All of us were in the living room. All but three. Fergus, who is dead. Riley, who is also dead and …

"Hugh," I say flatly.

"What?" Caleb says, sounding relieved he isn't dead after all. "That's impossible."

We had written off Hugh as dead, killed by hypothermia. We were guarding the doors to the lodge, but I didn't consider that he could have crept in through the basement window. Where is he now? Did he leave again through the window? If he did, he has probably already come back inside through the back door. As I think this, I hear loud noises coming from upstairs.

An array of thuds and screams. *Willow, Kaya, and Evelyn.* I grab Caleb, and we race up the basement stairs. When we get to the living room, I realize the noises are coming from

CHAPTER THIRTY-NINE

Shannon's room. The two of us creep towards the stairs, stepping over Arthur and Samuel's corpses. We ascend the staircase and put our ears against the double doors. I hear muffled speaking. Is it Kaya and Evelyn? Did they kill her? I really hope so. But I am, once again, let down as I open the door and see Willow and Hugh staring at us like deer in headlights.

I look to the floor and see Kaya and Evelyn dead. Two more victims of Willow's rampage. Kaya has been mutilated beyond recognition. Her face and hair are drenched in blood, and she has been stabbed so many times her intestines are drooping out onto the floor. Both the sight and stench make me want to vomit. Evelyn is bleeding heavily from her mouth. This is beyond self-defense. This was a crime of passion. How can't Hugh see through it?

"Back the fuck off!" Hugh threatens.

"Hugh, you have no idea what's happening. Stay out of it!" Caleb says.

"I do!" Hugh replies. "Willow told me everything."

I let out a chuckle. Of course, she did. I honestly want to hear her version of things. I'm sure it would make a great movie.

"Everything she told you is bullshit!" I scream. "But we don't have time to explain it."

I run at Willow with my knife gripped firmly in my right hand. Before I can reach her, Hugh throws his fist forward me and punches me square in the nose, sending me toppling to the ground.

"Willow, go!" Hugh shouts.

She does what she's told, and I watch as she runs to the door, pushes past Caleb and flees down the flight of stairs.

Chapter Forty

Hugh - 7:30 AM - Sunday, 30th January 2022

I stand in horror at the doorway of Caleb's parents' room. Yesterday, I was waking up in that bed next to Caleb, happier than I have been my whole life. Now, I know Caleb is probably a murderer, and I watched Willow viciously stab Kaya to death mere feet away from that same bed.

"Willow?" I say timidly. She leaps onto her feet and holds out her knife defensively. "What did you do?"

She slightly relaxes at the sight of me. She is completely saturated in blood.

"Shut the door," she whispers. I do, but as I turn back around, Willow walks towards me, still holding the knife. For a second, I think she is going to stab me, but instead, she embraces me in a long, tight hug.

"Thank God you're okay!" she cries.

I don't know what to think. I just watched her brutally murder somebody. If I hadn't just seen her tied to a chair, surrounded by all our "dead" friends, I would have run out of the room and never looked back. I have to believe that what she just did was out of self-preservation. But why were they targeting her?

"What the fuck is going on?" I ask her.

CHAPTER FORTY

She stops hugging me and takes a step back. She doesn't answer.

"Willow?" I pry.

She takes a deep breath before she starts speaking.

"It's all of them," she states. "They're all fucking crazy! They killed the groundskeeper, Riley, and Fergus."

I already know it's all of them. I want to know *why*. What did they tell her in the living room?

"Why are they doing this?" I ask.

She takes a few seconds to answer.

"Noa is insane. I think the murder of her family sent her spiraling," she claims. "They all are in it for different reasons. Kaya wanted to do it for fun, she hates me, and Caleb ... Caleb wants me to die so he can be with you."

What? That can't be true. That's not like Caleb at all. Well, not like the Caleb I *knew*. The Caleb I knew wouldn't pretend to be murdered and leave me outside for dead. I had been with him the whole night, and he was lying to me throughout all of it. When we went to the fire tower for help, he was the one we needed to be saved from. He betrayed me.

"Why did they reveal themselves to you?" I ask.

"I don't know," she says. Something about how she talks sounds like she's not telling the truth. "I think they want to pin everything on me! Hugh, they hate me. I knew I never should have come on this trip. Remember? I told you I never wanted to come!"

This information is making me feel dizzy. There are so many unanswered questions. Why are the rest of them involved? I know Willow isn't the most likeable of people, but why kill her?

"There was a woman in the basement," I say. "Who was

that?"

"Her name is Shannon," Willow answers. "This is her cabin. It was never Caleb's. He's a liar. We need to help her. Both of them. They can back up our story—they can back up the truth."

My eyes widen, and my stomach drops. Partly because I realize I have no idea who Caleb is, but mostly because I just killed her. Willow notices my facial expression.

"What, Hugh? What happened?" she asks.

I pause.

"She's dead," I inform her.

"What? No! We needed her, what happened?"

"I killed her."

Her face drops. She looks so mad.

"What the fuck, Hugh," she says as she pushes her hair out of her face, resting her hands on her head.

"It was an accident," I cry. "She jumped out at me! I thought it was the Wendigo!"

Willow looks taken aback by this comment. "What do you mean, the *Wendigo?*"

"The killer. It looks like a Wendigo," I explain. "I learned about them while researching for my play. I told you about them." As I say this, a thought tickles the back of my mind, but I can't pin it down.

Her face goes white, and she turns away from me.

"Oh sorry, I don't remember that," she states.

I know for a fact I told her. She was desperate to know what the play was about, so I told her about them. I have a feeling she remembers it, but why is she lying? Then I come to a sickening realization. The killings in Telluride began shortly after I started writing my play.

CHAPTER FORTY

"Wait," I say, but she doesn't turn around. "Didn't Noa say it was the same mask as the Telluride Maniac?"

Silence.

It could be a morbid coincidence that a killer wearing a Wendigo mask began a murder spree a few weeks after I showed Willow a photo of a Wendigo, but what if it isn't? Is Willow the … is this why she is being targeted? Is that why something about her explanation didn't sound right? My dizziness returns. It can't be true. I'm overthinking it. I want to think Willow isn't capable of murder, but I just saw what she did to Kaya. Willow finally turns around.

"I don't know," she says. "Nobody saw the maniac except Noa. She could have been making it up so we wouldn't think it was her, for all we know!"

"Okay," I say, barely concealing the quiver in my voice. She tilts her head.

"What?" she asks. "You think I'm the Telluride Maniac? You think I killed all those people? Hugh, come on. That is crazy."

I don't say anything. I'm scared of her for the first time since I met her. Afraid for my life. She approaches me and puts one of her hands over my cheek, her other still clasping the knife. I shudder at the feeling.

"I swear to you that is not true," she reassures me. "They're trying to pin this on me. Hugh, I love you."

She pushes my hair behind my ears.

"I love you too," I say unconvincingly.

I don't know if I believe her. I should, but this night has completely destroyed my ability to trust. Every single person has been lying, so why would Willow be any different? But then again, I have been awake for almost twenty-four hours. I'm exhausted, delirious, overly suspicious, and paranoid. I have no reason to believe that Willow is a serial killer. That's ridiculous. It's just a coincidence. Besides, Caleb and Noa were the ones wearing the killer's costume. Caleb is the one who brought us here, not Willow.

"Help shouldn't be too far away," she adds. "Noa and Caleb are the only ones left. We just need to avoid them and wait for the storm to pass."

She's right. However, avoiding them is no longer an option because, as she says this, the bedroom door slowly opens, and Noa and Caleb stand on the other side. I immediately become defensive as I shield Willow with my arm.

"Back the fuck off!" I scream.

I watch as Noa surveys the bedroom floor, taking a few seconds to comprehend what happened to Kaya and Evelyn. She appears queasy and looks as if she might barf. Caleb, on the other hand, doesn't look phased at all. Instead, he looks at Willow and me in annoyance. I don't think he was expecting us to be still alive.

"Hugh, you have no idea what's happening. Stay out of it!" he tells me.

I cannot believe him. I've been tormented all night along with Willow, and now I'm meant to *stay out of it*? How am I supposed to do that?

"I do!" I shout back. "Willow told me everything."

Noa lets out an agitated chuckle. "Everything she told you is bullshit!" she screams. "But we don't have time to explain it."

I want her to explain it, though. I have no idea what is going on, and it's intensely frustrating. Before I get the chance to speak up, Noa charges in our direction. *Willow's* direction. My fight or flight response kicks in when I see the knife in

CHAPTER FORTY

her right hand. When Noa gets close enough, I thrust my fist towards her and punch her in the nose. *Ouch.* Punching always looked so easy in the movies, but Jesus, that hurt.

Noa flies off her feet and falls to the ground, landing on her back with a loud thud. Although it hurt, I'm a little proud my punch was so effective.

This is our opportunity to escape. While shaking my hand, trying to ease the pain, I shout at Willow.

"Willow, go!"

Without hesitation, Willow bolts to the door. She shoves Caleb hard enough that he slams against the wall, and as she runs down the stairs, Noa slowly gets back to her feet. She has been covering her nose with her hand, but when she removes it, I can see blood is flowing from it. She looks at me, her eyes filled with rage.

"You have no idea what you've just done," she says menacingly.

Then she turns towards the door and slowly stumbles out of it, chasing Willow down the stairs. Caleb and I are left alone in the room. Caleb looks toward the doorway, clearly trying to avoid my stare, but I'm not doing this with him anymore. He can't just reveal himself to be a killer but be too shy to look at me.

"You're crazy," I tell him.

He turns his head sharply towards me. He looks offended.

"Hugh, you don't understand the circumstances—"

"What circumstances?" I yell. "You *murdered* people, Caleb. There are *no* circumstances where that is okay!"

"If only you knew," he says.

I'm getting so aggravated by constantly being left out. "Knew what?" I shriek. "Stop lying to me! I know you're doing this to Willow so we can be together!"

Caleb stops and stares at me, completely dumbfounded. "What?" he asks in disbelief.

He looks genuinely surprised, which in turn, throws me off guard.

"Willow told me why you're doing this," I inform him. "She told me how you killed the groundskeeper, Fergus, and Riley. She told me how you *kidnapped* the owners of this lodge! You lied to me!"

He looks guiltily to the floor. "In my defense, Willow killed Fergus. *She's* the liar! Technically, I never killed anybody." Then, he squints his eyes as he looks at me. "Can you say the same?"

Dammit. He must know it was me who killed Shannon. But that's only because I'm exhausted and paranoid from what *he* put me through.

"Oh, please!" I interrupt. "Everything about you is a lie! You were telling me how you wanted to spend the rest of your life with me, the same time you were plotting a killing spree!"

This comment catches Caleb's attention. His face turns sour, and he scoffs. He is no longer looking guilty. Instead, he looks furious.

"Everything about *me* is a lie?" he utters in disbelief. "Hugh, if you could just swallow your pride for once in your fucking life, you would see that me doing all of this 'just to be with you' is completely insane! Also, if I remember correctly, *you* were the one who wanted to spend the rest of your life with *me*. Then, you lied to Willow and everyone about it!"

"How is that relevant?" I screech.

"It's relevant because you fucking hurt my feelings! And because you're looking down at me for *being a liar* when you're

CHAPTER FORTY

the biggest liar here. Well, biggest liar after Willow. You lie to Willow. You lie to me. You lie to yourself about your sexuality," he says.

"Why do you keep calling Willow a liar?" I ask in irritation, completely ignoring the last part of his monologue. "What did she do?"

"You don't want to know," he responds.

"Yes, I do!" I scream. "I'm done with being kept in the dark! If you're not doing this to be with me, then tell me why the fuck you're doing this."

Caleb pauses. He takes a deep breath and then speaks.

"Because Willow is the Telluride Maniac."

My face goes numb, and my insides twist and turn. I already thought about that and dismissed it, but hearing somebody else say it without coercion, makes me rethink. But that theory is entirely ludicrous. There is no way a seventeen-year-old girl could kill that many people.

"Bullshit," I choke out.

"Fucking hell, Hugh, you have to believe me," Caleb pleads. "She murdered Noa's family! She's killed thirteen people! Eighteen including Fergus, Arthur, Samuel, Evelyn, and Kaya. She's using you, Hugh! You're blind!"

I don't want to believe him, but I almost do. Then I look at Caleb dressed in the killers' clothes and I can't help but doubt it.

"I am not blind! And, even if that is true, why wouldn't you go to the police?" I question. "You hurt people! You're no better than her!"

Caleb rolls his eyes. "See, this is why we didn't tell you about it," he groans. "We needed proof, and we got it. She admitted it!"

I am so disgusted by the sight of him. The person I am looking at now is not the Caleb I knew.

"Whatever she 'admitted' to, you forced her to say!" I yell. "And I will not let you get away with that."

Caleb looks down at the floor once again. However, this time it is not out of guilt. He looks disappointed. He glances at me, clicking his tongue on the roof of his mouth.

"I can't let you do that, Hugh," he says, sounding alarmingly calm. "You know, I really wanted you to survive. I hoped that maybe everything you said was true. But after you completely threw me under the bus, I don't give a shit what happens to you."

He then lifts his shirt, revealing the hunting knife tucked into his belt. He approaches me, but I run for the door. I only make it to the first step before Caleb grabs me by my hair and pulls me back towards him, making me stumble to the ground, hitting my head on the floor. The impact, mixed with my intense fatigue, is almost enough to make me pass out. But the sight of Caleb mounting me with the knife is enough to snap me back to reality. He tries to stab my chest, but I can grab his arm and delay him.

I can't help but think about us as we struggle with the knife. Almost exactly twenty-four hours ago, we were in this same position. But instead of an adoring display of affection, we're trying to kill each other. The knife gets closer and closer to my chest, but just before impact, I push Caleb's arm away forcefully, and he falls back into a sitting position. I hastily get to my feet, still keeping the weight off of my ankle, and he and I stand face to face in front of the stairs.

The *stairs.*

I know what I need to do. In a swift motion, I limp towards

CHAPTER FORTY

Caleb, pushing him back. He staggers until he has nowhere else to stand and falls. However, as he does, he grabs my arm and pulls me with him.

We topple down together, limbs intertwining. Every stair is a stab of pain, each worse than before. I feel what I can only assume is a bone snapping in my leg and I cry out. Caleb lets out a shriek of pain when we finally reach the bottom. I land on top of him but quickly roll off. My leg is in searing pain, and when I look down at it, my shin bone pokes through the skin. I try to sit up, but even the slightest of movements cause the most excruciating pain. I look at Caleb. He is turned away from me, but when he rolls over, I realize I got lucky because the hunting knife protrudes from his stomach.

I drag myself towards him, enduring the pain until I look down into his eyes. They are glazed over, but he's still alive. He lets out indistinct groans, and tears begin to form in his eyes.

"I'm sorry. I really did love you," he mumbles, mustering up the faintest of smiles.

Hearing it makes my heart break. I did too. I really, really loved him, but I was too ashamed to admit it. He deserved better than me. He deserved somebody who could love him to the fullest extent Somebody who could have given him a happy, *long* life. But that can never happen now.

"I loved you too," I whisper back.

A tear drops from my eye and lands on his cheek. He's in so much pain. I delicately grab the knife's handle and pull it out of his stomach. His mouth opens as he gasps for air. Then, he begins moving his hand. I thought he would hold me, but instead, he reaches into his pocket and pulls out a strange object. It's a device of some sort but when I grab and inspect it, I realize it's a tape recorder.

"What is this?" I ask. But he doesn't answer. "Caleb?" I call, looking back to him.

He lies motionless on the ground, his arm resting on my leg. "Caleb, please!"

Blood pools around him. He's gone. My lip starts quivering, but I stop myself. I can't grieve. I need to focus. I aimlessly fiddle with the recorder, trying not to think about my best friend lying dead next to me, until, finally, an audio clip starts playing.

It's Noa. She's talking to Willow. No, not talking, interrogating. It sounds incriminating against Caleb, Noa, and the rest of them, but I keep listening. That's when I hear it.

"How long have you known?" Willow's voice asks.

"Known what?" Noa's voice replies naively.

"Known ... known that I was the Telluride Maniac."

Oh my god. Willow wasn't forced to say anything. Caleb was telling the truth. I should have trusted my instinct. Willow is the Telluride Maniac.

As the audio finishes playing, a floorboard creaks in front of me. When I look over, Willow is standing in the living room, staring at me.

Chapter Forty-One

Willow - 7:45 AM - Sunday, 30th January 2022

I reach the bottom of the stairs within seconds of leaving the bedroom and am already pulling the back door open. The second I twist the handle, the wind tears it out of my hand, slamming the door against the wall. I'm so close to freedom, but I'm not there yet. There is still so much that needs to be wrapped up. Hugh almost figured out why Caleb, Noa, and the rest of our theater class were targeting me, but I was able to refute it.

I know that can't last long. He already protected me from Noa, but he's alone in the bedroom with them. They're going to start talking. I want to think I have given him reason to believe me over them, but they have proof, and I need to destroy it. I try to recall what the group had on me. Kaya had a video of me killing Fergus and Caleb had a taped confession, on a tape recorder rather than a phone. He always was one for theatrics. I hear a commotion upstairs, but I must do this now. I have no idea when the storm will end. It has already begun slowing down, and help can't be much further away. Surviving until help arrives will be pointless if they find evidence that incriminates me. I turn away from the outside and run into the living room, leaving the door wide open.

As I pass the couches, I see something on the coffee table. A phone in a lavender case. Kaya's phone. I grab it frantically, looking behind me to make sure I'm not being followed.

I don't know her passcode, so I try the basics.

1-2-3-4

4-3-2-1

2-4-6-8

2-5-8-0

0-0-0-0

None of them work, but I can't leave this here. I have to destroy the evidence in a different way. I hold her phone in my hand, raise it above my head, and then throw it to the ground, making it shatter. I turn my attention towards finding the tape recorder. It's nowhere in sight. Then, I remember, Caleb put it in his pocket. It's upstairs with them right now and could very well be being used to implicate me.

I consider returning to the bedroom and destroying it in front of them but I am thwarted by Noa coming down the stairs.

Surviving until help arrives will be pointless if they find evidence that incriminates me. But destroying evidence will be meaningless if I'm dead.

I stand up and return to the back door. I can feel Noa close behind me as I exit the lodge. Outside, I can tell that the storm has drastically slowed down. The police must be close. I start towards the tree line, hoping it can provide some cover. When I'm halfway there, I turn my head and realize that Noa is no longer chasing me, but I can't see where she went. I don't waste my time looking for her and instead continue running. I don't make it much further when I feel a stabbing pain in my left shoulder blade. I scream as I collapse in to the snow. I

CHAPTER FORTY-ONE

use my right hand to survey the painful area, and my fingers come across something long and thin sticking out of my skin. I yank it out, which causes a more intense pain than before, and hold it in front of my face. It's an arrow. Probably used to fake Evelyn's death. I turn to see Noa standing back at the lodge, holding a bow. Even from here, I can see the shocked look on her face. She did not expect to hit me.

She drops the bow and runs towards me, so I get to my feet and continue making my way towards the forest. I run aimlessly but like never before. I have no idea where I'm going, all I know is I don't want her to catch me. I zigzag, hoping she loses me, and terrified another arrow is heading my way. Everything looks the same and I can feel her gaining on me. Somehow in my desperate attempt to lose her, I have ended up back at the groundskeeper's cabin. I could lock the door and hide out from the cold and her. But I doubt anybody would find me all the way out her.

However, I barely make it ten feet when Noa tackles me. I hit the ground hard and lay face down on the ground as she sits on top of me. I desperately struggle to get free.

"Stop fucking moving!" she orders.

I don't stop. I struggle harder. I imagine the process of Noa trying to keep me pinned down is equivalent to riding a mechanical bull. She tries to grab her knife from her belt, but when she does, I wiggle harder, and it causes her left arm to slip off my shoulder and into the snow. Right in front of my face. I take the opportunity to bite down on her hand.

She lets out a grunt of pain and shoves her finger into the arrow wound on my shoulder blade. I squeal in agony as I thrash even harder. I manage to swing my foot behind me and I make impact on her back, making her fall forward onto me.

Those dance classes have made me extraordinarily flexible.

She lets go of my arms, and I swing my elbow backwards, smacking her in the temple. She rolls off of me, holding her head, and giving me enough leeway to crawl to freedom and race for the cabin. When I make it inside, I slam the door, but she is too close behind. She kicks it back open, and I stumble to the other side of the room, leaping over the solidified blood. She's in the doorway. I'm cornered.

We both stand up, looking at each other through narrowed eyes. She holds the knife. I am without a weapon and have no way to protect myself.

"Just fucking give up already," she says, breathing heavily. She clearly didn't expect me to put up this much of a fight. She's naïve.

"Fuck off," I say. "I'm not letting you get away with this." I look around the room for something to defend myself with, and my eyes land on a neat pile of chopped logs. They look thick, and I know one could pack a punch. I inch back, trying to grab it without her noticing me.

"Let *me* get away with it?" she echoes. "Are you utterly delusional? Or are you still putting on an act?"

I'm so close to them.

"You're the one who broke into a house and kidnapped the people who live here. You're the one who killed an innocent groundskeeper. You're the one who killed your own friend! I didn't do anything," I say. I know that isn't true, but I'm just trying to buy more time.

Noa looks livid. "I don't think my family would agree with you," she spits.

I've reached the logs, but I can't risk running at her. One slash from her knife would be enough to finish me off. She must come to me.

"Who cares what they think?" I ask, trying to get a reaction. "They're dead. And I had so much fun slaughtering them."

Her face goes red. "Shut the fuck up!"

"You should have seen the looks on their faces as the life drained from their eyes. And the sound that came from your mother flopping onto the pavement? It was beautiful."

I've done it. She lets out a battle cry as she charges me. I reach for the top log, and as she nears, I swing it at her, hitting her in the skull. She loses her grip on the knife, and it falls at my feet. She stumbles backwards dizzily until she knocks against the bed and slumps to the ground. I grab the knife and kneel beside her, raising it above my head. I think about when the two of us met on the first day of middle school. We had no friends, so we sat next to each other at lunch.

Then, as time went on, we became best friends. I think about what went wrong. When our friendship dissolved into nothing. I think about the pain of watching my soulmate become a stranger. How did we end up here? If only I could have controlled my murderous tendencies, this wouldn't be happening. But I couldn't, and I'm glad I couldn't. I love killing people. I've never felt more alive than I have these past two years. It's what I was put on this earth to do. I wish I could say I was sorry for what I did to Noa and her family, but I'm not. They got what was coming to them, whether she wants to admit it or not.

"Say hi to the family for me," I say with a smile.

I plunge the knife into her stomach and watch as her breathing slowly fades out and her eyes go blank. It's over. She's dead. I feel the knot in my stomach, which has been present since the night started, dissolve. I've done it. She can't hurt me anymore. I am free to tell whatever story I want.

I slowly get to my feet and start limping towards the lodge, still holding the knife. I have a newfound sense of freedom. Undoubtedly, Hugh was able to overpower Caleb, which means it's only us. Nobody knows who I really am. Nobody can turn me in. Nobody can ruin my life. Just Hugh and I, forever. This shared trauma may even bring us closer together.

That's what I thought, at least.

When I get back to the lodge, I hear a familiar sound. It's somebody speaking. No, it's *me* speaking. Then I see Hugh. Sitting on the floor clutching the tape recorder I was searching for. I step on a loose floorboard that lets out a small squeak, and Hugh darts his eyes towards me. He looks petrified.

"W-Willow," he stutters. "You're alive?"

Oh, Hugh. We were so close to being free, but you had to go and ruin it by listening to that recording.

"I am," I respond. "Are you surprised?"

He gulps loudly. His eyes are wide. He shakes his head.

"Why did you listen to that?" I sigh.

"Listen to what?" he replies. I'm sure he sees the knife in my hand. He'd say anything to stay on my good side.

"My confession," I say as I start moving closer to him.

He tries to crawl backwards, but he's in pain. Then I notice the bone sticking out of his leg.

"I won't say anything, Willow," he cries. "I swear! I'll say whatever you want!"

"I know you will," I say.

He looks so pitiful. I notice that his eyes are red and puffy, and then I see Caleb's dead body a few feet away from him and put the pieces together. There is one more thing I need

CHAPTER FORTY-ONE

to know.

"Hugh?" I ask.

"Yeah?" he replies shakily.

I walk closer to him.

"Did you love Caleb?" I ask.

He looks taken aback.

"What? No," he claims. "I loved you. I *love* you. I always have!"

I know he's lying, but I need him to confirm it.

"Hugh," I say reassuringly. "It's fine. I just need to know. Did you love him?"

He looks at me for a few seconds then tears start pouring down his face. He burrows his face into his hands and lets out a small cry. Then, he nods.

"Okay," I whisper before sinking my knife into his heart. The same way he did to me.

He quickly lifts his head, and his eyes open wide in shock. I pull out the knife, then planting it right into his throat. He gurgles blood as I pull it out and drop it to the ground. He covers his wounds, but blood sneaks through his fingers. I stand above him and watch as he tries desperately to cling to life until he finally can't. He lies still on the ground, blood seeping from his chest and neck and onto the floorboards and for the first time this trip, I am not being hunted. I am not being tormented. I'm just alone.

Completely *alone*.

Chapter Forty-Two

Willow - 8:30 AM - Sunday, 30th January 2022

I stand in the living room, soaking in the quiet. But soon, the relief I felt for being alive is gone and replaced with paranoia. I think about what my life will look like from now on. Will I get away with this? I can't stop thinking about what evidence the group has on me. Was it just the audio and video? Or is there more they didn't tell me about, just in case something like this happened? Knowing them, I don't think they planned this far. This whole weekend was messy. I think Noa should have taken up Kaya's offer in the school bathroom and waited a little longer to think this whole thing through.

I march to the tape recorder and examine it. It turns out it's not a tape recorder at all. It's a digital recorder that is designed to look retro. So tacky.

In one stomp, I destroy it. Will that do the trick? I look at Kaya's broken phone and begin to panic. What if they can still access the data? I start hyperventilating. I can't stop overthinking the situation.

I pace around the house, trying to devise a plan to destroy *all* the evidence—fingerprints, phones, recorders, photos, and whatever else. I'm stumped. The police could be here any minute, and there is evidence everywhere. I rip apart couch pillows, paranoid enough to think the place is bugged.

"Fuck!" I cry.

Out of frustration, I kick Caleb's body as hard as possible. I kick him again and again, screaming as I do. I quickly tire out and collapse on the floor. I feel much better after that and can now focus. I look across the room to see the garage door. I haven't been in there at all since we arrived, but if something is going to help me, that's where it will be. So, I stand up and head for the door. I was right. The second I enter the room, I notice three large, red gasoline tanks in the corner. There is no way of finding every piece of evidence and destroying it by hand before people get here but destroying the entire lodge should take care of it.

I grab a gas tank and walk to Shannon's bedroom. The tank is heavy, and my arrow wound is searing. But I can't stop now. Police could walk through the door at any time. I pour the gasoline over Kaya and Evelyn and then splash it all around the room. I walk out the doors and run it down the stairs. When I'm in the living room, I douse Caleb, Hugh, Samuel, and Arthur. By then, I have emptied the first can. I retrieve the second one from the garage and continue. I drench the couches and curtains, then move to the kitchen. A few splashes should do it. For good measure, I turn on the stove and blow out the flames, creating a flow of gas that should quickly fill the entire lodge. I cover the hallway and a few bedrooms with gasoline by the time the second canister depletes. I grab the last tank and walk to my bedroom. I shower my clothes and suitcase in the gas. I cover the bed and bathroom then head back downstairs and into the basement. I douse the body of Shannon and pour a little extra over the knife I used to kill Fergus, undoubtedly destroying all of my

DNA.

I walk back up the stairs, drizzling the last few pints of gas on the stairs and connecting it to the existing pool. I turn on the gas fireplace and smother the flames, leaving yet another gas stream filling the lodge. I find a box of matches in the top drawer in the kitchen. Bingo. I walk to the front door, move the barricade, and pull it open. I take one last look inside. It's funny. I genuinely tried to be a better person. I believed this trip could change me. I thought I had made friends. I thought I had a kind, honest boyfriend. But I was wrong. Nothing changed. They betrayed me. This only perpetuated my view of people. They will always let you down. They will always disappoint you. They will always villainize you no matter what. It's up to you to take control of your life. With a sigh, I strike a match and drop it to the floor.

The match makes contact with the gasoline, and within seconds, the floor of the lodge is covered in bright orange. Flames engulf Hugh, and shortly after, they take Caleb too. Then, the smell hits me—*burning flesh.* I turn around and walk onto the front lawn. There is still a slight wind, but there is no snow. The storm has ultimately passed, and a new day is breaking. The wooden walls of the lodge catch fire, and some windows shatter as flames erupt through them. Then, there is a loud explosion inside—the gas. The flames consume the lodge, and I watch on in amazement as they grow, taking every plank, nail, and brick with them. This represents a fresh start. A purge of my mistakes, like trusting the wrong people and opening myself up to be hurt. That all goes away with the lodge.

Then, out of nowhere, I am grabbed from behind by someone and stabbed in the lower back. My gasp is a mix of

CHAPTER FORTY-TWO

pain and shock and as I hit the ground, I see Noa standing over me.

Fuck.

She kicks me in the head repeatedly until I begin to lose consciousness. Every part of me hurts. She holds a knife in her hand, the one I dropped on the floor after killing Hugh. She's been inside. She's been following me. I try to fight back, but I can't. I'm in agony, but I'm also exhausted. Noa lowers herself to me. Her eyes are full of rage, but I can also see she's distraught.

"I guess you'll have to say hi to my family for me," she whispers in my ear. "Have fun in hell."

I almost laugh. Is that some kind of catchphrase?

"I'll see you there," I retort.

This is it. I put up a good fight. I did everything I could. I destroyed all the evidence. It's comforting to think about people not believing her when she walks out of here. I hope they throw her back in the asylum.

I close my eyes as she lifts the knife above her head and swings down. I brace myself for the stab, but instead, I hear gunshots. I'm confused because I feel nothing. Then, there are four more gunshots. I open my eyes and see Noa frozen in place, and then, the blood starts flowing from her chest. She collapses beside me and doesn't move again.

I turn to my left and see two police officers with their guns drawn. They run over to me to check if I'm alright, and when they see the bleeding, they call for help.

"It's okay, kid," one of the officers reassures me. "You're safe."

The last thing I see before I pass out is a helicopter flying over the mountain. I close my eyes and hear the police sirens get quieter and quieter, and the officers' voices become more distant.

It's okay.

I'm just going to sleep.

Chapter Forty-Three

Channel 15 - 10:00 AM - Sunday, 30th January 2022

"*Breaking News! We are getting word about an attack just outside the town of Telluride. Police shot and killed one teenage girl who is believed to be the attacker. Police only discovered one survivor. The lodge they were discovered at appears to have been burnt down, so anyone inside is presumed to be deceased. We do not have the names of the individuals yet, but once we do, we will share them with you, minors excluded. There isn't much detail surrounding the attack, but police say there have been multiple murders. Telluride is all too familiar with those. Could this be just another random act of violence? Or is this finally the end of the horrific Telluride Maniac killings? This has been Stacey Williams from Channel 15 news. Have a warm, safe night.*"

Epilogue

1 Year Later
Willow - 9:00 PM - Monday, 30th January 2023

It's been one year since I was rescued from the lodge by the police. My life has completely changed for the better. People love me. They are so fascinated by my story. The tale of The Telluride Maniac was already a popular true crime case, and now it's solved. People love it when the pieces come together. It gives them a sense of fulfilment—a win in their miserable lives.

When the police killed Noa and airlifted me to the nearest hospital, I passed out. When I woke up a day later, they told me it was from a mix of blood loss, head trauma, and exhaustion. I was badgered by the police, wanting to know what happened. Why Noa was trying to kill me and why the lodge was burning down. It was a few days before I started talking. They attributed it to me being in shock, and I went along with it, but really, I was trying to craft my story. I told them my version of events, which is now what everybody thinks really happened.

That is that Noa, Caleb, and Kaya were the Telluride Maniacs. They kidnapped the owners of the lodge and decided to construct the perfect horror movie setup. They were in it for the fame and wanted to frame me and walk away as survivors. Noa murdered her own family just to earn a buck. The media ate it up. They love a twist.

It turns out that Al survived. I suppose the fire didn't reach him all the way down there. He was unconscious when the firefighters got to him. He inhaled a sizeable amount of smoke, but as he was far down in the basement, it wasn't fatal. I'm glad it wasn't because he spoke about how *two* people attacked him and killed his wife. His comment, in addition to my story, made the claim that Caleb and the others kidnapped Shannon and Al and murdered our entire class undeniable. Caleb's parents said they had no idea of the plan, and they were flamed online for being terrible parents.

Hugh's parents were extremely opinionated. They despised Caleb for how he tried to, and I quote, "Tempt our baby boy with sin" and how "He has gone home to the lord." I mean, for Christ's sake, they're utterly delusional. They really didn't know their "baby boy" at all. I should have told them Hugh was the one tempting sin. He was a coward, and someone who didn't deserve to make it out alive. Now they've used Caleb's actions to spout homophobic rhetoric across social media and conservative news outlets. It's shameful. Let me be clear that I'm not homophobic.

I just didn't like Caleb.

Then, I went quiet. I couldn't be too outspoken. People needed to believe I was going through a hard time. If I went to the media straight away, people would think I was a fraud. My mother visited me in the hospital, and we finally talked. If there was one good thing to come from this whole experience, it was rekindling my relationship with her. Over the next six months, she put down the bottle and started acting like a parent.

She asked about dad and if they were the ones who killed him. I didn't know what to tell her. She has been grieving ever since I killed him. Part of me wants to give her imaginary closure, but I don't think killing my father would have been on Noa's to-do list. So, I told her I had no idea what had happened to him.

Worldwide, people believed me, but some were skeptical about it in Telluride. Noa's aunt spoke out, telling the world that the story was false, but the bodycam footage of Noa trying to kill me was published, and her story was invalidated. Classmates came forward and told stories about me being "mean." Boohoo. A few of them even said they were on Noa's side. That they supported her trying to kill me. Oh, how people can be cruel.

After about three months of living in Telluride, Mom and I decided to leave. I told her it was too hard to be there after what happened, but truthfully, I'd always hated it. I wanted to move to New York. I had earned a bit of money from small interviews, but it was enough to get a few months in a nice apartment. Because of how mainstream my story was, everybody knew I was a theater actress, and soon after moving, I was offered management, and I starred in my first Broadway musical a month later. I played Lydia Deetz in the *Beetlejuice* musical. In times like these, I wish Noa was still alive so she could see me succeeding.

After a while, I started writing a book. I wanted to eternalize *my* story—the truth. I already had dozens of publishers jumping down my throat for a book, offering me six-figure deals. I couldn't possibly turn those down. I called it *Requiem* to honor Hugh. A song for the dead, each chapter representing a section of the song. The Sanctus, The Kyrie, The Agnus Dei, etcetera. I always thought that was brilliant. And after a few months of writing, it was in the process of being published across the globe.

However, it had almost been a year, and I realized people's interest in my story was declining. That's when Oprah Winfrey reached out. She wanted to do an hour-long special to get the whole story. I would promote my book and answer her "hard-hitting" questions. God, I cannot stand her. But she offered me a shit-ton of money, so I graciously accepted.

I told her specific details nobody had heard. I told her the full truth about Shannon and Al and how Caleb and Kaya stalked them for days, and how I found them in that cellar, covered in piss. I told them about how Noa burnt the lodge down to destroy any evidence. The details about how Caleb wanted to be with Hugh and how he thought if I died, it would happen.

"There are some people who believe your story isn't true," she had said. "What would you say to those people?"

"My mother taught me that if you have nothing nice to say, don't say anything at all," I responded. "But if a stranger on the internet wants to repudiate somebody's trauma, they don't deserve to be spoken to with respect."

"But you have to agree that these attacks have, in some way, improved your quality of life," she said. "I mean, you've written a book, moved to New York, and starred on Broadway all in less than a year. You've really used this to your advantage. Can you understand why people could be skeptical?"

I felt my cheeks burn up. If millions of people weren't watching, I would have leapt off my chair and strangled the bitch. "I don't want to be defined by my trauma," I told her instead. "I need to move on."

The interview broke every single streaming and television record. I thought that was it. I had cemented myself as a celebrity. I was on par with Ms. H, who funnily enough, booked that job she auditioned for. She's up for an Academy Award this year.

Then, Oprah was over. My book was out. Months passed, and just like before, I faded into irrelevancy. The casting directors surmised that my singing and acting weren't great, and I couldn't book another job. I was washed up, and the rent quickly ate my entire fortune. I had to do something. Then I thought of it. There *is* something I could do and something I've been yearning for since I came back from the mountain. It made me famous once. It can make me famous again. I can guide the victims through it and be a mentor—the public face of the New York Maniac case.

So tonight, one year after the killings ended, I stand in front of an elegant three-story brownstone in the lower east side, looking in through a front window. A family sits on the couch, watching the TV. I watch as they laugh at whatever mind-numbing show is on. They look so happy. It's awful they have to sacrifice themselves, but it's for the greater good. They will have a legacy. One true crime podcasters and irrelevant influencers will speak about for years to come. I have given the performance of a lifetime since I came back from that mountain, but it wasn't enough.

With that in mind, I walk to another front window, pick the lock, and climb inside, all with a smile on my face.

Acknowledgments

There aren't many people to thank here, seeing as this book is self-published, which was a nightmare, by the way. I even made the cover design, which you cannot deny is a masterpiece.

Thank you to my incredible editor, Becky Wallace. Without her, this book would most definitely be incoherent. You were not afraid to tell me what worked and what was dumb as shit. I loved reading the *'?'* and *'this makes no sense,'* that you wrote next to a paragraph you thought was a tad far-fetched. Before, it just felt like I had written a silly little book for my friends, but you made this feel like a novel, and I am so thankful for that.

I would also love to thank my incredible friends Azzie, Sophie, Gina, Liv, and Aaron for reading and reacting to *Requiem chapter* by chapter. You all are the reason I even completed this book in the first place. I tend to start things and never finish them, but the thought of all of you reading the new chapter and then nagging me for the next one kept me going.

And thank you to my friends Trin, Ruby, and Kiara for reading Requiem on a trip to Albury, making sure to point out all the minor grammar mistakes. But, watching your faces as you read a twist more than made up for it.

And thank you to my parents, who helped me *(financially)*

edit this book and make it a finished copy. Even though you haven't read it yet, I'm sure you'll get around to it…

About the Author

Archie Myers has always been writing. At eight years old, he started writing terrible short stories, completely ripping off his favourite movies. Later, he advanced to writing terrible scripts for terrible movies. And now, finally, he's writing terrible novels.

Also by Archie Myers

Not Who You Say You Are
Every Family Has Its Secrets. Sometimes, They Should Stay Hidden.

The Quinn family have always been dysfunctional, and 21-year-old Theo Quinn has done his best to avoid them. But when Theo and his boyfriend, Miles, get invited to the Quinn Family Island for Christmas, they decide to go. However, what was meant to be a relaxing trip at his family's island estate quickly turns into a nightmare. With no escape off the island, somebody picking them off one by one, and dark family secrets being revealed, Theo must do whatever it takes to survive.

Lights Out, Campers
Coming 2024

The Last Summer of Their Lives.

Phoebe couldn't be more thrilled when she takes a job at a Michigan Summer Camp, so she packs up her life in Australia and heads for the States. She is excited to make new friends, explore different cultures and, most importantly, start fresh in a place where nobody knows who she is and what she has done. However, when she arrives at the camp, Phoebe quickly learns of its violent, haunted history. As children go missing and she continues seeing things that aren't there, she unravels the truth about the camp's past.

Requiem: Reprise

Coming 2025

It's been a year since the identities of the Telluride Maniac were revealed—at least, that's what the media and police think. Willow is living in New York City, revelling in her fame. She has gotten away with her crimes scot-free. However, her fame and attention soon die down, and Willow must search for them another way. Hence, the New York Maniac is born.

Balancing a killing spree whilst leading a support group for mass murder survivors seems to be more challenging for Willow than expected. However, she has no idea how hard it will get.

It's just getting started.

A new string of brutal murders shocks the nation, and Willow has nothing to do with it. But the person behind the mask knows the truth about her and will stop at nothing until it's revealed. Willow must find their identity and tie up all her loose ends before being outed to the public.

Printed in Great Britain
by Amazon